ANAGRAMS

ANAGRAMS

A NOVEL

Lorrie Moore

Alfred A. Knopf　New York 1986

THIS IS A BORZOI BOOK
PUBLISHED BY ALFRED A. KNOPF, INC.

Grateful acknowledgment is made to the following for permission to reprint previously published material:

Mills Music Inc.: Excerpt from the lyrics to "St. James Infirmary," by Joe Primrose. Copyright 1929 by Mills Music Inc. Copyright renewed. Used with permission. All rights reserved.

W. W. Norton & Company, Inc.: Excerpt from "Through the Looking Glass" from *Alice in Wonderland* by Lewis Carroll, Norton Critical edition, edited by Donald J. Gray. Copyright © 1971 by W. W. Norton & Company, Inc. Reprinted by permission of W. W. Norton & Company, Inc.

Library of Congress Cataloging-in-Publication Data
Moore, Lorrie.
Anagrams.
I. Title.
PS3563.O6225A8   1986   813'.54   86-45280
ISBN 0-394-55294-6

Manufactured in the United States of America
FIRST EDITION

Acknowledgments

For their helpfulness and support, many thanks go to the following: Victoria Wilson, Melanie Jackson, Joe Bellamy, Alison Lurie, Richard Estell, Margaret Moore, Mike Sangria, Sheila Schwartz, Gary Mailman, Kelly Cherry (and her typewriter), Ron Wallace, and my parents. My gratitude also to Yaddo, where part of this book was written.

The word *mammoth* is derived from the Tartar word *mamma* meaning "the earth" . . . From this some mistakenly came to believe that the great beast had always lived underground, burrowing like a big mole. And they were sure it died when it came to the surface and breathed fresh air!

—Roy Chapman Andrews
All About Strange Beasts of the Past

I shall be telling this with a sigh . . .

—Robert Frost
"The Road Not Taken"

I don't think there's anything in that black bag for me.

—Judy Garland
The Wizard of Oz

ANAGRAMS

I

Escape from the Invasion
of the Love-Killers

GERARD MAINES LIVED ACROSS THE HALL from a woman named Benna, who four minutes into any conversation always managed to say the word *penis*. He was not a prude, but, nonetheless, it made him wince. He worked with children all day, taught a kind of aerobics to pre-schoolers, and the most extreme language he was likely to hear seemed to him to be in code, in acronyms, or maybe even in German—*boo-boo, finky, peenick*—words that were difficult to figure out even in context, and words, therefore, from which he felt quite safe. He suspected it was not unlike people he knew who hated operas in translation. "Believe me," they would explain, "you just don't want to know what they're saying."

Today they were talking about families.

"Fathers and sons," she said, "they're like governments: always having sword fights with their penises."

"Really," said Gerard, sitting at her kitchen table, gulping at near-beer for breakfast. He palmed his beard like a man trying to decide.

"But what do I know." She smiled and shrugged. "I grew up in a trailer. It's not like a real family with a house." This was her excuse for everything, her own self-deprecating refrain; she'd grown up in a trailer in upstate New York and was therefore unqualified to pronounce on any of the subjects she continued to pronounce on.

Gerard had his own line of self-excuse: "I was a retard in my father's play."

"A retard in your father's play?"

"Yes," he said, realizing that faced with the large questions of life and not finding large answers, one must then settle for makeshift, little answers, just as on any given day a person must at least eat *something*, even if it was not marvelous and huge. "He wrote plays in our town. Then he did the casting and directing. It was harder to venture out through the rest of life after that."

"How awful for you," said Benna, pouring more near-beer into both their glasses.

"Yes," he said. He loved her very much.

Benna was a nightclub singer. Four nights a week she put on a black mini-dress and what she wearily called her Joan-Crawford-catch-me-have-me shoes, and went off to sing at the various cocktail lounges around Fitchville. Sometimes Gerard would go see her and drink too much. In the spotlight up front she seemed to him hopelessly beautiful, a star, her glass jewelry launching quasars into the audience, her laughter rumbling into the mike. He'd watch other men fall in love with her; he knew the fatuous gaze, the free drinks sent over between songs—he'd done that himself. Sometimes he would stay for all three sets and buy her a hamburger afterward or just give her a ride home. Other times, when it was crowded, he would leave her to her fans—the businessmen with loosened neckties, the local teenage girls who idolized her, the very musicians she hired to play with her—and would go home and sit in his bathroom, in his bone-dry tub, with his clothes on, waiting. The way their apartments were laid out, their bathrooms shared a wall, and Gerard could sit in his own tub and await her two-in-the-morning return, hear her enter her bathroom, hear her pee, hear the ruckle of the toilet-paper roll, the metal-sprung flush, the sliding shower door, the squirt, spray, hiss of the water. Sometimes he would call to her through the tiles. She would turn off the shower and yell, "Gerard, are you talking to me?"

"Yes, I'm talking to you. No. I'm talking to Zero Mostel."

"Listen, I'm tired. I'm going to bed."

Once she came home at three in the morning, completely drunk, and knocked on his door. When he opened it, she was slumped against the frame, eyes closed, shoes in hand. "Gerard," she drawled, thrusting her shoes at him, "will you make love to me?" and then she sank to the floor and passed out.

Every morning she downed a whole six-pack of near-beer. "You know, I'm a widow," she said, and then told him quickly about a husband, a lawyer who had been killed in a car crash.

"You're so young," murmured Gerard. "It must have been devastating."

"Nah," she exhaled, and then, peeling an orange, sang "O what a beautiful mourning," just that line. "I don't know," she said, and shrugged.

Near their apartment building was a large baseball field, rarely used. From Gerard's living-room window he could see the field's old rotting scoreboard, weathered as driftwood, its paint peeling but still boasting the neat and discernible lettering: HOME and

VISITOR. When he'd first moved into the apartment, the words seemed to mock him—scoring, underscoring, his own displacement and aloneness—so much that he would close the blinds so as not to have to look at them.

Occasionally now, however, late at night, he would venture out onto the diamond and, if it was summer and warm, would sprawl out on the ground at a place just to the left of the pitcher's mound and stare up at the sky. It was important to dizzy yourself with stars, he thought. Too often you forgot they were even there. He could stare at one star, one brilliant and fidgety star, so long that his whole insides seemed suddenly to rush out into the sky to meet it. It was like the feeling he'd had as a boy playing baseball, focusing on the pitched ball with such concentration that the bat itself seemed at the crucial moment to leap from him with a loud smack and greet the ball mid-air.

As an adult he rarely had those moments of connection, though what ones he'd had recently seemed mostly to be with the children he taught. He'd be showing them how to do reaches and bends—like trees, he would tell them—and when he put on music and finally had them do it, their eyes would cry "Look at me! I'm doing it!" the sudden bonds between them and him magical as home runs. More and more he was becoming convinced that it was only through children that one could connect with anything anymore, that in this life it was only through children that one came home, became a home, that one was no longer a visitor.

"Boy, are you sentimental," Benna told him. "I feel like I'm talking to a Shirley Temple movie." Benna was a woman who knew when she was ovulating by the dreams she'd have of running through corridors to catch trains; she was also a woman who said she had no desire to have children. "I watched my friend Eleanor give birth," she said. "Once you've seen a child born you realize a baby's not much more than a reconstituted ham and cheese sandwich. Just a little anagram of you and what you've been eating for nine months."

"But look at the stars," he wanted to say to her. "How does one get there?" But then he thought of her singing in the Ramada Inn cocktail lounge, her rhinestones flashing out into the dark of the place, and thought that maybe in a certain way she was already there. "Tell me why you don't want to have children," Gerard asked her. He had for a solid week recently allowed himself the fantasy of someday having a family with her, although she had shown no real interest in him after that one night in his doorway, and usually went out with other men anyway. He would sometimes hear them clunk up and down the stairs.

"You know me," she said. "I grew up in a trailer. Your own father made you a retard. You tell me why you want to have kids."

Gerard thought about the little deaf boy in his class, a boy named Barney, how just today Barney had said loudly in his garbled and unconsonanted speech, "Please, Mr. Maines, when you stand behind, can you stomp your feet louder?" The only way Barney could hear the music and the beat was through the vibrations in the floor. Gerard had smiled, kind and hearty, and said "Certainly, young man," and something raced and idled in his heart.

"Sometimes I think that without children we remain beasts or dust. That we are like something lost at sea."

Benna looked at him and blinked, her eyes almost swelling, as if with allergy. She took a long glug of near-beer, swallowed, then shrugged. "Do you?" she said. "I think maybe I'm just too exhausted from work."

"Yes, well," said Gerard, attempting something lighthearted. "I guess that's why they call it *work*. I guess that's why they don't call it *table tennis*."

. . .

"What are you watching?" Gerard had knocked on her door and sauntered in. Benna was curled under a blanket on the sofa, watching television. Gerard tried to smile, had even been practicing it, feeling the air on his teeth, his cheeks puff up into his vision, the slight rise of his ears up the sides of his head.

"Some science-fiction thing," she said. "Escape from something. Or maybe it's invasion of something. I forget."

"Who are those figures rimmed in neon?" he asked, sitting beside her.

"Those are the love-killers. They love you and then they kill you. They're from another planet. Supposedly."

He looked at her face. It was pale, without make-up, and the narrow planes of her cheeks seemed exquisite as bone. Her hair, pulled off her face into a rubber band, shone auburn in the lamplight. Just as she was, huddled in a blanket that had telltale signs of dog hair and coffee, Gerard wanted more than anything else to hold her in his arms. And so, in a kind of rush out of himself, he leaned over and kissed Benna on the mouth.

"Gerard," she said, pulling away slightly. "I like you very much, but I'm just not feeling sexual these days."

He could feel the dry chap of her lips against his, still there, like a ten-second ghost. "You go out with men," he insisted, quickly hating the tone of his own voice. "I hear them."

"Look. I'm going through life alone now," she said. "I can't think of men or penises or marriage or children. I work too hard. I don't even masturbate."

Gerard sank into the back of the sofa, feeling himself about to speak something bitter, something that tomorrow he would apologize for. What he said was, "What, do you need an audience for *everything*?" And without waiting for a reply, he got up to return to his own apartment where VISITOR and HOME, like a rigged and age-old game, would taunt him even through the blinds. He stood and went back across the hall, where he lived.

2

Strings Too Short to Use

ALTHOUGH I WAS BETWEEN JOBS and afraid I would slip into
the cracks and pauses of two different Major Medical policies, I
was pleased when they said I had a lump in my breast. I had
discovered it on my own, during a home check, had counted to
twenty and checked again, and even though Gerard had kept saying, "Where? *There?* Is *that* what you mean? It feels muscular,"
I brought it in to them.

"Yes," the nurse-practitioner said. "Yes. There's a lump in
your breast."

"Yes, there is," said the surgeon standing beside her like a
best man.

"Thank you," I said. "Thank you very much." I sat up and
put my clothes back on. The surgeon had pictures of his wife and
kids on the wall. The whole family looked like it was in high
school, pretty and young. I stared at them and thought, *So?* I
slipped my shoes on, zipped up my fly, tried not to feel somehow
like a hooker.

This is why I was pleased: The lump was not simply a focal point for my self-pity; it was also a battery propelling me, strengthening me—my very own appointment with death. It anchored and deepened me like a secret. I started to feel it when I walked, just out from under my armpit—hard, achy evidence that I was truly a knotted saint, a bleeding angel. At last it had been confirmed: My life was really as difficult as I had always suspected. "It's true. It's there," I said to Gerard when I got home.

"Who's there?" he muttered, preoccupied and absent as a landlord. He was singing the part of Aeneas in a local production of his own rock opera, and he was on his way downtown to shop for sandals "that sort of crawl up the leg."

"This is not a knock-knock joke, Gerard. The lump. The lump is there. It's now a certified lump."

"Oh," he said slowly, soft and bewildered. "Oh, baby."

I bought big stretchy bras—one size fits all, catches all, ropes all in and presses all against you. I started to think of myself as more than one organism: a symbiotic system, like a rhino and an oxpecker, or a gorgonzola cheese.

Gerard and I lived across the hall from one another. Together we had the entire top floor of a small red house on Marini Street. We could prop the doors open with bricks and sort of float back and forth between our two apartments, and although most of the time we would agree that we were living together, other times I knew it wasn't the same. He had moved to Marini Street after I'd been there three years, his way of appeasing my desire to discuss our future. At that point we'd been lovers for nineteen months. The year before he'd unilaterally decided to go on living on the other side of town, in a large "apartment in the forest." (He called my place "the cottage in the city.") It was too expensive, but, he said, all wise sparkle, "far enough away to be lovely," though I never knew what he thought was lovely at that distance —himself or me or the apartment. Perhaps it was the view. Gerard, I was afraid, liked the world best at a distance, as a photograph, as a memory. He liked to kiss me, nuzzle me, when I was scarcely awake and aware—corpse-like with the flu or struck dumb with fatigue. He liked having to chisel at some remove to get to me.

"He's a sexist pig," said Eleanor.

"Maybe he's just a latent necrophiliac," I said, realizing afterward that probably they were the same thing.

"Lust for dust," shrugged Eleanor. "Into a cold one after work."

So we never had the ritual of discussion, decision, and apartment hunting. It was simply that the Indian couple across the hall broke their lease and Gerard suddenly said during the Carson monologue one night, "Hey, maybe I'll move in there. It might be cheaper than the forest."

We had separate rents, separate kitchens, separate phone numbers, separate bathrooms with back-to-back toilets. Sometimes he'd knock on the wall and ask through the pipes how I was doing. "Fine, Gerard. Just fine."

"Great to hear," he'd say. And then we'd flush our toilets in unison.

"Kinky," said Eleanor.

"It's like parallel universes," I said. "It's like living in twin beds."

"It's like Delmar, Maryland, which is the same town as Delmar, Delaware."

"It's like living in twin beds," I said again.

"It's like the Borscht Belt," said Eleanor. "First you try it out in the Catskills before you move it to the big time."

"It's living flush up against rejection," I said.

"It's so like Gerard," said Eleanor. "That man lives across

the hall from his own fucking heart."

"He's a musician," I said doubtfully. Too often I made these sorts of excuses, like a Rumpelstiltskin of love, stickily spinning straw into gold.

"Please," cautioned Eleanor, pointing at her stomach. "Please, my B.L.T."

These are the words they used: *aspirate, mammogram, surgery, blockage, wait*. They first just wanted to wait and see if it was a temporary blockage of milk ducts.

"Milk Duds?" exclaimed Gerard.

"Ducks!" I shouted. "Milk ducks!"

If the lump didn't go away in a month, they would talk further, using the other three words. *Aspirate* sounded breathy and hopeful, I had always had aspirations; and *mammogram* sounded like a cute little nickname one gave a favorite grandmother. But the other words I didn't like. "*Wait?*" I asked, tense as a yellow light. "*Wait* and see if it goes away? I could have done that all on my own." The nurse-practitioner smiled. I liked her. She didn't attribute everything to "stress" or to my "personal life," a redundancy I was never fond of. "Maybe," she said. "But maybe not." Then the doctor handed me an appointment card and a prescription for sedatives.

There was this to be said for the sedatives: They helped you adjust to death better. It was difficult to pick up and move anywhere, let alone from life to death, without the necessary psychic equipment. That was why, I realized, persons in messy, unhappy situations had trouble getting out: Their strength ebbed; they simultaneously aged and regressed; they had no sedatives. They didn't know who they were, though they suspected they were the browning, on-sale hamburger of the parallel universe. Frightened of their own toes, they needed the bravery of sedatives. Which could make them look generously upon the skinny scrap of their life and deem it good, ensuring a calmer death. It was, after all, easier to leave something you truly, serenely loved than something you really and frantically didn't quite. A good dying was a matter of the right attitude. A healthy death, like anything—job promotions or looking younger—was simply a matter of "feeling good about yourself." Which is where the sedatives came in. Sedate as a mint, a woman could place a happy hand on the shoulder of death and rasp out, "Waddya say, buddy, wanna dance?"

Also, you could get chores done.

You could get groceries bought.

You could do laundry and fold.

Gerard's *Dido and Aeneas* was a rock version of the Purcell opera. I had never seen it. He didn't want me going to the rehearsals. He said he wanted to present the whole perfect show to me, at the end, like a gift. Sometimes I thought he might be falling in love with Dido, his leading lady, whose real name was Susan Fitzbaum.

"Have fun in Tunis," I'd say as he disappeared off to rehearsals. I liked to say *Tunis*. It sounded obscene, like a rarely glimpsed body part.

"Carthage, Benna. Carthage. Nice place to visit."

"Though you, of course, prefer Italy."

"For history? For laying down roots? Absolutely. Have you seen my keys?"

"Ha! The day you lay down roots . . ." But I couldn't think of how to finish it. "That'll be the day you lay down roots," I said.

"Why, my dear, do you think they called it *Rome*?" He grinned. I handed him his keys. They were under an *Opera News* I'd been using to thwack flies.

"Thank you for the keys," he smiled, and then he was off, down the stairs, a post-modern blur of battered leather jacket, sloppily shouldered canvas bag, and pantcuffs misironed into Möbius strips.

. . .

During rehearsal breaks he would phone. "Where do you want
to sleep tonight, your place or mine?"

"Mine," I said.

Surely he wasn't in love with Susan Fitzbaum. Surely she
wasn't in love with him.

Eleanor and I around this time founded The Quit-Calling-Me-
Shirley School of Comedy. It entailed the two of us meeting downtown for drinks and making despairing pronouncements about
life and love which always began, "But surely . . ." It entailed
what Eleanor called, "The Great White Whine": whiney white
people getting together over white wine and whining.

"Our sex life is disappearing," I would say. "Gerard goes to
the bathroom and I call it 'Shaking Hands with the Unemployed.'
Men hit thirty, I swear, and they want to make love twice a year,
like seals."

"We've got three more years of sexual peak," says Eleanor
crossing her eyes and pretending to strangle herself. "When's the
last time you guys made love?" She tried looking nonchalant. I
did my best. I sang, " 'January, February, June, or July,' " but
the waitress came over to take our orders and gave us hostile
looks. We liked to try to make her feel guilty by leaving large
tips.

"I'm feeling pre-menstrual," said Eleanor. "I was coerced
into writing grant proposals all day. I've decided that I hate all
short people, rich people, government officials, poets, and homo-
sexuals."

"Don't forget gypsies," I said.

"Gypsies!" she shrieked. "I despise gypsies!" She drank
chablis in a way that was part glee, part terror. It was always
quick. "Can you tell I'm trying to be happy?" she said.

Eleanor was part of a local grant-funded actor-poets group

which did dramatic and often beautiful readings of poems written by famous dead people. My favorites were Eleanor's Romeo soliloquies, though she did a wonderful "Stopping by Woods on a Snowy Evening." I was a crummy dancer with no discipline and a scorn for all forms of dance-exercise who went from one aerobics job to the next, trying to convince students I loved it. ("Living, acting, occurring in the presence of oxygen!" I would explain with concocted exuberance. At least I didn't say things like "Tighten the bun to intensify the stretch!" or "Come on, girls, bods up.") I had just left a job in a health club and had been hired at Fitch-ville's Community School of the Arts to teach a class of senior citizens. Geriatric aerobics.

"Don't you feel that way about dancing?" Eleanor asked. "I mean, I'd love to try to write and read something of *mine*, but why bother. I finally came to that realization last summer reading Hart Crane in an inner tube in the middle of the lake. Now there's a poet."

"There's a poet who could have used an inner tube. Don't be so hard on yourself." Eleanor was smart, over-thirty, over-weight, and had never had a serious boyfriend. She was the daughter of a doctor who still sent her money. She took our mutual mediocrity harder than I did. "You shouldn't let yourself be made so miserable," I attempted.

"I don't have those pills," said Eleanor. "Where do you get those pills?"

"I think what you *do* do in the community is absolutely joyous. You make people happy."

"Thank you, Miss Hallmark Hall of Obscurity."

"Sorry," I said.

"You know what poetry is about?" said Eleanor. "The impossibility of sexual love. Poets finally don't even want genitals, their own or anyone else's. A poet wants metaphors, patterns, some ersatz physics of love. For a poet, to love is to have no lover.

And to live"—she raised her wine glass and failed to suppress a smile—"is to have no liver."

Basically, I realized, I was living in that awful stage of life from the age of twenty-six to thirty-seven known as *stupidity*. It's when you don't know anything, not even as much as you did when you were younger, and you don't even have a philosophy about all the things you don't know, the way you did when you were twenty or would again when you were thirty-eight. Nonetheless you tried things out: "Love is the cultural exchange program of futility and eroticism," I said. And Eleanor would say, "Oh, how cynical can you get," meaning not nearly cynical enough. I had made it sound dreadful but somehow fair, like a sleepaway camp. "Being in love with Gerard is like sleeping in the middle of the freeway," I tried.

"Thatta girl," said Eleanor. "Much better."

On the community school's application form, where it had asked "Are you married?" (this was optional information), I had written an emphatic "*No*" and next to it, where it asked "To whom?" I'd written "A guy named Gerard." My class of senior citizens somehow found out about it and once classes got under way, they smiled, shook their heads, and teased me. "A good-humored girl like you," was the retrograde gist, "and no husband!"

Classes were held at night on the third floor of the arts school, which was a big Victorian house on the edge of downtown. The dance studio was creaky and the mirrors were nightmares, like aluminum foil slapped on walls. I did what I could. "Tuck, lift, flex, repeat. Tuck, lift, flex, now knee-slap lunge." I had ten women in their sixties and a man named Barney who was seventy-three. "That's it, Barney," I would shout. "Pick it up now," though I didn't usually mean the tempo: Barney had a hearing aid which kept clacking to the floor mid-routine. After class he would linger and try to chat—apologize for the hearing aid or tell me loud stories about his sister Zenia, who was all of eighty-one and mobile, apparently, as a bug. "So you and your sister, you're pretty close?" I asked once, putting away the cassettes.

"Close!?" he hooted, and then took out his wallet and showed me a picture of Zenia in Majorca in a yellow bathing suit. He had never married, he said.

The women mothered me. They clustered around me after class and suggested different things I should be doing in order to get a husband. The big one was frosting my hair. "Don't you think so, Lodeme? Shouldn't Benna frost her hair?" Lodeme was more or less the ringleader, had the nattiest leotard (lavender and navy stripes), was in great shape, could hold a V-sit for minutes, and strove incessantly for a tough, grizzly wisdom. "First the hair, then the heart," bellowed Lodeme. "Frost your heart, then you'll be okay. No one falls in love with a good man. Right, Barn?" Then she'd chuck him on the arm and his hearing aid would fall out. After class I would take a sedative.

There was a period where I kept trying to make anagrams out of words that weren't anagrams: *moonscape* and *menopause*; *gutless* and *guilts*; *lovesick* and *evil louse*. I would meet Eleanor either for a drink at our Shirley School meetings or for breakfast at Hank's Grill, and if I got there first, I would scribble the words over and over again on a napkin, trying to make them fit—like a child dividing three into two, not able to make it go.

"Howdy," I said to Eleanor when she arrived and flopped down. I had *lovesick* and *evil sock* scrawled in large letters.

"You're losing it, Benna. It must be your love life." Eleanor leaned over and wrote *bedroom* and *boredom*; she had always been the smarter one. "Order the tomato juice," she said. "That's how you get rid of the smell of skunk."

. . .

Gerard was a large, green-eyed man who smelled like baby powder and who was preoccupied with great music. I'd lie there in bed explaining something terrible and personal and he'd interrupt with, "That's like Brahms. You're like Brahms." And I'd say, "What do you mean, I'm old and fat with a beard?" And Gerard would smile and say, "Exactly." Once, after I'd shared with him the various humiliations of my adolescence, he said, "That's kind of like Stravinsky."

And I said, annoyed, "What, he didn't get his period until the ninth grade? At least it's consoling to know that everything that's happened to me has also happened to a famous composer."

"You don't really like music, do you?" said Gerard.

Actually, I loved music. Sometimes I think that's the reason I fell in love with Gerard to begin with. Perhaps it had nothing to do really with the smell of his skin or the huge stretch of his legs or the particular rhythm of his words (a prairie reggae, he called it), but only to do with the fact that he could play any instrument that had strings—piano, banjo, cello—that he composed rock operas and tone poems, that he sang pop and lieder. I was surrounded by music. If I was reading a newspaper, he would listen to Mozart. If I was watching the news, he'd put on *Madame Butterfly*, saying it amounted to the same thing, Americans romping around in countries they didn't belong in. I had only to step across the moat of the hallway and I would learn something: Vivaldi was a red-haired priest; Schumann crippled his hand with a hand extender; Brahms never married, that was the biggie, the one Gerard liked best to tell me. "Okay, okay," I would say. Or sometimes simply, "So?"

Before I met Gerard, everything I knew about classical music I'd gleaned off the sound track record of *The Turning Point*. Now, however, I could hum Musetta's Waltz for at least three bars. Now I owned all of Beethoven's piano concertos. Now I knew that Percy Grainger had been married in the Hollywood Bowl. "But Brahms," said Gerard, "now Brahms never married."

It's not that I wanted to be married. It's that I wanted a Marriage Equivalent, although I never knew exactly what that was, and often suspected that there was really no such thing. Yet I was convinced there had to be something better than the lonely farce living across town or hall could, with very little time, become.

Which made me feel guilty and bourgeois. So I comforted myself with Gerard's faults: He was infantile; he always lost his keys; he was from Nebraska, like some horrible talk show host; he had grown up not far from one of the oldest service plazas on I-80; he told jokes that had the words *wiener* and *fart* in them; he once referred to sex as "hiding the salami." He also had a habit of charging after small animals and frightening them. Actually, the first time he did this it was with a bird in the park, and I laughed, thinking it hilarious. Later, I realized it was weird: Gerard was thirty-one and charging after small mammals, sending them leaping into bushes, up trees, over furniture. He would then turn and grin, like a charmed maniac, a Puck with a Master's degree. He liked also to water down the face and neck fur of cats and dogs, smoothing it back with his palms, like a hairdresser, saying it made them look like Judy Garland. I realized that life was too short for anyone honestly and thoroughly to outgrow anything, but it was clear that some people were making more of an effort than others.

In my early twenties I got annoyed with women who complained that men were shallow and incapable of commitment. "Men, women, they're all the same," I said. "Some women are capable of commitment, some are not. Some men are capable of commitment and some are not. It's not a matter of gender." Then I met Gerard, and I began to believe that men were shallow and incapable of commitment.

"It's not that men *fear* intimacy," I said to Eleanor. "It's that they're hypochondriacs of intimacy: They always think they have it when they don't. Gerard thinks we're very close but half the time he's talking to me like he met me forty-five minutes ago, telling me things about himself I've known for years, and asking me questions about myself that he should know the answers to already. Last night he asked me what my middle name was. God, I can't talk about it."

Eleanor stared. "What *is* your middle name?"

I stared back. "Ruth," I said. "Ruth." Hers, I knew, was Elizabeth.

Eleanor nodded and looked away. "When I was in Catholic school," she said, "I loved the story of St. Clare and St. Francis. Francis gets canonized because of his devotion to vague, general ideas like God and Christianity, whereas Clare gets canonized because of her devotion to Francis. You see? It sums it up: Even when a man's a saint, even when he's good and devoted, he's not good and devoted to anyone in particular." Eleanor lit a Viceroy. "Why are we supposed to be with men, anyway? I feel like I used to know."

"We need them for their Phillips-head screwdrivers," I said.

Eleanor raised her eyebrows. "That's right," she said, "I keep forgetting you only go out with circumcised men."

Gerard's and my courtship had consisted of Sunday chamber music, rock concerts, and driving out into the cornfields surrounding Fitchville to sing "I Loves You, Porgy," loud and misremembered, up at the sky. Then we'd come back to my apartment, lift off each other's clothes, and stick our tongues in each other's ears. In the morning we'd go to a coffee shop. "You're not Czechoslovakian, I hope," he would say, always the same joke, and point to the sign on the cash register which said, SORRY, NO CHECKS.

"He'd look great, legless and propped in a cart," said Eleanor.

Actually Eleanor was pleasant when he was around. Even flirtatious. Sometimes they talked on the phone: He asked her questions about *The Aeneid*. I liked to see them get along. Later he would say to me in a swoon of originality, "Eleanor would be beautiful if she only lost weight."

"It's in the wing of your breast," said the surgeon.

I hadn't known breasts had wings, and now I had something waiting in them. "Oh," I said.

"Let's assume for now that it's cystic," said the surgeon. "Let's not immediately disfigure the breast."

"Yes," I said. "Let's not."

And then the nurse-practitioner told me that if I had a child it might straighten out my internal machinery a bit. Prevent "Career Women's Diseases." Lumps often disappear during pregnancy. "Can I extend my prescription on the sedatives?" I asked. With each menstrual cycle, she went on to explain, the body is like a battered boxer, staggering back from its corner into the ring, and as the years go by, the body does this with increasing difficulty. Its will gets broken. It screws up. A woman's body is so busy preparing to make babies that every year that goes by without one is another year of rejection that is harder and harder for it to recover from. Soon it could go completely crazy.

I suspected it was talk like this that had gotten women out of the factories and started immediately on the baby boom. "Thank you," I said. "I'll think about it."

One problem with teaching aerobics was that I didn't like Jane Fonda. I felt she was a fickle, camera-wise, overconfident half-heart who had become rich and famous taking commercial advantage of America's spiritual crises. And she had done it with such self-assurance. "You just want people to be less convinced of themselves," said Gerard.

"Yes, I do," I said. "I think a few well-considered and

prominently displayed uncertainties are always in order." And uncertainty and fuzziness were certainly my mirrors then.

Barney adored Jane Fonda. "That woman," Barney'd say to me after class. "You know, she used to be just one of those sex queens. Now she's helping America."

"You mean helping herself to America." Oddly enough Jane Fonda was one of the few things in the world I did feel certain about, and she made me prone to such uncharacteristically bald pronouncements. I should beware of such baldness, I thought. I should think hedge, think fuzz, like the rest of my life.

"Aw go on," said Barney, and then he filled me in on the latest regarding Zenia, who was chairing a League of Women Voters committee on child abuse.

I packed up my tape deck, took a sedative at the urinal-like water fountain in the hall, trudged downstairs and home. I went into Gerard's apartment and spread out on his bed, to wait for him to come home from work. I looked at a black and white print he had on the wall opposite the bed. Close up it was a landscape, a dreamily etched lake, tree, and mountain scene, but from far away it was a ghoulish face, vacant and gouged like a tragedy mask. And from where I was, neither close nor far, I could see both lake and face, one melting into the other and then back again, competing for my perception until finally I just closed my eyes, tight so as to see colors.

Loving Gerard, I realized, was like owning a tomcat, or having a teenaged son. He was out five nights a week and in the day was sleepy and hungry and sprawled, eating a lot of cold cereal and leaving the bowls around. Rehearsals for *Dido and Aeneas* were growing more frequent, and on other nights he was playing solo jazz gigs in town, mostly at fern bars (one was called The Smokey Fern) with four-armed ceiling fans torpid as winter insects, and ferns that were spidery and crisp. He played guitar on a platform up front, and there was always a group of women at a ringside table who giggled, applauded adoringly, and bought him drinks. When I went out to see him at gigs, I would come in and sit alone at a table way in the back. I felt like a stray groupie, a devoted next-door neighbor. He would come talk to me on his breaks, but he talked to almost everybody who was there. Everyone got equal time, equal access. He was public. He was no longer mine. I felt foolish and phobic. I felt spermicidal. I drank and smoked too much. I started staying home. I would do things like watch science specials and Bible movies on TV: Stacy Keach as Barabbas, Rod Steiger as Pontius Pilate, James Farentino as Simon Peter. My body became increasingly strange to me. I became very aware of its edges as I peered out from it: my shoulders, hands, strands of hair, invading the boundaries of my vision like branches that are made to jut into the camera's view to decorate and sentimentalize the picture. *The sea turtles' need to lay eggs on land,* said the television, *makes them vulnerable.*

Only once, and very late at night, did I run downstairs and out into the street with my pajamas on, gasping and watering, waiting for something—a car? an angel?—to come rescue or kill me, but there was nothing, only streetlights and a cat.

At The Shirley School we wondered aloud about male hunters and female nesters. "Do you think there's something after all to this male-as-wanderer stuff?" I asked Eleanor.

She made something of a speech. She said she could buy the social diagram of woman as nestmaker (large, round, *see* ovum) and man as wanderer, invader, traveler in gangs (*see* spermatozoa), but that if she were minding the fort, she wanted some guests, a charging, grinning cavalry. Her life was misaligned, she said. The cavalry bypassed her altogether, as if the roadmaps were faulty, and she was forced to holler after them, "Hey, where's everybody going?" Or a few deserters managed to stroll by, but then mostly just sat on the curb to talk about how difficult it was to save money nowadays. Her D.N.A. was in danger of extinction. What lovers she'd had had always depressed her. She preferred being with friends.

"Sex used to console me," I said. "It was my anti-coma coma."

Eleanor shrugged, gulped vermouth. She liked to yell out her car window at couples holding hands on the street. "Cut it out! Just cut it out!"

"How's Gerard?" she said.

"I don't think he loves me anymore." I bit my fist in mock melodrama.

"Give that man a mustache to twirl and a girl to tie down to the railroad tracks. Look, you're going to be fine. You're going to end up with Perry." Perry was a man she'd invented for my future. He was from Harvard, loved children, and believed in Marriage Equivalents. The only problem was that he was an epileptic and had had fits at two consecutive dinner parties. "Me," said Eleanor, "I'll probably end up with some guy named Opie who collects Pinocchio memorabilia and says things like 'Holy-moley-pole.' He'll want me to dress up in sailor suits."

In the senior citizens' class it was hard to concentrate. One of the women there, Pat, had stained and streaked her legs orange with Q-T or something. Barney kept having trouble with his hearing aid. Lodeme spent a lot of time in the back row taking everyone's pulse the way I had shown them: two fingers placed on the side of the neck. "Holy Jesus," she shouted at them. "You must be hibernating!"

This was my fear: that someone would have a stroke in there and die.

"Okay," I said. "Let's begin with the 'Dance Madness' routine. Remember: It's important not to be afraid of looking like an idiot." This was my motto in life. I slapped in the cassette and started up with some easy lunges, step-digs, and a slow Charleston.

"Are we healthy yet?" yelled Pat over the music, her legs like sepia sunsets, her face the split-apple face of an owl. "Are we healthy *yet*?"

"Let me feel your breast again," said Gerard. "Is this the lump?"

"Yes," I said. "Be careful."

"It's not muscular?" His fingers pressed against the outside wall of my breast.

"No, Gerard. It's not muscular. It's floating like fruit in Jell-O. Remember fruited Jell-O? There's no muscle in Jell-O." Although of course there was. I'd learned that long ago from a friend in junior high school who'd told me that Jell-O was made from horses' hooves and various dried bones and muscles. She had also told me that breasts were simply displaced buttocks.

Gerard slipped his hand back out from beneath my bra. He leaned back into the sofa. We were listening to Fauré. "Listen to the strings," Gerard murmured, and his face went beatific. The world, all matter, I knew, was made up of strings. I had learned this on television. Physicists used to believe that the universe was made up of particles. But recently they had found out they'd been wrong: The world, unsuspectedly, was made up of little tiny strings.

"Yes," I said. "They're lovely."

The women in the class were suggesting that I get my face sanded. I had had acne as a teenager, a rough slice of pizza face, and it had scarred my skin. Gerard had once said he loved my skin, that it didn't look pitted and old, but that it looked sexy, a tough, craggy sexy.

I sunk into one hip and fluttered my eyelashes at Betty and

Pat and Lodeme. "Gee, I thought my face looked sort of scrappy,"
I said.

"You look like a caveman," said Lodeme, her voice half
gravel, half gavel. "Get your face sanded."

In bed I tried to be simple and straightforward. "Gerard, I need
to know this: Do you love me?"

"I love being with you," he said, as if this were even
better.

"Oh," I said. And then he reached for my hand under the
covers, lifted his head toward mine, and kissed me, his lips
outside then inside, back and forth like polyps. The heel of
his hand ran up my side beneath my nightgown, and he moved
me, belly up, on top of him. His penis was soft against my buttocks and his arms were clasped tight around my waist. I didn't
know what I was supposed to do, offered up to the ceiling like
that. So I just lay there and let Gerard figure things out. He lay
very still beneath me. I whispered finally: "What are we supposed
to be doing, Gerard?"

"You don't understand me," he sighed. "You just don't
understand me at all."

The senior citizens' class was only eight weeks in duration but by
about the sixth week the smallness of the class, and whatever
makeshift intimacy had sprung up there, became suddenly oppressive to me. Perhaps I was becoming like Gerard. Suddenly I
wanted the big, doughnut-faced anonymity of a large class, where
class members did not really have faces and names and problems.
In six weeks with Susan, Lodeme, Betty, Valerie, Ellen, Frances,
Pat, Marie, Bridget, and Barney, I felt we'd gotten to know each
other too well, or rather, brought to the stubborn limits of our
knowability, we were now left with the jagged scrape of our differences, our unknowability laid glisteningly bare. I developed a

woodlands metaphor—"swirls before pine," I told Eleanor. Aerobics in front of a forest took much less courage than the other way around, aerobics before a few individuated trees. A forest would leave you alone, but trees could come at you. They witnessed things. When you could see them, they could see you. They could see there were certain things about you. You were not a serious person. You were not a serious dancer. I didn't want my life to show. At a distance, I was sure, it couldn't possibly.

Moreover, it was hard being close to these women who, I realized, had exactly what I wanted: grandchildren, stability, a post-menopausal grace, some mysterious, hard-won truce with men. They had, finally, the only thing anyone really wants in life: someone to hold your hand when you die.

And so the sadnesses started to ricochet around and zap me right in the heart, right in the middle of the Michael Jackson tape. I was, I knew, unconvinced of myself. I wanted to stop. I wanted to fall dead as a leaf. Which I tried to turn into a move for the rest of the class: "One-two and crumple, one-two and crumple." Once in Modern Dance class in college one sunny September afternoon we had been requested to be leaves tumbling ourselves across the arts quad. I knew how to perform it in a way that prevented embarrassment and indignity: One became a dead leaf, a cement leaf. One lay down on the dying grass of the arts quad and refused to blow and float and tumble. One merely crumpled. One was no fool. One did not listen to the teacher. One did not want to be spotted fluttering around on campus, like the others who were clearly psychotics. One did not like this college. One wanted only to fall in love and get a Marriage Equivalent. One just lay there.

I looked up into the mirror. Behind me Lodeme, Bridget, Pat, Barney, everyone was stiffly though obediently crumpling. I loved them, in a way, but I didn't want them, their nippled fist-faces, their beauty advice, their voices old, low, and scratchy. I wanted them to recede into some lifeless blur. I didn't want to hear about Zenia or about how I could use a good pair of hips. I didn't want to be responsible for their hearts.

We got back up on our tiptoes. "Good! Good! Punch the air, three-four. Punch the air." In the mirror we looked as if we had melted—puddles that shimmered and shimmied.

Afterward, Barney came up and told me more about Zenia. I tried to be minimally attentive, packing up the cassettes, waving good night to the other women who were leaving. Barney's voice seemed to have a new sort of gobble and snort. "I saw a program on child abuse," he was saying, "and now I realize I was an abused child myself, though I didn't know it." I looked at him and he smiled and shook his head. I didn't want to hear this. Christ, I thought. "My sister Zenia was fourteen and I was six and she climbed into bed with me once and we didn't know no better. But technically that's abuse, that. And funny thing is is that I . . ." He wanted badly to be telling someone this. He followed me around the studio as I switched off lights and locked windows. "I never would have watched that show but for the committee she's heading. She's my sister, I've got to love her, but—"

"No you don't," I snapped at the old man. The world was a carnival of fiends and Zenia was right in there with everyone else. "Good night, Barney," I said, locking the studio door and leaving him standing at the top of the stairs. "Good night," he mumbled, not moving. I did a fast bounce down the three flights, the cassettes rattling in my bag, out into the cool drink of the night. If only this were some other city, I would go exploring in it! If only this were someplace, if there were someplace, new in the world.

In a single week four things happened: Barney stopped coming to class; Gerard announced he was thinking of spending a year in Europe on a special fellowship ("Sounds like a good opportunity,"

I said, trying to keep my voice out of his way, like a mother); I got a letter from a friend asking me if I wanted to come to New York and work in a health club that she and her husband were partners in; I did a home-kit pregnancy test, which came out positive. I tried to recall when last Gerard and I had even made love. I double-checked the kit. I re-read the instructions. I waited, hopelessly, as I had in the ninth grade, for my period to come like a magic trick.

"New York, eh?" said Eleanor.

"I'd be teaching yuppies," I complained. Despite our various ways of resembling yuppies (Eleanor was a wine snob, and I owned too many pairs of sneakers), we hated yuppies. We hated the word *yuppie*, though we used it. Eleanor would walk down the street looking at people she passed and deciding whether or not they qualified for this ignominy. "Yup, yup, nope," she would say out loud, as in a game of Duck, Duck, Goose. Yuppies, we knew, were greedy, shallow, and small. They made their own pasta. They would rather play racquetball than read *Middlemarch*. "Go home and read *Middlemarch*," Eleanor once shouted at a pastel jogger, who glanced sideways to see Eleanor and me zipping by in Eleanor's car. We renamed the seven dwarves: Artsy, Fartsy, Cranky, Sleazy, Beasty, Dud, and Yuppie.

"Well," said Eleanor, "if you're in New York, it's either yuppies or mimes. That's all New York's got. Yuppies or mimes."

I loved *Dido and Aeneas*. It had electric guitars, electric pianos, Aeneas in leather and Dido in blue sequins, sexily metallic as a disco queen. The whole thing resembled MTV, replete with loud guitar solos. Aeneas shouldered his guitar and riffed and whined after Dido throughout the whole show: "Don't you see why I have to go to Europe? / I must ignore the sentiment you stir up." Actually it was awful. But nonetheless I sniffled at her suicide, and when she sang at Aeneas, "Just go then! Go if you must! /

My heart will surely turn to dust," and Aeneas indeed left, I sat in my seat, thinking, "You ass, Aeneas, you don't have to be so literal." Eleanor, sitting next to me, nudged me and whispered, "Shirley's gonna turn her heart to dust."

"I doubt it will be Shirley," I said.

Gerard, as Aeneas and director, got a standing ovation and a long-stemmed rose. In my mind I gave Dido a handful of tiger lilies, a bouquet of floral gargoyles.

Afterward, Eleanor had to go home and nurse a headache, so I went backstage and shook hands with Susan Fitzbaum. She was out of her sparkles and crown. She was wearing a plaid skirt and loafers. She had a large head. "So nice to meet you," she said in a low, tired voice.

I kissed Gerard. He seemed anxious to go. "I need a beer," he said. "The cast party's not until midnight. Let's go and come back."

In the car he said, "So what did you *really* think?" and I told him the show was terrific, but he didn't necessarily have to leave someone just because they told him to, and he smiled and said, "Thanks," and kissed my temple and then I told him I was pregnant and what did he think we should do.

We sat for a long time in a nearby bar with our fingers drawing grids and diagonals in the frost of the beer glasses. "I'm going back to the cast party," Gerard eventually said. "You don't have to go if you don't want to." He got up and put down cash for half the check.

"No, I'll go," I said. "If you want me to."

"It's not that I want you to or don't want you to. It's up to you."

"Well, it would be nice if you wanted me to. I mean, I don't want to go if you don't want me to."

"It's up to you," he said. His eyes were knobby, like knuckles.

"I get the feeling you don't want me to go."

"It's up to you! Look, if you think you'll have things to say at a party full of music-types, fine. I mean, I'm a musician, and sometimes even I have trouble."

"You don't want me to go. Okay, I won't go."

"Benna, it's not that. Come along if you—"

"Never mind," I said. "Never mind, Gerard." I drove him to the cast party and then drove home, where I got into my pajamas and in my own apartment listened to the sound track from *The Turning Point*, an album, I realized, I had always loved.

There was one main reason I didn't tell Eleanor I was pregnant, although once, when we both had gone into the ladies' room together, a not unusual occurrence of synchronized plumbing which allowed chit-chat between the stalls, I almost told her anyway. I attempted it. I stared at the crotch of my underwear and said, "You know, I think I'm pregnant." There was no response, so when I was finished, I stepped out, washed my hands slowly, and then just said to the feet in Eleanor's stall, "Welp, see you out in the real world." I looked in the mirror; the glare and precision of it startled me. I had that old look: that look where you look—old. When I got back to our table, Eleanor was already sitting there lighting one of my Winstons. "You took a long time," she said.

"Oh, my god," I laughed. "I just confessed my entire life story to someone in black boots."

"I would never wear black boots," said Eleanor.

Which was some residual thing, she said, having to do with Catholic school. Which was why I never finally told her about the pregnancy: She still had weird, unresolved strings to Catholicism. She was sentimental about it. She once told me about a frugal, lapsed Catholic aunt of hers who, when she died, left two large, mysterious boxes in her attic, one full of various marital and contraceptive devices, and one labeled "Strings Too Short to Use," which was a huge collection of small pieces of string, multicolored and inexplicable, matted together in large coils and nests. *That*, I realized, was both Eleanor's and her aunt's relationship to Catholicism: ties too short to bind and therefore stowed away in a huge and secret box. But Eleanor clearly liked to lug her box around, display her ties like a traveling waresperson.

"You can't really be a fallen Protestant," she said. "How can there be any guilt?"

"There can be guilt," I said. "It's my piety, I can cry if I want to."

"But being a fallen Catholic—that's skydiving! Being a fallen Protestant—that's like mugging an old lady, so easy why bother."

"Yeah, but think how awful you'd feel after you'd mugged an old lady."

Eleanor shrugged. She liked lapsed Catholics; I think the only reason she managed to like Gerard at all was that they both had been Catholics. Sometimes when Gerard got on the phone to ask her things about Virgil, they would end up talking about Dante and then about nuns they'd known in Catholic school. They'd both attended parochial schools called The Assumption School, where, they said, they had learned to assume many things. More than once I sat at Gerard's kitchen table and listened while he talked on the phone with Eleanor, uproarious and slap-happy, exchanging priest stories. I had never known a priest. But it was curious and lovely to see Gerard so taken up by his own childhood, so communed via anecdotes with Eleanor, so pleased with his own escape into an adulthood that allowed him these survivor's jokes, that I would sit there, floating and transfixed as a moon, laughing along with him, with them, even though I didn't really know what the two of them were talking about.

"I've made an appointment," I said to Gerard.

We were in my apartment. He thought he might have left his keys there.

"Christ, Benna," he said. "You stare at me with those cow eyes of yours—what am I supposed to say? I've got to go off to a gig in a half hour and you say, 'I've made an appointment.' It's like what you did the night of the cast party: cow eyes and then 'I think I'm pregnant.'"

"I just thought you'd want to know." I kept thinking of that horrible saying mothers tell you about getting the milk and buying the cow.

"You make me feel like I'm in a tiny store and all I want to do is relax, look, and enjoy, but because I'm the only potential customer there, you keep coming over and pressuring me."

"I don't pressure you," I said. I have a lump in my breast, I wanted to say but didn't. Maybe I will die.

"Yes, you do. You're like one of those ladies that just keeps coming over to say, 'Can I help you?'"

I stared at his square chin, his impossibly handsome unshaven chin and then I looked off at the Mary Cassatt print on the wall, mother bathing child, why did I own such a thing, and it was at that moment I really truly understood that he was in love with Susan Fitzbaum.

Things, however, rarely happened the way you understood them. Mostly they just sort of drove up alongside what you thought was the case and then moved randomly down some other way.

Gerard kept repeating himself. "You're like one of those ladies that just keeps coming up to you—'Can I help you, this is nice, let me know'—over and over and over. You won't leave me the hell alone."

I thought about this. Finally I said very quietly, "But you're *in* the store, Gerard. If you don't like it, get out of the goddamn store."

Gerard picked up a magazine and hurled it across the room; then, without looking further for his keys, he left early for his gig at The Smokey Fern.

I was not large enough for Gerard. I was small, lumpy, anchored with worry, imploded. He didn't want me, he wanted Macy's; like Aeneas or Ulysses, he wanted the anonymity and freedom to wander purchaseless from island to island. I could not be enough of the world for him. A woman could never be enough of the world, I thought, though that was what a man desired of her, though she flap her arms frantically trying.

Eleanor had said she was staying home to watch *The Sound of Music*, so I stayed in and read the abortion chapter in my women's health book. On TV I watched a nature documentary. It was on animal species who, due to a change in the landscape, begin to produce unviable eggs, or are chased into the hills.

I wandered into Gerard's apartment and fetched back some of my stuff that had ended up there: shoes, dishes, magazines, silverware. It was like some principle of physics: Things flowed naturally back and forth between the two apartments until the maximum level of chaos was reached. I had his can opener, but he had my ice-cube trays. It was as if our possessions were embarked upon some osmotic, conjugal exchange, a giant french kiss of personal effects, which had somehow left us behind.

On Monday I met Eleanor for breakfast at Hank's. I wanted to discuss hopeful things: the job in New York, how she might feel about coming with me. Perhaps she could start up a reading group there. I would promise not to die of Globner's Disease.

"We should stop smoking cigarettes. Do you wanna stop smoking cigarettes?" said Eleanor as soon as I sat down.

Despite my degenerating health, I enjoyed them too much. They were sororal. "But they're so cysterly," I said, and stuck out a breast. No idiocy was too undignified for me. I might as well have sat in a corner and applied Winstons directly to my lymph nodes, laughing and telling terrible jokes.

Eleanor's mouth formed a small, tough segment of a smile. "I have something to tell you, Benna."

Something to do with *cysterly;* I said, "What?"

"Benna, I asked Gerard to go to bed with me."

I was still smiling, inappropriately, and my breast was still stuck out a bit. "So, when was this?" I said. I pulled back my breast, realigned my torso. Something between us had suddenly gone pale and gray, like a small piece of meat one dislodges hours late from between the teeth. I lit up a cigarette.

"Saturday night." Eleanor's face looked arranged in anxiety, the same face she used when reading Romeo's speech to the County Paris he's just killed: *O, give me thy hand / One writ with me in sour misfortune's book.* She looked pink and beseeching, though essentially she looked the same, as people do despite the fact they have begun to turn into monsters and are about to tell you something that should require horns or fangs or vaulted eyebrows but never apparently does.

"I thought you said you were staying in to watch *The Sound of Music*," I said in the same voice I always used when blowing cigarette smoke out my nostrils.

"I, uh, ended up not doing that. I went to see Gerard play instead. He said you'd had a fight, Benna."

And suddenly I knew this was only a half-truth. Suddenly I knew there'd been more than this. That there always had been.

"Benna, I thought at first we were kidding," she continued. She kept saying my name. "I sat down next to him and said, 'Hey, let's ruin a beautiful friendship—' "

"You hated each other," I insisted.

"—and he said, 'Sure why not?' and Benna, I'm convinced he thought at first he was kidding . . ."

Kidding? That was what my Mary Cassatt print was a picture of. A woman with kids.

"Benna, I'm sure it's not . . ."

Eleanor's skin was smooth and poreless. Her hair was frosted
golden like some expensive, marbley wood. I wanted her to stop
saying my name.

"But you didn't actually sleep together, did you?" I asked,
though it sounded pathetic, like a tiny Hans Christian Andersen
character.

Eleanor stared at me. Her eyes started to fill with water. She
felt sorry for me. She felt sorry for herself. I could feel my heart
wither like a hand. I could feel the lump in my breast rise into my
throat, from where perhaps it had fallen to begin with.

"Oh, Benna, he's such a shit." They did hate each other.
That was why she was telling me this: We all hated each other.
"I'm so sorry, Benna. He's such a shit. I knew he would never
tell you."

She was fat. She didn't know anything about music. She was
a child. She still received money from her parents in Doc Country. *No animal is as problematic in captivity as the elephant*, I
thought meanly, like an aerobics teacher who watches too much
PBS. *Every year around the world at least one zookeeper is killed.*

Something in Eleanor now began crumbling and biting.
"How long do you think I could have been a sounding board for
the two of you, Benna?"

This was horrible. This was the sort of thing you read about
in magazine advice columns. *O, give my thy hand / One writ with
me in sour Ms. Fortune's book.*

". . . I deserved a love affair, and instead I was spending all
of my time being envious of you. And you never noticed me. You
never even noticed I'd lost weight." She knew nothing about
music. She knew none of the pieces from *The Turning Point*.

"Don't you see, sisterhood has to be redefined," she was saying. "There are too few men in the world. It's a heterosexual depression out there!"

What I finally managed to say, looking at the Heimlich Maneuver poster, was, "So, is this what's called *sociobiology?*" She smiled weakly, hopefully, and I started to laugh, and then we were both laughing, teary-eyed, our faces falling into our arms on the table, and that's when I took the ketchup bottle and cracked it over her head. And then I got up and wobbled out, my soul numb as a crossed leg, and Hank yelled something at me in Greek and rushed out from behind the counter over to Eleanor who was sobbing loudly and would probably need stitches.

For nine days Gerard and I didn't speak to each other. Through the walls I could hear him entering and exiting his apartment, and presumably he could hear me, but we didn't speak. On the very first day I had refused to answer his knock.

I went out at night to all the really bad movies in Fitchville and just sat there. Sometimes I brought a book and a flashlight.

I missed him. Love, I realized, was something your spine memorized. There was nothing you could do about that.

From across the hall I could hear Gerard's phone ring, and I would listen and wait for him to pick it up and speak into it. The words were always muffled. Sometimes I could hear him laugh, as if he were quite ready to be happy again. A few times when he stayed out all night, his phone rang until three in the morning.

I stopped taking sedatives. The days were all false, warm-gray. Monoxide days. Dirty bathmat. Shoe sole. When I went downtown the stores all bled together like wet magazines. There was a noise in the air that changed with the wind and that could have been music, or roaring, or the voices of children. People were looking up into the trees for something, and I looked up as well and saw what it was: Not far from Marini Street thousands of dark birds had landed, descended from their neat, purposeful geometry into the mess of the neighborhood, scattered their troubled squawking throughout trees and on rooftops, looking the rainbowy, shadowy black of an oil spill. There were scientists, I knew, who did studies of such events, who claimed to discern patterns in such chaos. But this required distance and a study that took no account of any single particle in the mess. Particles were of no value. Up close was of no particular use.

From four blocks away I could see that the flock had a kind of group-life, a recognizable intelligence; no doubt in its random flutters there were patterns, but alone any one of those black birds would not have known what was up. Alone, as people live, they would crash their heads against walls.

I walked slowly, away from Marini Street, and understood this small shred: Between large and small, between near and far, there was no wisdom or truce to be had. To be near was to be blind; to be one among so many was to own no shape or say.

"There must be things that can save us!" I wanted to shout. "But they are just not here."

I got an abortion. Later I suffered from a brief heterosexual depression and had trouble teaching my class: I would inadvertently skip the number three when counting and would instead call out, "Front-two-four-five, Side-two-four-five." Actually that happened only once, but later, when I was living in New York, it seemed to make a funny story. ("Benna," said Gerard, the day I left. "Baby, I'm really sorry.")

Because of the pregnancy, the lump in my breast disappeared, retracted and absorbed, never to sprout again. "A night-blooming-not-so-serious," I said to the nurse-practitioner. She smiled. When she felt my breast, I wanted her to ask me out to dinner. There was a week in my life when she was the only person I really liked.

But I believed in starting over. There was finally, I knew, only rupture and hurt and falling short between all persons, but, Shirley, the best revenge was to turn your life into a small gathering of miracles.

If I could not be anchored and profound, I would try, at least, to be kind.

And so before I left, I phoned Barney and took him out for a drink. "You're a sweet girl," he said, loud as a sportscaster. "I've always thought that."

3

Yard Sale

THERE ARE, I'VE NOTICED, THOSE IN the world who are born salespeople. They know how to transact, how to dispose. They know how to charm their way all the way to the close, to the dump. Then they get in their cars and drive fast.

"Every time I move to a new place," Eleanor is saying, "I buy a new shower caddy. It gives me a nice sense of starting over." She smiles, big and pointed.

"I know what you mean," says Gerard, bending over in his lawn chair to tie a sneaker. We are in the side yard of the house, liquidating our affections, trading our lives in for cash: We are having a yard sale. Gerard straightens back up from his sneaker. His hair falls into his face, makes him look too young, then too handsome when he shakes it back. My heart hurts, spreads, folds over like an omelette.

It's two against one out here.

Eleanor is trying to sell her old shower caddy for a quarter, even though the mush of some horrible soap has dried to a green wax all over it. Eleanor is a good friend and has come to our yard sale this weekend with all of the mangy items she failed to sell in her own sale last weekend. I invited her to set up her own concession, but now I wonder if she's not desecrating our yard. Gerard and I are selling attractive things: a ten-speed bike, a cut-glass wine decanter, some rare jazz albums, healthy plants that need a healthy home, good wool sweaters, two antique ladderback chairs. Eleanor has brought over junk: foam rubber curlers with hairs stuck in them; a lavender lace teddy with a large, unsightly stain; two bags of fiberglass insulation; three seamed and greasy juice glasses, which came free with shrimp cocktail, and which Eleanor now wants to sell for seventy-five cents. She's also brought an entire crate of halter tops and an old sound track of *Thoroughly Modern Millie.* She spreads most of this out on one of the low tables Gerard and I have constructed from cement blocks and two old doors hauled from the shed out back. Magdalena, our dog, has a purple homemade price tag somehow stuck ("like a dingleberry," says the ever-young Gerard) to her rear end. She sniffs at the shrimp glasses and knocks one of them over. Gerard smooths her black coat, strokes her haunches, tells her to cool it. Eleanor once described Magdalena as a dog that looked exactly like a first-grader's drawing of a dog. Now, however, with her ornamented rear end, Magdalena looks a bit wrong—dressed up and gypsied, like a baby with pierced ears. Her backside says "45 cents." Magdalena has the carriage of a duchess. I've always thought that.

Eleanor places various articles of clothing—some skirts, a frayed jacket, the wounded teddy—in the branches of the birch trees next to us. Now we are truly a slum.

"That is just lovely, Eleanor," says Gerard, pointing to the birch trees. Magdalena has run over and started woofing up at Eleanor's clothes.

"Oh, go off and be a yuppie puppy," says Eleanor to the dog. Sometimes, like a spooky ventriloquism act, Eleanor assumes, and overassumes, my anger. Gerard is a tired lounge pianist who is leaving in two days to start law school in California. He is taking Magdalena. He is not taking me. He says he needs to make *Law Review* so he can get some wonderful job somewhere. Eleanor likes to define yuppies as people who buy the expensive mustard and the cheap ketchup, while the rest of the world gets it the other way around. "Gerard, you're too old to become a yuppie," she says, though she is wrong. Gerard is one year younger than Eleanor, and almost two years younger than I.

Eleanor strolls over with a paper bag and sits down. "A watershed moment!" she announces, and reaches into the bag and pulls out an opened box of Frost 'N' Tip for Brunettes Only and places it on the table next to my beautiful Chinese evergreen and my wine decanter, which my brother gave me; I'm willing to pawn more than I realized. "My entire past, right here, and I'm only asking a dime." Eleanor grins. She has recently rinsed her hair red. She and her husband, Kip, are moving in ten days to Fort Queen Anne, New York, where Kip got a better job, and Eleanor wanted to start over. "Dead town," she said, "but you can't beat the money with a stick."

I stare at the frost kit. The lettering is faded and there are coffee cup rings, like an Olympics insignia, on the front. "Eleanor," I say slowly. People walk by, look at the clothes in the trees, smile, and keep walking. I'm about to tell her her sense of retail is not ours. "Eleanor," I begin again, but then instead I dig a dime out of my change cup and give it to her. "How do you think I'll look?" I smile, and hold the frost kit next to my face like a commercial. I'm the only one here who's not moving out of town, though I am taking a vacation and going to Cape Cod for two weeks to think about my life.

"The terror of Truro," she says. "You'll dazzle." She rips off a hangnail with her teeth. "Gerard'll rue the day."

It's two against one out here.

Gerard sits back down next to me on the other side. Eleanor, suspecting she's been overheard, reaches over and pats Gerard on the thigh, tells us again about the ketchup and mustard.

Gerard isn't smiling. He stares off at the trees. Magdalena has settled at his feet. "Looks like someone was murdered in that thing, Eleanor," he says, pointing at the lace teddy.

I reach next to me, under the table, and clasp Gerard's hand, in warning, in rescue. It's two against one out here; we just keep taking turns.

"No, we're not getting married," I told my mother on the phone when she asked. "He's going to California and I'm staying here." Usually she doesn't phone. Usually she just does things like send me notes with histrionic scrawlings that read, "Well, you know, *I* can't use these," and along with the notes she encloses coupons for Kotex or Midol.

"Well," said my mother. "The advice I hear from my women friends nowadays is don't get married until you're thirty. Just take your time. Have fun gallivanting around while you're young. Get everything out of your system."

Gallivanting is a favorite word of my mother's. "Mom," I said slowly, loudly. "I'm thirty-three. What on earth do you think I'm getting out of my system?"

This seemed to stump her. "You know, Benna," she said finally. "Not every woman thinks like you and I do. Some just want to settle down." This yoking of mother and daughter was something she'd taken to doing of late—arbitrarily, without paying attention. "No, you and I are kind of exceptional that way."

"Mother, he said he thought it would be hell to live with me while he was in law school. He said it already was a kind of hell. That's what he said."

"I was like you," said my mother. "I was determined to be single and have fun and date lots of men. I didn't care what anyone thought."

. . .

Everyone keeps asking about Magdalena. "Dog's for sale?" they say, or "How much ya asking for the dog?" as if it's their own special joke. Then they laugh and stay around and poke through our belongings.

The first thing to go is my ten-speed bike. It is almost new, but it's uncomfortable and I never ride it. "How much?" asks a man in a red windbreaker who has read about our sale in the classifieds.

I look at Gerard for assistance. "Forty-five?" I say. The man nods and gets on the bike, rides it around on the sidewalk. Gerard scowls at his sneakers, walks off, circles back. "Next time," he whispers, "ask for sixty-five." But there isn't a next time. The man comes back with the bike. "I'll take it," he says, and hands me two twenties and a five. Gerard shrugs. I look at the money. I feel sick. I don't want it. "I don't think I'm good at these things," I say to Gerard. The man in red loads the bike into his Dodge Scamp, gets in and starts the ignition. "It was a good bike, but you didn't feel comfortable with it. The guy got a great deal," says Gerard. The Scamp has already lumbered off out of sight. Now I own no bike. "Don't worry," says Eleanor, putting her arm around my shoulder and leading me off toward the birch trees. "It's like life," and she jerks a thumb back toward Gerard. "You trade in the young spiffy one and then get yourself an old clunker and you're much happier. The old clunker's comfortable and never gets stolen. Look at Kip. You have the old clunkers for life."

"Forty-five dollars," I say and hold the money up in front of my face like a Spanish fan.

"You'll get the hang of it," says Eleanor. There is now something of a small crowd gathering by Eleanor's box of halter tops, by Gerard's records, by my plants. Not the plants, I say to myself. I'm not sure I should be selling the plants. They are living things, even more so than Eleanor's halter tops.

Eleanor is being a saleswoman by the birches. She indicates the black skirt. "This is a Liz Claiborne," she says to a woman who may or may not be interested. "Do you know who she is?"

"No," says the woman, annoyed, and she moves off toward the jazz records.

"We'll take the plants," says a teenaged girl with her boyfriend. "How much?"

There's a small ficus tree and the Chinese evergreen. "Eight dollars," I say, picking a number out of the air. The sick feeling overtakes me again. The Chinese evergreen is looking at me in disbelief, betrayed. The couple scrounge up eight dollars, give it to me, and then take the plants in their arms, like kindly rescuers of children.

"Thanks," they say.

The branches of the ficus tree bob farewell, but the Chinese evergreen screeches, "You're not fit to be a plant mother!" or something like that all the way out to the couple's car. I put the eight dollars in my cup. I'm wondering how far you could go with this yard sale stuff. "Sure," you might say to perfect strangers. "Take the dog, take the boyfriend, there's a special on mothers and fingers, two-for-one." If all you wanted to do was to fill up the cash cup, you might get carried away. A nail paring or a baby, they might all have little masking-tape price tags. It could take over you, like alcoholism or a religion. "I'm upset," I say to Gerard, who has just sold some records and is gleefully putting cash in his cup.

"What's the matter?" Again I've unsweetened his happiness, gotten in the way, I seem to do that.

"I sold my plants. I feel sick."

He puts one arm around my waist. "It's money. You could use some."

"Gerard," I say. "Let's run off to New Hampshire and wear nothing but sleeping bags. We'll be in-tents."

"Ben-na," he warns. He takes his arm away.

"We had a good life here, right? So we ate a lot of beans and rice."

"Take your eight dollars, Benna. Buy yourself a steak."

"I know," I say. "We could open a lemonade stand!" The evergreen still shrieks in the distance like a bird. In the birch trees the stain on Eleanor's teddy is some kind of organic spin art, a flower or target; a menstrual eye bearing down on me.

I know what will happen: He will promise to write every other day but when it turns out to be once a week he will promise to write once a week, and when it becomes once a month and even that's a postcard, he'll get on the phone and say, "Benna, I promise you, once a month I'll write." He will start saying false, lawyerly things like "You know, I'm extremely busy" and "I'm doing my best." He will be the first to bring up the expense of long distance calls. Words like *res ipsa loquitur* and *ill behooves* will suddenly appear on his tongue like carbuncles. He will talk about what "some other people said," and what he and "some other people did," and when he never specifically mentions women it will be like the Soviet news agency which never publicizes anything containing the names of the towns where the new bombs are.

"Sure, I'll take a check," Eleanor is saying. "Are you kidding?" Miraculously, someone is buying *Thoroughly Modern Millie*. A man with a swollen belly and a checkbook but no shirt. The hair on his chest is like Gerard's: a land very different from his face, something exotic and borrowed, as if for Halloween. He picks up the wine decanter. It's ugly, a hopeful gift, expensive and wrong, from my lonely and overweight brother. "You can have it for a dollar," I say. Once I found a fairly new book of poems in a used bookstore, and on the inside cover someone had written, "For

Sandra, the only woman I've ever loved." I blushed. I blushed for the bitch Sandra. Betrayals, even your own, can take you by surprise. You find yourself capable of things.

The man writes checks to both Eleanor and me. "Is the dog for sale?" he chuckles, but none of us responds. "My wife's crazy about Julie Andrews," he says, holding up the record. "When she was little she wanted to grow up to be a nanny, just so she could sing some of her songs. Doe a deer and all that."

"Ha! me too," I say, a ridiculous nanny, a Julie Andrews with a toad in her throat. The man toasts me with the wine decanter, then takes off down the sidewalk.

"The taste of a can opener," mutters Eleanor.

And on the phone in California, in one final, cornered burst of erotic sentiment, he will whisper, "Good night, Benna. Hold your breasts for me," but the connection won't be very good and it will sound like "Hold your breath for me," and I'll say "You're out of your mind, baby doll," and hang up with a crash.

There is a lull in our yard sale. I go inside and bring out beers, pouring one into a dish for Magdalena. "Well," says Gerard, leaning back in his lawn chair, exploding open a can and eyeing the birches. "No one's gone for the lavender teddy yet, Eleanor. Maybe they think it's stained."

"Well, you know, it's not really a whole stain," Eleanor explains. "It's just the outline of a stain—it's faded in the middle already. Bruises fade like that, too. After a few more washings the whole thing'll be gone."

Gerard blinks in mock seriousness. I gulp at my beer like a panicked woman. Gerard and Eleanor count their money, rolling it and unrolling it, making cylindrical silver towers. It's two against one. People stroll by, some stop and browse, others keep on going. Others say they'll come back. "People are always saying

they'll come back, and then they never do," I say. Both Eleanor
and Gerard look quickly up at me from their money cups, as if I
have somehow accused them, one against two. "Just noticing," I
say, and they return to their money.

A very beautiful black-haired woman in a denim jumper
walks by, and, noticing our sale, stops in to poke and rearrange
the merchandise. She is tan and strikingly gray-eyed and all those
things that are so obviously lovely you really have to give her
demerits for lack of subtlety. "Oh, is the dog for sale?" She laughs
rather noisily at Magdalena, and Gerard laughs noisily back (to
be polite, he'll explain later), though Eleanor and I don't laugh;
he is closer to her age than we are.

"No, the dog's not for sale," says Eleanor, recrossing her
legs. "But you know, you're the very first person to ask that
question."

"Am I?" says the beautiful woman. The problem with a
beautiful woman is that she makes everyone around her feel hopelessly masculine, which if you're already male to begin with poses
no particular problem. But if you're anyone else, your whole sexual identity gets dragged into the principal's office: "So what's
this I hear about you prancing around, masquerading as a
woman?" You are answerless. You are sitting on your hands. You
are praying for your breasts to grow, your hair to perk up.

"A clunker," whispers Eleanor, noticing Gerard. "Get yourself a clunker."

I'll probably watch a lot of TV specials: Sammy Davis singing
"For Once in My Life," Tony Bennett singing "For Once in My
Life," everybody singing "For Once in My Life."

"Can I interest you in a Liz Claiborne?" says Eleanor, pulling
down the black skirt from the tree. "I don't know much about
designer clothes, but supposedly Liz Claiborne is good stuff."

The beautiful raven-haired woman in the denim jumper smiles only slightly. "It's okay except for the lint," she says, gingerly lifting the hem of the skirt, then dropping it again. Eleanor shrugs and puts the skirt back up in the tree. "No one knows anything about *character* anymore," she sighs, and lurches back toward the tables where she piles up old complimentary airlines magazines and back issues of *People* and *Canadian Skater.*

"Just this, then, I guess," says the woman, and she hands Gerard a dollar for a record album. I look quickly and see that it's a Louis Armstrong record I gave him last Christmas. When the woman has left, I say, "So what's this, you're selling gifts? I gave you that record last Christmas and now it's in our yard sale?"

Gerard blushes. I've made him feel bad and I'm not sure whether I intended it. After all, *I* have sold the wine decanter my brother gave me last year, his foot jiggling, his entire impossible life printed on his face like a coin.

"I've got it on tape," Gerard says. "I've got the Louis Armstrong on tape."

I look at Eleanor. "Gerard tapes," I say.

She nods. She's looking through some old *People* magazines that she wants to sell for a dime apiece. "So, Billy Joel's getting married to a fashion model," she is saying, flipping pages. "What can you expect from a guy who writes 'I don't want clever conversation' and calls that a love song." Pretty soon Eleanor has lost it and is singing "I don't want clever conversation, I just want gigundo buzooms." "Kip loves Billy Joel," she adds. "The man's got the taste of a can opener."

It's every man for himself out here.

I will move to a new apartment in town. I will fill it with new smells—the vinyl of a shower curtain, the fishy percale of new sheets, the peppery odor of the landlord's pesticides. I will take too many hot baths—a sex and alcohol substitute and an attempt to get reoriented.

At work, suddenly, no one will seem to understand when I'm joking.

We are actually doing fairly well in the yard sale, though the sweaters aren't a big hit since the weather's warm. "I'm sorry about the record album," says Gerard, putting his hand on the part of my thigh where the shorts end.

"That's okay," I say, and go into the house and bring out a lot of junky little presents he's given me in the last two years: crocheted doilies, Crabtree and Evelyn soaps, a drawer sachet that says, "I Pine for You, and Sometimes I Balsam." They are all from other yard sales. They have sat for years in someone else's drawers, and then in their yards, and now I'm getting rid of them. I suppose I'm being vengeful, but I never really liked these presents. They are for an old maid, or a grandmother, and now's my chance to dump them. Perhaps I'm just a small person. Sometimes I think I must love Magdalena more than I love Gerard, because when they both take off for California, I want Magdalena to be happy and I want Gerard to mope and lose his hair into his water dish. I don't want him to be happy. I want him to miss me. That is not really love; I suppose I understand that. But perhaps it is like a small girl who for one baffled and uncharmed instant realizes her rigid plastic doll is not a real baby—before she resumes her pretending again. Perhaps it is like a football player who, futile and superfluous, dives in on top of the manpile, even after he knows the tackle's over; even after he knows the play's completed and it all had nothing to do with him; he just leaps in there anyway.

"Oh my god," cries Eleanor, picking up the balsam sachet. "I've seen this in at least two other yard sales."

"I got it down on Oak Street," says Gerard. "Is that where you saw it?"

"I don't think so." She holds it up by two fingers and eyes it suspiciously.

For a while I'll find myself talking to myself, which will be something I've always done, I'll realize, it's just that when you're living with someone else you keep thinking you're talking to them. Simply because they're in the same room, you assume they're listening. And then when you start living alone, you realize you've developed a disturbing habit of talking to yourself.

As medication, I will watch a lot of HBO and eat baked apples with sour cream. The whites of my eyes will chip and crack with scarlet. Only once or twice will I run out into the street, in the middle of the night, with my pajamas on.

By three-thirty-five business really winds down. I have already sold my ladderback chairs and my Scottish cardigans. I'm not even sure now why I've sold all these things, except perhaps so as not to be left out of this giant insult to one's life that is a yard sale, this general project of getting rid quick. What I really should have brought out is the food Gerard and I still have: potatoes already going bad, growing dark intestines; parsley and lettuce swampy in plastic bags; on the shelf above the stove, spices sticking to the sides of their bottles. Or I should have brought down all the mirrors—the one in the bathroom, the one over the dresser. I'm tired of looking into them and putting on so much make-up I look like a prostitute. I'm tired of saying to myself: "I used to be able to get better-looking than this. I know I used to be able to get better-looking than this."

It all gives me a stomachache. "There goes my dowry," I say when a ten-year-old girl actually buys the "I Pine for You" for a quarter. I feel concerned for her. She is mop-haired and shy, with a small voice that whispers "Thank you." She walks with tiny steps and holds the sachet against her chest.

I'm looking at the sky and hoping it will rain. "This gets

dull after a while, doesn't it," I say. "I'd like to close up, except we advertised in the paper we'd stay open until five." Very few cars drive past on Marini Street; some slow down, check us out, then rev up their engines and speed away. Eleanor shakes a halter top and shouts, "Same to you, buddy."

"If we closed," I continue, "could we get sued for false advertising? Perpetrating a public fraud?"

"Littering," says Gerard, and he points to the lavender teddy again.

"Boy," says Eleanor, oblivious. "I hate it when someone comes by and pokes through a box of clothes that you always thought were kind of nice, and they just poke and stir and sniff and then move on. I mean, I wasn't even sure I wanted to get rid of the Liz Claiborne skirt, but now that it's been pawed over, forget it. There's no way it's going back inside my closet."

I go inside and Magdalena follows, stays, lies down on the linoleum of the kitchen floor where it's cool. I grab the remaining six-pack in the refrigerator and bring it outside. The pop and hiss of cans comforts me, the starchy bitterness bubbling under my tongue. Gerard strolls around the yard with his beer can. He is pretending to be a customer. He struts past the tables, past the birch trees, spins, and in some Brooklynesque, street-kid voice he picked up from the movies, he says, "Hey. How much will *you* pay *me* to take this stuff off your hands?" We laugh, resenting him for being cute. I swallow beer too quickly; carbonation burns and cuts my throat.

Eleanor jumps up, deciding it's her turn. She grabs the fiber-glass insulation and models it like a stole. She scuddles and swishes up and down the sidewalk, a runway model on drugs. "Dahlinck, don't vurry about tuh spleentairs," she is saying. "So vut, a leetle spleentairs."

Gerard and I applaud.

·   ·   ·

My new apartment might be in a place where there are lots of children. They might gather on my porch to play, and when I step out for groceries, they will ask me, "Hi, do you have any kids?" and then, "Why not, don't you like kids?"

"I like kids," I will explain. "I like kids very much." And when I almost run over them with my car, in my driveway, I will feel many different things.

"Your turn, Benna," Eleanor and Gerard are saying. "Be somebody," they are saying. "Do something," they are saying. "Some feat of characterization. Some yard sale drama. We're bored. No one's coming."

The sky has that old bathmat look of rain. "Some daring dramatic feat?" I don't feel quite up to it.

"Three feats to a yard." Gerard grins, and Eleanor groans and smacks him on the arm with a *People* magazine.

I put my beer can, carefully, on the ground. I stand up. "All right," I exhale, though it sounds edged with hysteria, even to me. I know what hysteria is: It is your womb speaking up for its own commerce. "This is your sex speaking," it says. "And we are getting a raw deal."

I walk over and pretend to be interested in the black skirt. I yank it down out of the tree and hold it up to myself. I step back and dance it around in the air. I fold back the waistband and look at the tag. I point at it theatrically, aghast. I glance over my shoulders, then look front at Gerard who is waving and at Eleanor who is laughing. I make a horrible face. "Liz Claiborne?!" I yell, pretending to be outraged. "*Liz Claiborne?!*" I toss the skirt off toward the street; it lands on the curb. "Liz Claiborne's nothing but a hooker!"

And then there is a guffawing, hiccuping sort of laughter, but it seems to be coming mostly from me, and I have collapsed, squatted on the grass, holding my stomach, this thing that might be laughter coming insistently, in gulps and waves. I lift my head, and in the distance I see Eleanor and Gerard—Eleanor worried and coming toward me, Gerard afraid and not coming toward me, and jutting into my line of vision is the edge of my own body, fading from the center first like a bloodstain or a bruise, only my outlying limbs, my perimeter lingering. That is all I can see, the three of us, here, small and vanishing, and caught in the side yard, selling things.

4

Water

"So, YOU DON'T LIKE THE LIFE you're leading?" asks Gerard, unbelieving as the police. He is an art history graduate student, a teaching assistant of Benna's, although they are about the same age. They are sitting in Benna's office, which could use some potted plants and more books. The art history department, she thinks, must be wondering about her empty shelves, whether this suggests an attitude problem. She has tried to joke and say that she's going to fill the shelves with Hummels and porcelain horses with gold chains connecting their hearts. But no one seems to find it funny. "You're Impressionist scholarship's new golden girl," Gerard is saying. "I don't get it."

Benna considers this. *Leading a life* always makes her think of something trailing behind her in a harness, bit, and reins. "You can lead a life to water, but you can't make it drink." She smiles at Gerard. Her books are all at home, still in boxes.

Gerard's grin is a large plastic comb of teeth, the form his fury has taken. "You're being ungrateful," he says. Benna has

what he hopes someday to have: free pencils, department sta-
tionery, an office with a view. Of the lake. Of the ducks. Not the
glamour bird, she has said. How can Benna suggest she's unhappy? How can she imply that what she's really wanted in her
life is not this, that her new position and her oft-quoted articles on
Mary Cassatt have fallen into a heap in her lap like, well, so many
dead ducks. How can she say that she has begun to think that all
writing about art is simply language playing so ardently with itself that it goes blind?

"Maybe I'm being ungrateful," bristles Benna, "but you're
being insubordinate." Yet she likes Gerard, is even a bit attracted
to him, his aqua sweaters and his classroom gift for minutiae;
like a Shakespearean's pop quiz, he surprises everyone with years,
dates, the names of dogs and manservants. Now Benna regrets a
bit having said what she's just said. Even if Gerard is behaving
badly. Perhaps she drives men away. Perhaps, without even being
able to help herself, she just puts men into her ill-tempered car
and drives them off: to quarries, dumps, small anonymous
bodies of water.

"Well, I guess that's a signal I should leave," says Gerard,
and he gets up and does a stiff swagger out of her office, without
even saying good-bye, the blues and greens of him bleeding like
Giverny lilies.

Benna takes a bus home, which she usually resents, tending, as
she does, to think of buses as being little more than germs-on-
wheels. But today, because of the October chill, the peopled
humidity of the ride is comforting. In the city back east where
she went to graduate school, everything was within walking distance: school, groceries, laundry. She lived in a house with a large
group of friends and was known for her carrot soup and her good,
if peculiar, sense of humor. Then in August, she packed up her
car and drove out here alone, feeling like a map folded back

against its creases. She stopped overnight at motels in Indiana, Nebraska, and Montana (where she danced in the cocktail lounges with truckers), and blinked back tears through prairie after prairie and towns that seemed all to have the same name: Watertown, Sweet Water, Waterville. She came to this California university for one reason, she reminds herself: the paycheck. Although every time the paycheck arrives the amount taken out in taxes for a single woman with no dependents is so huge it stuns her. The money starts to feel like an insult: For this, she thinks, I've uprooted my life? Whatever money she might save, moreover, she usually spends trying to console herself. And it is hard to make any job financially worth its difficulties, she realizes, when you're constantly running out to J. C. Penney's to buy bathmats.

Benna misses everyone.

Benna misses everyone she's ever known and spends her weekends writing long letters, extravagant in their warmth, signed always, "Lots of love, Benna." She used to pay attention to how letters people wrote her were signed, but now she tries not to notice when the letters she receives close with "Take Care" or "Be Well" or "See you Christmas"—or sometimes simply "Moi." Look for "Love," she jokes to herself, and you will never find it.

It is the eating dinner home alone that is getting to her. At first, because she had no furniture, she ate sandwiches over the kitchen sink, and in ways that was better than sitting down at her new dining-room table with a pretty place setting for one and a carefully prepared meal of asparagus and broiled chicken and pasta primavera. "I quickly exhaust my own charms," she writes in a letter to her friend Eleanor, who has begun to seem more imagined than real. "I compliment myself on the cooking, I ask myself where I got the recipe. At the end I offer, insincerely, to do the dishes. I then tell myself to just leave them, I'll do them later. I find myself, finally, quite dull."

"Things are going well," she writes to her father, who lives in a trailer and goes out on dates with women from his square dance club. "I think you would be proud."

There are children, beautiful, bilingual, academic children, who leave their mudpies on her porch, mud in Dixie cups with leaves and sticks splayed out at all angles. They do not know quite what to make of Benna, who steps out of the house and often onto one of their mudpies, and who merely smiles at them, as if she just wanted to please, as if they, mere children, had some say in her day's happiness.

Where she often goes is to the all-night supermarket, as if something she urgently needed were there. And in a kind of fluorescent hallucination, she wanders the aisles with a gimp-wheeled shopping cart, searching, almost panicked, for *something*, and settles instead for a box of glazed doughnuts or some on-sale fruit.

At home, before bed, she heats up milk in a saucepan, puts on a nightgown, looks over her lecture notes for the next day— the old familiar notes about the childless Mary Cassatt giving herself babies with paint; the expatriate Mary Cassatt, weary and traveling, dreaming homes for herself in her work; woman Mary Cassatt, who believed herself no woman at all.

Benna sifts through this, sipping the milk and half-waiting for the inevitable eleven o'clock phone call from an undergraduate who has been delinquent in some way and who wants very badly to explain. Tonight the phone rings at ten forty-five. She brings it into the bathroom, where the air is warmer, and gazes into the medicine cabinet mirror: This way at least she'll feel as if she's talking to an adult.

"Hello?" she says.

"Hi, Benna. This is Gerard. I want to apologize for this afternoon." His voice is careful, slow.

"Yes, well, I guess we got a little tense." She notices her face has started to do what her mother called *bunch*—age making pouches at her mouth and eyes: Are there such things as character *bags*? Benna opens the medicine cabinet mirror so she can look instead at the aspirin, the spearmint dental floss, the razor blades.

There is some noise on Gerard's end of the phone. It sounds like a whimpering child. "Excuse me," says Gerard. "My daughter's wiping something on my pant leg." He covers up the phone, but Benna can still hear him say in a patient, Dad voice: "Now, honey, go back to bed. I'm on the phone right now."

"Sorry about that," he says when he gets back on.

"You have a *daughter*?" Benna exclaims.

"Unfortunately, tonight I do," he says. "My wife's at the library, so it's my turn to stay home."

I didn't even know you were married, Benna almost says. A *daughter*? Perhaps he is imagining it. Perhaps he has only an imaginary daughter.

Her finger traces the edge of the cold water faucet.

"So . . . hello? Are you still there?" calls Gerard.

"Yeah," says Benna finally. She envies the spigot in her hand: solid, dry, clear as a life that has expected nothing else. "Sorry. I was just, uh, hemorrhaging."

She hears Gerard laugh, and she looks straight into the toothpasted drain and laughs too. It feels good to laugh. "Give to seizure what is seizure's," she adds, aiming for hilarity.

"You're crazy, Benna," Gerard says merrily.

"Of course," she says, "I'm here," though it sounds stale, like the hard rock of bread a timid child hurls into duck ponds, less to feed than to scratch at the black beads of the eyes.

"Things flow about so here!" she said at last in a plaintive tone, after she had spent a minute or so in vainly pursuing a large bright thing, that looked sometimes like a doll and sometimes like a workbox, and was always in the shelf next above the one she was looking at.

—Lewis Carroll, *Through the Looking-Glass*

Everyone says, stay away from ants. They have no lessons for us; they are crazy little instruments, inhuman, incapable of controlling themselves, lacking manners, lacking souls.

—Lewis Thomas, *The Medusa and the Snail*

And—you say to yourself—what's the harm? Who's to say what happened really? What's the truth, anyhow?

—*Jerry Lewis in Person*, with Herb Gluck

5

The Nun of That

IN THE DICTIONARY *lumpy jaw* comes just before *lunacy*, but in life there are no such clues. Suddenly, for no reason, you might start to dribble from the mouth, to howl peevishly at the moon. You might start quoting your mother, out loud and with conviction. You might lose your friends to the most uninspired of deaths. You might one day wake up and find yourself teaching at a community college; there will have been nothing to warn you. You might say things to your students like, There is only one valid theme in literature: Life will disappoint you. You might say things to your students like, There is only one valid theme in literature: Life will disappoint you.

Dub the imagination *pharmacist*, and then we can talk turkey.

These are things you might find yourself saying.

There is a crack moving around my house—from ants on the inside eating the beams. It fractures an inch every week or so, zigging across the stucco, steady as lead. It's four feet off the ground, beginning at the northeast corner of the house, and it moves west like Lewis and Clark. You could pull up chairs in the driveway and just watch it, turn it into a sort of apocalyptic theme party: a crack potluck. "Ha!" squawks my imaginary friend Eleanor in the FVCC faculty lounge, where we correct freshman writing together. I have given her an unusual double appointment: Gym and Anguish-as-a-Second-Language. FVCC is the third-largest community college in the country and still we have no office. We are what are called Junior Instructors. We never finished our dissertations. One day in graduate school we looked at what we had done so far and decided to face facts. "This isn't writing," said Eleanor, "this is drinking." We dropped out of graduate school, worked for a while as legal secretaries in New York, and then moved here. We pretend the lounge is ours—and it's true: No one else comes in here. "Crackpot luck! Ha!" squawks Eleanor again. She usually has snappier retorts than this, but sometimes the unfinished thesis affects her brain. Every time she passes the department sign for "outgoing mail," for instance, she mutters, without fail, "I've had enough of those; I need a wan poet type." Eleanor is overweight and can't seem to convince her phys ed students (at whom she shouts aerobics instructions from a chair in the corner by a cassette box) that exercise does anything for your life but prolong it. Her students need the credits but obtain them insincerely. Eleanor herself doesn't do a single exercise and instead spends too much time looking at her watch to see when she can go have a cigarette.

"Ha, ha!" Eleanor slaps her knee and dumps her papers onto the floor in a flamboyant gesture of despair, leans back in her chair and laughs some more. (These are pre-semester "orientation" papers; we are weeding out the illiterates in advance so that the department can herd them together, into their own classrooms, like a doomed and leprous people. We do this for extra, end-of-summer money.) Eleanor gets up and goes out to get a drink of

water from the corridor fountain. Ten seconds later, still swallow-
ing, and wiping her mouth, she comes back in, picks the papers
back up, sets them in her lap. She begins reading student sentences
aloud. "Benna, get this: 'He had lost his composer, and he put his
hand to his borrowed forehead.' I think they mean *furrowed
brow*."

"It's video games," I say. "Or maybe it's more than that.
Maybe it's tap water."

"Here's another one," says Eleanor. " 'The man began to
speak in a sarcastic manor'—m-a-n-o-r."

Things do overwhelm her. "Come on, we've got to do
this," I say, trying to concentrate. Meticulousness, I think.
Compassion.

Eleanor puts her pen down, all histrionics, and gazes out the
lounge window at the parking lot and the one tree. "You know,
I just hate it when I lose my composer," she says.

My imaginary daughter, Georgianne Michelle Carpenter, is six
and will soon be in the first grade. She watches too much TV
news, even for someone who's not a kid, which has resulted in her
adoption of one giant new fear a week. The house will burn up
and cook her to a nugget. Soon she will be laid off and living in
an abandoned car in Maryland. "Geeze, George. At least have
interesting fears," I tell her. I have ants, dogs, unemployment
checks—I only pretend to be a fear snob. "Or switch to cartoons.
When I was growing up there were cartoons on at this hour.
Aren't there any cartoons on?"

She digs a finger into her shoe to get at something itching
there. She suspects I am only trying to have my way with the TV.
"I dunno," she says, eyes glued to Dan Rather, who looks like her
school principal. I sip my beer. Perhaps he even *is* her school
principal. Perhaps there are really only a hundred people in the
whole world and they all have secret jobs as other people, rushing

to airports, switching outfits, chowing down small, packaged fruit pies in taxicabs. I press the chilled bottle against my temple. I gnaw a cuticle. I wonder who else is me, who else is George.

George bites into a strawberry so huge it looks painful to itself. Juice spurts down her fingers. I hand her a napkin. We are sitting together on a quilt on the living-room floor. "Even if I had to, Mom," says George, staring at her strawberry, "I would never lay you off."

Machinists are picketing in Ohio. Once when George was younger I made the mistake of telling her that her father and I had broken up because he hadn't been doing his job and I had had *to lay him off*. At the time it seemed like the right thing to say, nifty with clarity, like a new mop. Then the economy got a giant, moaning cramp, and the phrase took on connotations, intimations, power; it buzzed troublesomely around our cracking house. "Would you lay *me* off?" she asks, both sad and hopeful.

I put my nose in her ear. She smells of sweet, fruity children's shampoo. "Nope. Never, never, never." She giggles and butts her head into my underarm. This is our language of reassurance. I've always imagined it would work quite well at summit talks, weapons negotiations. You could never dislike a nation whose ambassador kept giggling, nudging, bumping his head into your armpit.

The ants are crawling all over everything, dusting themselves in spilled Nestlé's Quik, measuring the faucets and cabinets, squiggling over chrome and wood. I zap them with paper towels. I find one stomach-up in the toilet bowl, drowned from overzealous bathrooming, a fate I once feared for myself when I was a toddler and skinny and forced to sit on toilet seats that didn't go all the way around. This ant must have slipped, and now it floats there on the skin of the water, a tiny, tragic, triptychtic leaf. I've found that you can best entrap ants with the corpse of another ant. A squashed one of their own in the middle of the floor, and boom, like stubborn Antigones, they rush out to bury their dead brother and get nabbed.

That's probably why they're called *ants*, says Eleanor.

Maybe I'm using up too many paper towels.

Maybe I'm actually enjoying this, this carnivorous hunting and trapping. The slow, inevitable rending of my house and theirs. I reach into the toilet bowl and lift out the ant body and place it on the floor under the sink.

On the first day of class the teacher, Benna Carpenter, marched into her classroom, flicked on the light, clunked over to the front desk, and heaved her briefcase up onto it. She removed her gray, baggy blazer and put it on the back of the chair, then remained standing, staring one by one at the twenty pale and attentive faces collected in the horseshoe of desks and chairs in front of her. They looked younger every year. Already she could feel herself spotting the types: the quiet redhead who would write not-bad sonnets; the curly-haired woman who was there for Benna's jokes (she'd heard about them in bio lab); the guy in the Nike t-shirt who was there for his own jokes, ethnic and protracted (What do you call WASP foreplay? Washing dishes. What do you call Jewish foreplay? Begging. What do you call Irish foreplay? "Brace yourself, Bridget"); and two very clean Johnson & Johnson types who were there for an easy A-minus for their moms and dads. "Well," she began. "This course is called The Reading and Writing of Poetry. I have one thing to say to you at the start: Ya wanna read and write poetry? You're gonna have to go home and goddamn read and write poetry!" It came out in a shout.

Nobody moved. Two women exchanged glances.

The teacher opened her briefcase. She took out the Xeroxed class list and looked back up at their confused stares.

"The Reading and Writing of Poetry!" she barked again,

loudly. "That's why we're here. We're all a bunch of crazy people!" And then she looked down, called the roll, even the middle
names and initials, her hands fidgety through her hair, at her side,
around her pencil, her handwriting on the attendance sheet a
shaky, old woman's scrawl.

"I start off determined, but they make me nervous," I tell my
friend Gerard, a part-time carpet salesman and local jazz pianist
who gigs in the motel-hotel nightclubs around town. He boasts
privately of playing an exquisite broadloom. We are sitting in
Hank's, a favorite junk coffee shop downtown, a place where I
join him almost daily in ceremoniously sending month-old grease,
cigarette smoke, and mind-blitzing coffee in the direction of vital
organs. Gerard has a way of alchemizing what is essentially self-
destructiveness into a sort of quaint, homely charm. The world
seems okay with Gerard; it seems comfortable even when sitting
in the very "kitchen of its poisons," Gerard's phrase for Hank's,
the Pentagon, and certain parts of Queens, where he's from.
    Gerard sticks one whole fried egg into his mouth and speaks
with his mouth full, as if with tempera paint. Yolk lines his lips.
"Tell them they mustn't bring their shotguns and machetes to
class."
    "Gerard, you just stuffed one whole egg into your mouth." I
glance over at the waitress, who is new. It's not Patti anymore. It
used to be Patti.
    "What can I say, I'm a gastronomical illiterate. You should
see what I do when you're not here." He pushes toast into his
mouth and grins.
    Gerard has unusual eyes. He can only see out of one eye at
a time, and often his sight will hop to the other eye without warning, always leaving the eye it has fled sitting in his head like a
dead lightbulb. A fake window. A tiddly wink. He had eye operations when he was little, even woke up in the middle of one, he

said, and, glimpsing the startled surgeons, screamed "The Bug Men, the Bug Men!" Until he was ten he had to do exercises to get the muscles in each of his eyes to work together, to get the good eye to lead the blind eye, so that the blind eye, whichever one it happened to be, didn't stray off in some odd, independent direction, like a kid in Woolworth's. He has no depth perception, yet has twenty-twenty vision. I often wonder when his vision switches eyes whether the storage and retrieval capabilities of his brain switch hemispheres. Perhaps whole experiences—dinners, songs, girl friends, entire books—are lost, unavailable to him, depending on which eye he's looking out of. Sometimes I even try to imagine it for myself: I close one eye, imagine my corpus callosum frayed as an old jumprope, and try to wipe out things.

Gerard has bright crumbs in his beard. I smile. "How did the gig go last night?" I light my daily cigarette. One a day, I'm convinced, helps build antibodies.

"Same as always. I'm still competing with the bartender's blender. I'll be in the middle of 'Somewhere Over the Rainbow,' and it'll start crushing ice or something."

"Christ," I say, both my word and Gerard's word of disgust and commiseration. I remember when it used to mean a person.

"Yeah, do you need a brown pile?" This is the punch line of a sick, old scatological joke of his. Gerard throws it out every time he wants to change the subject. It has become a kind of symbol of how much he hates what he does for a living, as if it were his very life he was offering you.

"Gerard, please."

Georgianne came out of the bathroom this morning and said, "Ugh, Mom, don't go in there yet. You'll get *dung lung*." I don't know where she picks these words up from. She said she thought she'd "pumigated" things, sent the ants packing.

"Sorry," says Gerard.

.   .   .

The teacher had been assigned two additional sections of the same course. "My name is Benna Carpenter," she shouted and turned and spelled it out on the board. "This course is called The Reeling and Writhing of Poetry, and I'm gonna pass out these index cards and on them I want your name and address and phone number. In the upper left-hand corner I want you to write down the name of your favorite poet, no friends or relatives, and on the back I want you to draw, as best you can, a picture of your soul as you imagined it when you were a child." She told them, with mock solemnity, that for the rest of the semester they would be attempting to craft with words what they were right now drawing on their cards.

"You've gotta be kidding," Gerard says later. "You told them *that?*"

Renoir's Madame Charpentier and her daughters stare at me from over the sofa, all of them, even their cranky dog, a bit cross-eyed. Gerard calls the print "sentimental, prostituting schlock." I smile and say, "Isn't it wonderful?" Then I usually make fun of his Greece posters. He's got about ten. His apartment looks like a coffee shop.

In the faculty lounge with Eleanor I look through the cards to see how my students had once imagined their souls. There were things that looked like flying saucers, like Oreo cookies, like milk bottles, like teardrops, ghosts, heads of ghosts, fire, tongues of fire, a television set, a bowl, a black ball, an anonymous "This class sucks," a chair, a flower, several lightbulbs.

"I like the big cookie one," says Eleanor with a cigarette in her mouth.

Before she was even all the way in the classroom, a student anxiously approached her from the back of the room. "Do you have the class list?" he asked. "I want to see if I'm here."

Clearly an ontological question. She looked quickly at him and said, "You're here." Then she stumped over to the front desk, heaved her briefcase up onto it, looked out at the wall at the other end, and said, "Good afternoon." The anxious student returned to his seat. "This is The Reading and Writing of Poetry, if I'm not mistaken," announced the teacher for the third time that day. "My name is Benna Carpenter and—"

"Donna who?"

"Benna. B. As in beer or bug or B-minuses. Which reminds me: No one is to hassle me about grades in here. If you're afraid of C-pluses, take the course pass-fail or take sedatives. And I'm adamant about attendance; it's mandatory. I'm going to be small, niggling, and unwavering on this."

A guy with a gold chain: "We heard you were an easy grader. You're just talking tough because it's the beginning of the year."

"I am talking tough," the teacher said slowly, raising her voice, then bringing her fist down hard on the desk in front of her. Someone in the back gasped. "And yes, it is the beginning of the year."

"These are their souls," I show Gerard later that night. I pull out the index cards and spread them across the coffee table. He looks at each one thoughtfully, sipping scotch. He finally swallows and looks up, a look of tremendous seriousness.

"And you're going to go on and try to work with these kids?"

I shrug. "Only fourteen more weeks. They're not all kids. I have an escaped housewife and a Vietnam vet. It's better than all eighteen-year-olds."

Gerard shakes his head. "Look at this one, Benna." He reaches to his left and holds up one of the cards. I look and see a big blue-inked cube with wavy lines coming out of it, swastikas at the end of each squiggle. "You're gonna try to teach poems to this guy?"

"Hell, it's only community college, Gerard."

"Sounds like one of the circles Dante forgot to put in the Inferno." Gerard believes the other forgotten circles are Carpet Town and the Ramada Inn.

"Look, if all else fails, I can always sing almost any Emily Dickinson poem to 'The Yellow Rose of Texas.' " I smile and flutter my eyelashes.

"You know so much about literature," twinkles Gerard out of one eye. He grabs me for a fast tango about the room, the citrusy beard of him against my face. The tango isn't quite right for "I Heard a Fly Buzz When I Died," which I am now singing, country-western style, but we pretend not to notice.

"Yeah, I know," I sigh. "Aren't I devastating?"

Georgie's first day of school is tomorrow. She needs cheering up so I drive us downtown to Children's Clothes so that she can pick out a dress to wear. The store is small and the three saleswomen are all sisters, widows with different last names. The rods against the walls are loaded with dresses.

Mrs. Hazelstein knows Georgianne. "Well, Georgianne. Looking for something to wear to school tomorrow? I've got just the ticket. In fact, I've got many tickets." Mrs. Hazelstein winks at me, and George follows her, silent, obedient, over to the size sixes, which, for some reason, are hanging from the highest, not the lowest, rod on the wall. Georgie looks up at the dresses, head dumped back, mouth hung flaccidly ajar like a kid in the first row of a movie theater.

Mrs. Hazelstein pushes clear the size eights and size fives and proceeds to glide each size six, one by one, slowly from left to right across the rod so that Georgie can view them.

"Oh, now here's a nice one," she says and lifts a very adult-looking purple knit dress down off the rack, holding it in front of George.

"Ya like that, George?" I ask dubiously.

George steps back, suddenly afraid of Mrs. Hazelstein. She hides behind my legs and slips a hand inside the rear pocket of my jeans. "I dunno," she says softly.

Mrs. Hazelstein looks at me for advice. I have none. "Perhaps that's a little warm for September, anyway. Tell me, Georgianne, if you see something you like." Mrs. Hazelstein continues the slow sliding parade across the rod.

"That one," whispers Georgie, finger in her mouth.

"Did she say something?" Mrs. Hazelstein asks me.

"Which one, honey?"

"That one," she points. "The one with the babies."

"This one?" Mrs. Hazelstein takes down a cotton dress printed all over with little peach-colored babies, their heads haloed in bonnets.

Georgie is entranced. She tries it on in the dressing room, comes out to get buttoned and tied, and swirls around shyly in front of the three-way mirror. It's a hideous mud of pinks, blues, and yellows. Something's crooked with the collar. George, however, is smiling, touching the little babies on her dress.

"Are you sure now? You're the one that's going to have to wear it." My mother: That is what my mother always said to me.

"Yup."

Mrs. Hazelstein shrugs.

We put it on my charge account there, and Georgie wears it home, her old shirt and jeans in a plastic Children's Clothes bag that draws shut with a string. She fastens her seat belt carefully and continues staring at her dress.

When we get home she takes the dress off, lays it carefully on her bed, looks at it awhile, and then takes a Mr. Bubble bath. "Don't forget your ears!" I call and then go into the kitchen to fry chops, boil potatoes, make a salad. Ten minutes later, however, there is a howling. "Georgie?" I call and dash to the bathroom, push open the door. Not since my husband left have we ever really latched it.

Georgie is sitting in the tub amidst quickly dissipating suds. She has lather on her face, her eyes squinted shut, and is blowing her nose into a washcloth, but stops and begins to wail as giant soap bubbles bloom forth from her nostrils. I grab a clean towel and wipe soap off her face. "What's going on here? Didja get soap in your nose?"

Georgie nods. She holds up a little soap chunk she has broken off the bar. She is crying. "I put it up my nose," she sobs. "I wanted to be all clean for tomorrow for school and now it won't come out."

"A friend of mine put soap bits up her nose last night," the teacher told her ten o'clock class. "So I didn't get a chance to memorize your names. I know some of you have these reversible jobs like James Russell or Jay Kim, so you're going to have to help me out a bit here, okay?"

My husband was a lawyer. I met him at the firm I worked for in New York, right after I dropped out of grad school. I got married, not because I'd met Mr. Right, but simply because I felt like getting married. That was also back in the days when I would shave one leg and not the other, just to see what would happen. But I had, I thought, figured it out. People didn't get married because they had *found* someone. It wasn't a treasure hunt. It was more like musical chairs: Wherever you were when the music of being single stopped, that's where you sat. I was twenty-six when the notes started winding down and going minor. A dark loneliness, in a raincoat and fedora, scuffed in instead. Or maybe I was just

tired of saying I was twenty-six years old and having it sound like
"I am a transsexual." Also, two different people in the office had
asked me if I was married. When I said no, they acted very surprised. To me it was a preposterous question, like grown-ups at a
wedding, trying to be funny and asking the flower girl if her
husband's in town. But these people were serious. They asked me
if I'd *ever* been married. I had, they said, some sort of married
look. The thought burrowed in me like a fever tick: a married
look. When I met my husband, the old musical-chair music had
already begun to skitter to a halt. I clutched and sat. He was new
at the firm and liked me because I typed his briefs faster than anyone. ("Yeah, I'll bet you did," says Eleanor, still.) After work he
and I would head out for drinks. He knew a lot about food, fish,
planets—he was an information fetishist, and I was impressed. He
knew that a pound of a certain smoked fish in Iceland was the
equivalent in benzopyrene to four thousand cigarettes. He was the
first person I'd ever heard pronounce *Reykjavik* out loud. He knew
that human beings never dream smells. Later, of course, I discovered the dust bunnies under the bed of his soul: He liked to do
weird things with cameras; he could never say anything sweet or
romantic; his heart was frozen as a winter pipe—it was no wonder he knew so much about Iceland. By the end of our marriage
I was sitting in our house in outer suburbia, wondering, Where
does love go? When something you have taped on the wall falls
off, what has happened to the stickum? It has relaxed. It has
accumulated an assortment of hairs and fuzzies. It has said *Fuck it*
and given up. It doesn't go anywhere special, it's just gone. Energy
is created, and then it is destroyed. So much for the laws of physics.
So much for chemistry. So much for not so much. Three days
after my husband walked out of the house, his rented Mazda
veered off into a wall of blasted-out rock, on his way to the air-
port. He'd been planning a trip to the Caribbean somewhere. I got
the house in outer suburbia and an imaginary ankle-biter. Actu-

ally, once I thought we'd brewed up a real ankle-biter and when I phoned my husband at work to tell him that it looked like the rabbit had died, he'd started cursing and shouting because he thought I meant our car, our VW with the RUST IN PEACE, the POETIC LICENSE, and THE MORAL MAJORITY IS NEITHER bumper stickers. Later he took me for a drink—"a drink with milk in it," he insisted—and spent a lot of time joking around with the waitress. This is what happens to a marriage.

"You're full of shit," says Gerard. "He always loved you. I'll bet he thought you were the most beautiful woman in the world."

"Christ, Gerard. You don't know anything about it." Gerard has done this before, seemed to imply that my husband must have driven his car deliberately into the Fallen Rock Zone. I spin the coffee cup around on the saucer. "You never met him, even. I don't know why you think you know what you're talking about."

"I don't know what I'm talking about. But I *am* smart."

"You're smart. That's rich." The words hover in the air like helicopters. In graduate school Eleanor and I used to say, "If we're so smart, how come we're not rich?" Then I got the house in outer suburbia, and I sat in it and wondered, "If I'm so rich, how come I'm not smart?" There's more and more tension between me and Gerard these days. I keep wishing it would go away. I try to wipe out the last five minutes in my mind. I try to switch eyes.

"Benna. Look. I'm sorry." Gerard suddenly feels bad. He gets up, comes around next to me on my side of the table. He puts his arms around me.

"Gerard," I say quietly, pulling away. "Believe me. You just don't know."

Gerard picks up a lock of my hair, brings it straight up toward the ceiling, then lets it drop. "Let's go," he says.

. . .

"Okay, now I hope all of you have purchased or acquired by some legal and ethical means the poetry anthology for this course. It's in the campus store under English 210." Because the book seemed sexist to her, the teacher sometimes referred to it as "The Ralph and Norton Anthology" and supplemented it with handouts. A young woman in a pink cardigan raised her hand.

"Yes?" the teacher asked hesitantly, afraid of contradictions, reluctance, insubordination.

"I looked yesterday and it wasn't there. So I asked somebody working in the store and they showed me. It's under English 120, not 210."

"Oh, really," said the teacher. Was the world dyslexic or was it trying to demote her. "Well, you've all heard what . . . what is your name?"

"Sharon Humphrey."

"What Sharon has said and should consider yourselves edified or redirected or born again or whatever. Now—"

"The course itself is still 210, though, right?" interrupted the boy sitting closest to her. "Cuz I need a 200-level."

"Yes, no matter what the store has done to us, we are still what we are." The teacher sounded disheartened.

"How was school, honey?" I call to George when I hear her push open the front door. I am stirring cookie batter, trying to get the shortening to blend with the brown sugar and flour, single-handedly, I'm sure, defying several important scientific laws.

Unlike last year I will be home before her every day now, her school day running from eight-fifteen to three-thirty. Last year she went to kindergarten in the morning, then stayed at Mrs. Kimball's down the street in the afternoon. Mrs. Kimball showed George how to draw pictures of farms and lighthouses and let George watch news on the TV all day.

"Rick Riley's in my class. He thinks he's so great."

In my first-grade class, too, I remember, there had been a Riley.

"Why does he think he's so great?" I ask, hoping to encourage the rationalization of irrational responses—you should learn these things early in life.

"Feats me," she says, something she has taken to saying.

"George, it's 'beats me,' not 'feats me.' "

"Beats me?"

"Yeah. How do you like your teacher, Mrs. Whatsername?"

"Mrs. Turniphead." George throws her sweater and pencil case on the kitchen table. She is wearing her babies dress.

"Geeze, George, you're beginning to sound like one of *my* students. Quick, say: 'That's dumb, why do we have to do that?' "

"That's dumb," she says. "Why do we have to do that?"

"Very good," I say, still stirring cookie dough, arm aching. "Now you can go to college."

The teacher shuffled through stacks of papers, called the roll, then distributed Xeroxed copies of "The Song of Solomon." "This is love poetry of the highest order: 'The Song of Songs, which is Solomon's.' It's not in the anthology and pre-dates by many, many—"

"How many?" There was always one smartass, in the back playing with the window-shade pull.

"—many years the poems that are. In the anthology." The teacher glanced apprehensively at the boy in the back by the window. His name was Steven. His soul was a ghost with a mustache. His favorite poet was Pink Floyd. "You can read this religiously, if you want, as a metaphor for the church or whatever, but that's really more for institutional purposes, like those huge jars of mayonnaise you see in cafeterias." She glanced at her notes. "As with all love poems, this is also a despair poem. I like to read it as the most powerful articulation available of a hormone-induced consciousness. How many people have read this before?"

One person raised his hand.

"How many people have read the Bible?"

The same person raised his hand, plus Sharon in pink again.

"Only two?" The teacher murmured to herself, weighing various diatribes. "Well, let's at least read this. Would someone like to volunteer his or her voice?"

The boy in the front volunteered, stumbling through some of the lines because some of the photocopying was faint or smeared illegibly. At the line "I am a Rose of Sharon" someone nudged Sharon-in-pink and there were a few giggles. Christ, thought the teacher. I'm teaching congenital morons and savages.

"They haven't read the Bible," I say later to Gerard at breakfast at Hank's. Hank is at the grill today, a bald, impish man, plowing homefries to one side with a huge spatula, making room for eggs. "Only two of them have."

"Have *you* read it?"

"What is this, a quiz? Of course. Well, most of it. Have you?"

"Four times."

"Oh come off it. Four whole times?"

"I camped in the Smoky Mountains one summer when I was nineteen. I only brought one book and that was it. I read it three times."

"That's only three."

"I've read it once through since, as well."

"Liar. Tell me. What is your favorite book in the Old Testament."

"Habakkuk."

"You're just being cute." That is Gerard's way, cuteness. Also drunkenness.

"No, really. The first line of Habakkuk is 'O Lord, how long shall I cry for help, and thou will not hear?' The last line is the standard note to the choirmaster: 'with stringed instruments.'"

"A thousand violins."

"Yeah. It pretends to be about violence, but it's really only about violins. I've met people like that."

"It sounds like a disease. He's in advanced stages of Habakkuk. Or a casserole: Ham Habakkuk. Or a rock band: just plain Habakkuk. Live. Tonight." I do my imitation of a badass guitarist.

"Had a rough morning, Benna?"

"God, I guess."

I try to calm down. Gerard wants to quote some more. "'Woe to him who says to a wooden thing, awake; to a dumb storm, arise!'"

"Now you know what teaching's all about. Like Saint Francis preaching to the birds."

"But Benna, dearie, sweet, you used to love teaching," Gerard says in his put-on smarmy voice. It's also his Aunt Emmadine's voice and his impression of certain dental assistants.

I cross my eyes and tear off corners of napkin, shove them in my mouth, and chew on them to amuse Gerard, and Hank, who looks over at me from behind the counter and shakes his head. "She teaches college, this woman," says Gerard, pointing at me.

"What is this?"

The teacher cleared her throat. "It's 'The Song of Songs.' A sort of play, really, a—" She looked at her notes. "A passionate dialogue that reaches an emotional pitch so intense that if it were to continue for even one more stanza it would tumble out of itself and collapse. Its sharpest points are its most fragile." She looked quickly around at the class, the little marble eyes, the tucked chins, the temples angled onto fists. "It dips in and out of an erotic despair, which it's lifted finally out of by the very hope imparted by its sensuousness." She looked out the window and winced.

The minutes were long highways. The teacher began to pace, three steps each way, back and forth in front of the blackboard, which was really a greenboard; she remembered when they all had been black, not too long ago though long enough. These kids had probably never seen a blackboard, probably wouldn't know who Jim Morrison was, or Huey Newton, or the song "Cherish." They probably wouldn't remember Colleen Corby, a fashion model whose career barely made it into midis. They probably had no idea that greenboards had once been black, that Mia Farrow had once been married to Frank Sinatra, that life had not always been like this. "For Friday I want you to bring in one of your own love or despair poems. If you don't have one already, I want you to write one."

Amos White, his name emblazoned across his t-shirt, shot up his hand, grinning wildly. "What if we're virgins, man, and we've never known no real love or no despair?"

The teacher had taught community college too long. "See me after class," she said.

The teacher's last class of the day was in another building on the opposite side of the Fitchville Community College campus. It was a five-minute walk. This particular day she noticed that signs had been spray-painted: DO NOT ENTER at the truck-loading drive by the administration building had become DO NOT ENTER U.S. WARS; DEAD END had been cleverly trans-mogrified to read GRATEFUL DEAD HEAD; one STOP sign now read STOP IN THE NAME OF LOVE; another read simply STOP, YOU BITCH.

. . .

" 'Thy hair is as a flock of goats that appear from Mount Gilead'? Who is this asshole?" Somebody else in the back, dressed all in orange burlap, frowned.

The teacher had already passed out the photocopies and given the assignment. "It's God," she said. "Would someone like to read this aloud for us?" She looked around the classroom. Twenty faces with the personalities of cheeses and dial tones. "Well, then," she continued. "I'll read it." And she began, dangerously: " 'The Song of Songs, which is Solomon's. O that you would kiss me with the kisses of your mouth / For your love is better than wine . . .' " The teacher raised her eyes slightly to note any squirming, any gasps. They looked inert, frozen as fish sticks.

It took a long time to read, though people did seem finally to be listening, silently reading along.

" 'Make haste, my beloved, and be like a gazelle or a young stag upon the mountains of spices.' " The bell rang on "stag." "Okay," she commanded, damp with perspiration. "Don't forget: *Your* poems next time." There was a clumping and galumphing, a sliding of chairs across the floor. The teacher looked down, shuffled papers. A black student named Darrel Erni paused by her side as everyone drifted past him.

"Ms. Carpenter?" he said.

The teacher looked up. The student was smiling. She had noticed him before, on Monday. He seemed older or wiser or was it merely that he was more battered and less worried about it. It was all the same, she guessed.

"I just wanted to say that I liked the poem very much. And I liked the way you read it."

The teacher knew asskissers from way back. They lingered after the period was over, they separated themselves from the rest of the huge cryogenic experiment that was the class, they cooed, they beamed, they twinkled. They wanted you to make them your assistant. Yet something was different here. He nodded. She liked nodders. His eyes were slightly pink, slightly shiny. Had he really been moved? Or was he on drugs like the rest of the class? "Well," she said, all helpful teacherliness. "I'm glad you enjoyed it."

"It's beautiful, you know, just beautiful." He had an old fatigue jacket on and the anthology tucked up under one arm. He hunched up his shoulders, put his hands in his pockets, and sauntered backwards toward the door. He winked and gestured with his head. "This is a neat class."

"Glad you're enjoying it," she said, something almost happy rushing to her face. She liked this Darrel Erni. But then he turned and was off down the hall with a quick padding and bounce of sneakers.

George and I send out for pizza. When it arrives, we eat in front of the TV, watching the news. "So what did you talk about in class today, George?" Cheese stretches like delicate tusks from bitten wedge to mouth.

She sighs. "We did reading groups—redsies and greensies. Then we talked about going to a dairy farm to see the cows." George picks off the bits of green pepper and anchovies. "No cat food pizza for me," she says. The commercial is Oil of Olay and everyone in it, though old, is happy and smooth.

"You should eat the peppers, George. They have vitamin A in them. They help you get A's."

She ignores me, continues vegetableless through her piece.

"I get it. You're a redsie not a greensie, is that it?"

"Redsies are the dumb ones," she says. "I'm a green for green light. That's what Mrs. Turners said."

"What's the red? Red for *red* light?" How unsubtle of Mrs. Turniphead. How meanly self-fulfilling, like a churlish fortune cookie.

"No. They're red for tulips." And she puts her two lips together and makes a joke, a big pizza kiss in the air.

Dan Rather speaks of a volcano in the Dutch Antilles. Two-thousand-degree lava flows and bubbles thick as chowder across our TV screen.

"Poor Beruba people," mispronounces George. Then she switches the subject. "We do fire drills next week. Lauren says there's never any fire and all you do's get yelled at by teachers for talking in line."

"Didn't you have fire drills last year in kindergarten?"

"Uh-uh."

"No fire drills?"

"Nope." She shakes her head then stops. "Opes. That's right, I forgot."

An ant is checking out the oil stains on the pizza box. I pinch it between a napkin and the cardboard.

"Can we go to Beruba someday?" asks George with her mouth full. I have taken George on two vacations—once to Toronto, a city of manufactured whimsey suited only to shoppers, and once to Cape Cod to see the ocean, at which she was much astonished and at the age of three raced exuberantly up and down the beach, arms spread, shouting at the water, "Juice! Juice! Look at all the juice!"

To me the ocean, so loaded with seafood, is more like a loud and giant bouillabaisse.

"To all that lava? Into the eye of the potato? You want to?"

"Yeah. We could be hula girls."

"That's Hawaii, George. We would have to be Beruba girls." I stand up to throw the ant napkin away but instead wave my arms and wiggle my hips. George stands up and pulls the bottom of her shirt up through the neck so that her belly button and midriff are bare. She sways and rimples and giggles around the pizza box. Dan Rather is signing off, getting the hell out of our living room, a living room of Beruba girls. Sometimes I wonder if I try too hard to be George's playmate, or if it comes naturally to me, if it comes like the easiest thing in the world.

"They'll never learn that *a lot* is two words," mutters Eleanor. "Or *no one*. Or *another time*. I had three students spell *another time* as if it were a season. Give me Gym class any day."

"Anothertime and the living is easy."

"Yeah. That's for when Harry the Dean of Sophomores calls you up to go to the movies. 'Thanks—*anothertime*.'" I had gone to the movies once with Harry, Dean of Sophomores. Afterward we ate chocolate sundaes and he told me about the Baltimore medical student he was engaged to. "She works hard," he said. When Harry first came to FVCC, he was a music professor. "I teach Canon and Fugue," he had said, and all I could think of was detectives, a TV show like *Starsky and Hutch*. Then he became Dean of Sophomores. Eleanor had gone out with him once, too, to a poetry reading. "Medicine is a fascinating profession nowadays," he had said three times in the car on the way home. When she got out at her house, so did he, following her, attempting to kiss her. She didn't know what to do, so she made some crack about the Taco Bell Canon and then electronically lowered the garage door onto one of his shoulders. Though he wasn't seriously hurt, he never called her again. "A damn poor sport," said Eleanor.

"By the way, didya hear we might get fired?" Eleanor's expression is a cross between urgency and marijuana.

"Huh?" She's switched subjects too quickly for me.

"Budget cuts. Distribution changes. Curriculum overhaul. They're looking around at all of us non-tenured folk. They're looking at the courses we're teaching. They got cyanide in their eyes, sugar shoes."

"*Sugar shoes?* When's this supposed to happen?" I ask it

wearily. A woman named Phillie McCabe has put a poem in my department mailbox. It is about losing weight. "Oh diet, diet, they said / and I looked at the bread / trembling with dread / and said, 'What color?' / and then went to bed." "Dye-it—get it?" she has scribbled at the bottom.

"Shortly before Christmas I guess they're supposed to have it all squared away. Or us all squared away." Her eyes are all bruisey turquoise. She can inhale a cigarette like no one I know. If Cleopatra had smoked Winstons she would have smoked them exactly like Eleanor. "Listen to this sentence," she says. " 'They decided to go sledding on their rear ends where the incline was less steep. Then an audible burp sent a shudder from her pleated and powdered chin down to her buttocks, which hung inertly over the struggling and baffled chair.' "

"Is that Stacy or Tracy?"

"No, that's Howard."

"Eleanor, what are we going to do?"

Because the teacher didn't have an official office, she had to have what she euphemistically called "office hours" in the Student Union Snack Bar on Thursdays from two to four. On this particular Thursday she trudged into the Union with way too much stuff, books crammed into bag and briefcase, department memos she had yet to read clutched with haphazard violence in one fist. She spotted an empty table in the back—not the one she usually liked, but close—and she trudged over and unloaded, books and papers on the table, briefcase on the floor. She put her rumpled gray blazer on the back of one chair, then got in the snack bar line, paid forty cents for a Styrofoam cup of coffee, grabbed some plastic half & halfs for her smarting, tripish stomach, and then wended her way back to the table. Sitting was a relief. She let the steam from the coffee float up and into the itchy, chalky corners of her eyes. She breathed. It felt good. She gingerly slurped her coffee and stared out the window for a little while at the small hill which slid gently from the Union's outer wall toward a stream at the bottom. There was an asphalt promenade built on either bank, which gave the stream a captive look, as if without the walks, someone had thought it would leap maniacally outward, take off through campus like a mad motorcyclist. Paths and roads always followed water—rivers, shorelines—but this promenade, thought the teacher, seemed so ugly, so senselessly competitive with nature. And because the walk took all the bends of the river, it was never the fastest way to get anywhere. It was usually frequented by students and teachers interested in a leisurely stroll. The teacher turned her attention back to her coffee and papers. She began reading through memoranda. New, more rigorous faculty review procedures, some department gatherings—both social and business, though who could really distinguish—some offers for small magazine subscriptions, and then someone was standing beside her.

"Hi, Ms. Carpenter. Do you mind if I join you?"

It was Darrel Erni, all laughlines and teeth, knitted hat and green fatigues.

"Sure, have a seat," she said, a bit scattered and harebrained, trying to clear a place, frantically making one towering pile of papers and books, which, finally, slipped, tumbled, crashed into the Styrofoam cup of coffee, milky brown spreading out, over, onto things, like a yearning but stagnant pond.

"Oh my god, *my nightmare!*" howled Eleanor from three tables away, having a conference with a student but obviously not engrossed. She had caught this accident of caffeine and cream and paper and was clearly enjoying it. The teacher crossed her eyes, shook her head, and began mopping things up with napkins yanked from the dispenser on the table. Darrel, like Eleanor, was brimming with harmless bemusement, giving him a power over the situation, which the teacher couldn't help but resent. He pulled over a chair and sat down. "Would you like a cup of coffee?" she asked, some zany displaced hostess with soggy napkins.

Darrel placed a full Styrofoam cup on the table. "I already have one, thanks," he smiled.

The teacher stared at his cup for a second. "Right," she said.

The teacher already knew that one student of hers was a Vietnam vet. He was in her ten o'clock class, a quiet blond named Robert, whom she would probably never get to know. He had written a synopsis of his life on the index card, along with the picture of his soul (a striped bowl) and his favorite poet (Jesus). Robert had a tendency to dash out of class the minute it was over, alone, like a man who has to go to the bathroom.

She hadn't known it about Darrel, though he, too, had been in the war. "A million years ago," he said. They spoke about it carefully and the teacher hoped he would not tell her stories about ears and eyes—about pendants made from the shriveled leather of ears, how in the rain they changed from dried fruit to soggy recognizable flesh, how gouged eyes were placed on the foreheads of the dead, about how there were cash prizes. Anemically, she would have to muster that old horror and alongside it, another horror would not require mustering at all—the very familiarity of the tale, the survivor's tale edged always with other survivors' tales who got there first and told. Told first. Those who don't get there first, before the books and poems and television shows, had stories no one ever really heard. Please not the eyes and ears, I won't listen, I won't hear, thought the teacher to herself, and shame leaped in like a commercial. This is a flaw in my character, she would think to herself later. This is what is known as peacetime.

But he didn't tell her about eyes and ears. He told her a long, complicated story about an officers' party in Saigon, where he'd hurled a bottle of cognac against the wall and stomped out imperially. And though she didn't catch exactly why he'd done it, she could imagine this tall, strong man, capable of such astonishing gestures, such huge moments, such moral angers. He also told her he wanted to be a dentist.

"A dentist," she repeated dumbly, and her tongue fished back into her molars for crumbs, for the rot-nuggets of cavities.

"Probably an orthodontist." He grinned. He had perfect teeth. As a kid, growing up in a trailer in Tomaston, she had nightly pressed her front teeth hard against the heel of her hand, to push them back: orthodontia for the poor and trailered.

"Braces," she said.

"Yeah," and he smiled like a king. He said he'd been doing mostly odd jobs for years, that he'd recently divorced.

"Me, too," said the teacher. "Actually, uh, my husband died several years ago." A sign by the window said PLEASE KEEP WI DOWS CLOSED.

"I know. I heard."

"Huh?"

"Things get said. Students talking about the teachers and all."

"Yes, I suppose," said the teacher.

The black Vietnam vet student Darrel who wanted to be a dentist smiled again and said how about dinner sometime. The teacher's office hours were almost over, he noted, and they still hadn't discussed poetry very much. The teacher felt tense and moronic and smiled and said, "All right." What did she know about poetry, about dinner, all her smarts tiny and jammed in the back of her mouth like a tooth. Impacted as wisdom. "Why not."

"I think he's cute."

Gerard doesn't say anything.

"I guess I'll have dinner with him. What do you think?"

Gerard still doesn't say anything, doesn't give me even a look. He has a hangover, gulps orange juice like a dying plant.

He also has a cold, and has pulled the hood of his sweat shirt up over his head and tied it. "You look like the Little League version of *The Seventh Seal*," I say. "How was the gig last night?" I was part of the first generation to grow up on television. I've learned how to change channels, switch stations, search through the snow for a new program.

"The Ramada," Gerard says. "Rough place."

"Gerard, are you okay?"

"Last night," he says, "I got two requests from people moving through the salad bar: the theme from *Chariots of Fire* and the theme from *Rocky*. Plus, the Ramada has a chimpanzee tune their piano. It breaks my heart."

"Why don't you quit that place, Gerard? You don't really need the money that badly, do you?"

With two fingers he picks up a spoon by its middle and twiddles it up and down, a fast, stainless seesaw. "You know when I first wanted to be a professional musician?"

"When the fifteen-year-old moss in your navel started talking back."

Gerard scowls, it isn't funny. I trust his assessments of my jokes. When his eyebrows come together in a single quick caterpillar, I know it's dumb. When he falls helplessly back against the booth, says "Christ, Benna," and laughs out loud with a sort of pain, I know it's still dumb. But I use it in class.

"It was when I first met this aging hippie on the beach. I was just out of the ninth grade and had nothing to do. He was ten years out of graduate school and had nothing to do. His name was Buff. I went back with him to this old ramshackle beach house with creaky plank floors all covered with orange peels and sand. He had an old Steinway upright and he sat down and played and I thought he was God, man, I did. He could do everything from Kabalevsky to "Moon River." I never saw him after that. I went home and convinced my mother to rent a piano. We were the only ones in our building with a piano. I even tried to change my name to Buff, but it didn't catch on. Everyone at the school still kept calling me Gerard."

"Imagine that."

"Am I boring you?"

"No."

"At any rate, the point is, well, if you promise not to laugh..."

"I promise," I say, planning a guffaw for no matter what he says. I am, essentially, a fourteen-year-old.

"I want to sing opera. I'm trying to figure out how I can swing it."

The guffaw doesn't materialize. I just stare at him, the anxious hope of his cheek and eye muscles. I see his vision switch eyes, one eye now going off slightly to one side.

"You're serious, aren't you?" Gerard, I think, does have a nice tenor voice, but so does my father. So does my Uncle Bob.

"Do you think I'm crazy?"

"It's not that, Gerard. It's just that, well, you're thirty-three years old."

"No," he smiles. "*You*'re thirty-three years old. I'm thirty-two." He has a face like a parking meter.

I slump, sigh loudly, look at the table, play with my spoon. "Gerard," I say, syllables deliberate, tidy as needlepoint. "We should talk about this. Want to have dinner tonight?"

I do some reading at the library and then, noticing it's almost time for George to be let out of school, dash off to pick up a few groceries and get home before she does. When I get in, however, she is already home sprawled out on the living-room sofa, her babies dress on again, wrinkled and untied. "George, my goodness, how come you're home so early?"

"I don't feel so good," she says.

"You don't feel very *well?*" I ask, pedagogy in me like a burglar. "What's wrong, honey? Is it your stomach?" I put my things down on the piano bench and go sit next to her, stroke her hair. She is flushed red and her hair is in damp strings against her temples. I press my wrist to her forehead and can feel she is hot.

"Do I have a temperature?" she asks.

"Yup," and though she is big and six-and-a-half already, I pick her up, legs dangling, lug her upstairs to her room, to her white room splotched pink with animals and dolls. I help her take off her dress, then tuck her into bed with just her slip on. I pull the shades. I sit on the bed's edge, in the dark, rosy lap of the afternoon. I hold her hand.

"Was school okay? Was it the nurse that sent you home?"

George nods. "She had to fill out a form first. Then the nurse's aide drove me." Her fingers knead the satin edge of the blanket. "Mom," she whispers. "What was my father's name?"

I'm always startled when she asks about him. Once she asked me where he went after I'd "laid him off and he went and got killed." I was stunned at her phrasing and simply said, "He went to Heaven," though I've never believed it for a minute.

"What do you mean? His name was Mr. Carpenter."

"No, but what was his first name?"

And here I hesitate. She has a fever. She shouldn't ask about these things, she shouldn't think, she should sleep. I pull the quilt up over her. "I've invited Gerard over for dinner tonight. But I'll bring you up some of what we've had, and I'll make sure he stands in the doorway and says hi." George has always liked Gerard. "In the meantime, Miss Sickie, you get some rest."

"But what was his name?" she whimpers. Sleep is pulling on her face.

I pause for a long time. "George. It was George," I say.

"George Carpenter? Like me?"

"Yes," I say, and it makes me sad, though I can see her smile a little, seeming to find something nice in this news, this new news. The sing-song of an ambulance on the street hollers and fades. I sit there and say nothing. I watch George. I watch George's eyes close.

I make a special kind of macaroni and cheese. It has three kinds of cheese and doesn't turn out quite right, but Gerard doesn't seem to mind, although he doesn't want seconds. I give him some more anyway. He is talking about amateur competitions at the Met; applications to voice programs; the voice teacher he has now, a guy named Gil who has one arm; trying to sing Loggins and Messina at the Holiday Inn while the football game on the TV over the bar drowns him out. I try to listen fairly. I don't want necessarily to discourage him. He says he has always loved Verdi and Puccini, Buff had tempted him astray, he needs to be in touch with serious music. "At least what you're doing," he says, "has something to do with what you're serious about, something to do with poetry."

My mouth is full of macaroni. I try not to choke. "What I'm doing," I say between swallows, "has very little to do with poetry." And the remark, the truth of it, sits there in front of me, shivering, like a funny old Italian man with no clothes, like a tepid macaroni from my lips.

"Gerard and I have decided to go out dancing for an hour or so," I whisper to Georgianne. I have brought her juice and a small cup of pasta and placed them on the night table without turning on the light. She is mumbling something in her sleep. She turns toward me, eyes closed, and puts her face against my hand. I brush her dark hair off her forehead. She is not as feverish as before. "Mrs. Kimball is downstairs if you need anything. I'll give you more aspirin when I get back." Mrs. Kimball does crossword puzzles, eats Kraft caramels, and wears tangelo-colored pantsuits.

She has a constant crinkle about her, perhaps from the Dacron or the caramel wrappers. She has a terrific red mouth, a huge crocket of a nose, and one very serious strawberry mole. She loves my daughter. She adores her.

Moths hang on the screen like bats. George has begun snoring, a small rattly whistle in one nostril. I kiss her and get up quietly, like someone leaving church.

I first met Gerard three years ago at the movies, a bad science-fiction thing about an electric guitar that takes over the universe. I was there with my friend Verrie, who viewed the whole thing as a Hitler metaphor, and has since gone to Palo Alto to teach. Gerard was there with his friend Maple. They sat in front of us. Verrie and Maple knew each other from dance class. Verrie was stunning—tall, blonde, Plantagenet-looking—and so was Maple, though he was male and fond of earrings and Verrie was neither. Apparently they both had the same color leotard in class, some weird sort of crimson, and often they stood next to one another at the barre, cracking jokes and knees. They looked illegal together. Gerard and I were necessarily darker and scruffier than they, and had a certain small but immediate understanding of each other which came simply from that fact.

After the movie ended, while we were standing to go and Maple and Verrie were oh-helloing it, Gerard and I introduced ourselves. "Can you believe how much alike these two look alike?" asked Gerard, under his breath.

I've always been drawn to people who misspeak. I consider it a sign of hidden depths, like pregnancy or alcoholism.

"Maybe we shouldn't talk about it," I said. Gerard kept looking at Verrie. I think he was attracted to her. He leaned against the back of a theater seat and for a long moment, while I was talking about when the electric guitar had taken over the army, he regarded her legs. I decided he was a jerk.

Afterward we all went for drinks. We sipped whiskeys in a booth made from two church pews, in a smokey fern bar called The Smokey Fern. The place was noisy and had too few waitresses. I don't know precisely how we got on to it—I guess we were talking about the necessity for gun-control legislation—but suddenly Gerard was wildly insisting on government tanks in the streets of New York, automatic searches and arrests of anyone and everyone in order to enforce, effectively, gun-control and curfew regulations.

"Curfews?" I hooted. "What do you want? A city-sized version of Annette Funicello's dormitory?"

He ignored me. He was inexorable, generally advocating the transformation of the entire metropolitan area into a police state. Anyone with a gun should be shot on sight.

"That'll show them," I said. Who was this guy? He was so crudely fascistic, I didn't know whether we were to take him seriously. Perhaps it was the movie. Surely he was being ironic. Verrie looked at me and shrugged. I was speechless, though I tried to speak anyway and it came out in vehement splutters and thought bubbles as in comic books: loaded with the upper register of a typewriter's top row. How could he presume the incorruptibility of such a state? What liberties did we enjoy that totalitarianism would subsume? He didn't care, he said (though I saw Maple wink at me); the government was for the protection of citizens and their property and if it didn't perform that function it didn't do anything at all. I was aghast. What sort of property did he own?

Maple leaned forward, smiled, put his hand on mine. "Gerard likes to try out extreme positions on people he's just met, just to see how the words sound."

Verrie was quiet. She was watching me.

Gerard shook his head. "No, I mean this. I've had a gun at my ass and at my head, and that should never happen in this country, no matter what has to be done to ensure it. It should never happen."

Maple chewed on his bottom lip and there was a morguish lull, a murderous wave arching back getting ready to break and strike, and then Gerard was quickly up, saying, "Who would like another round?" waiting for the nods, and "I would's," and then bounding across the room toward the bar.

"You'll have to excuse Gerard," Maple said to me and Verrie, though mostly to me. He knew I was tense, inarticulate with rage. "Do you remember last winter reading about a restaurant on Fifty-ninth Street getting held up by some stockinged men with sawed-off rifles?"

"Vaguely," I said.

"I remember," said Verrie.

"Gerard was there. Two people had their heads blown off. Gerard was forced to strip and have sex with the woman he was with. He had a gun butt up his ass the whole time." Maple paused. I suddenly felt sick. I looked up at the bar and could see the back of Gerard, the sweater, the patched corduroys, waiting for drinks. "The worst thing, in Gerard's mind, was that she was the first woman he'd gone out with in years who really interested him, and afterward they couldn't speak to each other, they were too reminded of the incident. He called her a few times, but they finally never saw one another again."

"Holy shit," said Verrie. I pressed a hand over my mouth and kept it there.

Far away Gerard was joking with the bartender about something, putting away his wallet. A tiny waitress, all spritely flirtatiousness, came up and placed a hand on the small of Gerard's back, up and down the sweater, and asked him something. Gerard smiled and nodded and picked up the four whiskeys and began making his way slowly back to the table.

Maple continued quickly. "He's all Hobbesian hobbledy-hoy

one day and the next it's something else. Gerard is really one of the most wonderful and one of the most unlucky people I know."

Gerard arrived and expertly placed four glasses down on the table. We all reached for our wallets. A hundred years had gone by.

"No, this is all on me," said Gerard. He pulled out the largest glass in the quartet and placed it in front of me. "And this is for you. Old freedom-at-any-price." It was a double. He slid Maple and Verrie theirs and sat down across from me.

"Thank you," I murmured. I looked down at the drink.

"You're welcome," he murmured back.

Gerard and I never really became lovers, though we almost did. A few weeks after the night at The Smokey Fern we ran into each other at the Fitchville public library, standing in line to have our library cards cybernetically transmutated. The library was switching over to a computer system which involved a final Fitchville disbanding of Dewey Decimals. It made me sad. As a kid I had loved simply the sound of the name: Dewey Decimals. It sounded like cartoons. It wasn't Library of Congress, slick and federal.

"It's the end of an era," I said to Gerard.

"You've had an earache?" he asked. "Me, too."

After we got our new computerized library cards, we walked out the door together, then stood on the granite steps, exchanging perfunctory information about how our lives were going. It was cold and we were shivering.

"Do you have time to have coffee?" he asked.

That was our first coffee together at Hank's. We exchanged phone numbers, and later in the week he called and asked me out to dinner and I said yes, although it wasn't without some apprehension: This was a man unlucky in restaurants. We went, however, to a small Greek one, ate souvlaki in peace and drank house wine. We smoked too many cigarettes. "The liter and the pack," quipped Gerard, and I laughed loudly because I had drunk a lot and because, despite everything, I liked him much. He leaned over the table, touched my hair, and kissed me. Life is sad, I thought. Here is someone.

We ended up in my bed together, sort of, spastic and looped, doomed for failure, like two senile inventors in an upstairs room, lonely as spoons. The whole business finally seemed less an expression of mutual attraction than a soft, noodly act of existentialism.

After a long parade of kisses and other things, Gerard rolled over, blitzed with wine, and collapsed. "Impudence is very common," I said to him in the dark, hoping he would smile. I didn't want to pat his hand and say, "It's okay," the way they do in television movies. "Sorry," he murmured into the ribbony edge of the blanket, and we kept on drinking—cheap cream ale in cans. We talked about childhood, and he told me how when he was little he thought he had Superman hearing, how he thought he could hear for miles. Then he got up and went home.

Miraculously, we became the best of friends, moving on to other romantic flailings, but having regular breakfasts at Hank's, comparing sordid life-notes, having dinner, going disco-dancing for the exercise. (Although Gerard usually tries to meet women, his recent success rate hasn't been wonderful and he has taken to greeting attractive disco women with the opener "Why have I never seen you before, and why will I never see you again?") Often I go hear him play at one of the local cocktail places. I love Gerard, even if he is a lounge act.

The walls of The Grounded Star, the only disco in Fitchville, beat like a migraine. It is packed, even on a Thursday night. The music hurts my *eyes* for some reason, and I wonder if I'm getting old, somebody's great-aunt at a disco. Perhaps soon I'll have dyed hair and cheap black underwear you can see the shadow of through tight, peach-tone pants. I saw a woman like that yesterday. George was with me. "If you ever notice me starting to wear things like that," I told her, "you have permission to send me away forever on a bus." I am getting the thunder thighs of my Aunt Ivy. The lumpy oatmeal buttocks. When Georgianne is fourteen she will be embarrassed to be seen with me in public places like hosiery aisles and church. She will stand in the doorway of the bathroom, while I'm getting ready to go out, and will cluck her tongue and groan, "Oh, god, Mo*ther*" and then show me how to wear make-up, hauling out her own slick tubes, unrecognizable gels, sneering at my dusty compacts, my fuddy-duddy wands.

The strobe-light show over the dance floor looks like something that could bring on epilepsy.

"Hey. Exercise. Good for you," I grunt at the door, Tonto to Gerard's masked stranger: He has put on silvery New Wave sunglasses. "You're very cool," I reassure him.

"You either have it, Benna, or you don't," he says.

We pay the five-dollar cover, take our two wooden nickels over to the bar and get two "free," fancy German beers, which we glug theatrically from their bottles, our heads back, hands jammed into ass pockets, like juvenile delinquents. Before we are quite finished, Gerard puts his beer down on the bar, and for no reason but comedy, says "Excuse me" to the bewildered person next to him, grabs my arm and together we poke and strut our way out to the dance floor, which we locate mostly by noticing where the carpet underfoot gives way to wood. It is that crowded. We dance with our knees and elbows, all angles from the joints. We are warm and spinning in place, imitating each other's movements: fake boxing, fake karate, fake roller derby. I look at Gerard: We are in charge; we are the best people here, whether we really are or not.

I accidentally step on someone's foot and she turns around shrieking, "A cripple, you've made me into a cripple!"

"Sorry," I call over the music.

The next song is a slow, hug-your-honey number. "I've got to go to the bathroom," I shout at Gerard. He nods.

In the bathroom someone has written I WANT TO BE FUCKED.

Beneath it someone else has added, in a red, searing scrawl, YOU ARE FUCKED.

At the bar with Gerard, I glug more beer, warm, unfizzled, sweet. The room is pounding and airless. "You could die of White Shoulders poisoning in here," says Gerard, absently gazing at a group of women by the dance floor, all pretty, all young. I look off in some other direction, but think I see someone I know smiling at me. I look away; it's probably a student—I dread seeing students. I look back and someone else, a handsome black man in a white silk shirt, is standing next to me. It is Darrel, sans army greens.

"Darrel," I say. "Hi."

"Dr. Carpenter," he says. Why do students do that? Add the oppressive and unprophetic *Dr.*

"Benna. Please. It's Benna. Call me Benna. This is my friend Gerard. Gerard-Darrel, Darrel-Gerard."

Gerard proffers a hand and shakes more warmly than he usually manages with strangers. Sometimes when new people enter the picture, he growls inside himself. Like a groundhog seeing his shadow, or like a thief, you see all of his features abscond, close, a window shade pulled down behind his face.

"I hope I'm not interrupting anything," says Darrel, turning toward me, "but would you like to dance?"

It's another hug-your-honey number.

"Gee, I'm not sure." I look at Gerard for advice. He nudges me gently, is probably winking at me behind his glasses.

"Go on," he says quietly. "Go on, go on, go on."

"All right, already." I like saying that. It's something I picked up in New York City, when I lived there. Like a sinus condition, or something on sale. I follow Darrel out onto the floor. It's less crowded now, the lighting dimmed to a television blue, couples pressed close as toast. Darrel smiles, very tall, very much at ease here, lightly taking my waist and my right hand and moving me surefootedly around the small corner of floor that is, apparently, ours. Where are Darrel's sneakers? He is wearing what my brother Louis used to call "hard shoes"—leather shoes. And a slick shirt, slippery and nice. It has a dry, sweet smell, like bubblegum and cedar.

Whenever I have danced this way with Gerard, it's always been sort of a joke: I lead and he pretends to swoon. With Darrel, there's no joking. I try to catch Gerard's eye every 360 degrees. To be reassured? Encouraged? Gerard lifts his glasses up onto his head and flutters his eyelids at me. His eyebrows wriggle up and down, crazed and wooly. Maple has turned up here and the two of them are leaning lazily against the wood lip of the bar and talking. A couple to one side of them are watching Darrel and me dance. I turn back, look up at Darrel, and feel my heart fluttering. It's a Tennessee Williams heart. A bad Tennessee Williams heart. I don't know what to say. The music urges love on you like food. I say, "Well, waddya know. Here we are." I shout it. I'm out of breath. My feet are like turtles, my armpits ponds.

Darrel grins, listening to the music, not saying anything. He spins me around, pulls me close, then steps back, then moves close again. What is this jazz? I grew up in the country, in a trailer. We did things like stand far apart and ripple our stomachs in and out.

When the song ends, moving subtly into a faster one, we let go and I wipe my palms on my jeans and say, "Well, Darrel, thanks for the dance." I thrust my hand at him and he shakes it, warm and dry. I follow him off the dance floor. When he turns around to say good-bye, I gaze up at his sad laughlines, the lashes, the perfect keyboard of his teeth, and I say, "Let's have dinner this week."

"Absolutely," says Darrel.

"He has a kind face," I say to Gerard, riding home in his Datsun.

Gerard shrugs and then there is silence, the dark sky pricked with stars, dotted lines in the headlights pulled under and to the left of us, the black of trees running footlessly by. Gerard is speeding.

Finally he asks, "Why do you always sleep with your students?"

My vision leaves me for a minute, my brain grinds against my skull. I turn and glare at Gerard's profile. "Fuck off, Gerard! I don't always sleep with my students." Gerard doesn't say anything. We are approaching a stoplight. "Once. Once before, that's all." And only as I say it do I realize I've said "before." "Goddamn it, Gerard. What are you trying to make me out to be? You know how many people I've slept with in my whole life? Six! Up until a year ago I could count them on one hand. I've had six lovers and I'm thirty-three years old, and I still send all of them Christmas cards and birthday cards. Still! And that's even counting my husband and *you*, Gerard, which I think is rather generous of me." Meanness flies around my brain like a spluttering balloon. "I don't always sleep with my students."

Gerard doesn't say anything.

I slept with one of my students about a year ago. His name was Scott Hayden, a thin, pale, insensitive blond, and he stayed at my house twice and ate all the shredded wheat in the morning. Georgianne didn't like him; she is into cereal monogamy—like me—and was annoyed about the shredded wheat. Eleanor, too, thought I was crazy. Verrie, in a postcard from Palo Alto, a color-ful aerial view of strips and strips of motels and car dealerships, had simply written, "Honey, do what you want." When I suggested to Scott that we stop seeing one another, he stopped coming to my class. I gave him an Incomplete for the course and in June sent him a card for his birthday. At the end of August I saw him in the grocery store near campus and said, "Hey, you've got an outstanding Incomplete still, you know," and he looked at me and said, "Oh, Benna, it's not *that* good," and charged up the soup aisle, turned left, and disappeared.

"Whatever you say," chimes Gerard, all false conciliation, turning the corner onto my street.

"Gerard, why are you being such a bastard? You know I don't sleep around. In fact"—I punch him in the arm—"you know what they called me in high school? Do you know what they called me in high school?"

"What did they call you in high school?" Gerard sighs, drags one palm down across his face, puts the car into park.

"The Nun of That. That's what they call me. The Nun of—"

"You're repeating yourself."

"—That. Do you honestly think six men is a lot to have slept with in your whole life?"

Gerard tries not to smile. "Of course I don't. But you do. That's why you send them all cards." We've stopped; we're at my house. "And I'm not talking about numbers," he continues. "That's *your* weird little department. I'm just talking about the fact that you're a teacher."

"Leave me alone, Gerard." I get out, slam the door. I'll have to take Mrs. Kimball home myself. "Get the hell out of here." The car hesitates, hiccups backward then lurches forward, whirrs away, past bushes and streetlamps, into the night, his VIRGINITY IS FOR LOVERS bumper sticker lit up like a fiery Band-Aid.

"Georgianne was crying a little there," says Mrs. Kimball, all orange crinkle. "But she wouldn't say why. She wanted to wait up for you."

"Could be her fever," I say, helping Mrs. Kimball on with her all-weather coat.

"She's a sweet girl," smiles Mrs. Kimball. I give her five dollars and drive her home, though it's only six houses away, as she chats about her sister's children, how day in day out they just listen to that noise.

When I get back home, George is standing at the top of the stairs in her nightgown. "Mommy?" she calls. I stand at the foot of the stairs, in the dark. To me, she is like an angel, a beautiful child ghost, looking down at me, for me, scared but hopeful, creamy with tears and sleep. I turn the front porch light off, lock the door, and go upstairs to be with her. I take her hand and walk her to her bed.

"How do you feel, honey?"

She presses suddenly against me, puts her arms around my waist, and crumples into inexplicable sobs. "We need to have some more babies in this house," she cries. "Will you have another baby?" I lift her, and her arms circle my neck, her legs clamp around me. When I put her into bed, I climb in next to her, the covers over both of us, the nightstand lamps on low.

I have done this before. Sometimes I do this.

Sometimes as I'm drifting toward sleep, in the beginnings of that dissolution, I wonder where I am, when this is, and realize that at these moments I could be anywhere, anytime, for all I know: eight and napping in the trailer, my broken arm in a cast, or thirteen at night clutching a pillow to my neck, or twenty in the arms of my boyfriend, or twenty-seven in the arms of my husband, or thirty-three next to my imaginary daughter; at every place in the whole spinning shape that is my life, when I am falling asleep, I am the same person, the identical awareness, the same fuzzball of mind, the same muck of nerves, all along the line. I forage through my life and everywhere—there, there, and there—it is only me in it, the very same me, the same harmless lump, the same soggy weirdo, the same sleeping, breathing bun.

Georgianne, too, perhaps, even when she's old, will be the same flanneled muffin as now, this snoring puff, this snoozy breath and heart always.

"Humans are the voice boxes of life," the teacher told her classes that Friday. "They are protein's means of speaking about itself. We owe the dumb, the inarticulate—the grass, the snails—that much." What rot, she thought. What could be more articulate than a blade of grass, a lovely blade of grass scaled by an ant, what could be more superfluous than words, ghoulish and life-eating, for a snail, for a tree, for a wise man in a robe in a cave in Tibet? "I want you guys to keep notebooks. Record anything you want in them, any word or phrase or poem, but write! The difference between a poet and a non-poet is that a non-poet believes he will remember everything the next day without getting up, switching on the light, and writing it down."

The weekend appeared before her like a lovely hammock slung between two wide weeks. The teacher had coffee alone and went home.

Saturday mornings in Fitchville the college radio station from eight-thirty to eleven plays only songs from Broadway musicals. I usually make it out of bed by nine, pull down the shredded wheat for Georgianne, then head back upstairs, turn on the shower, and scrub my back to something by Cole Porter, shampoo to Jerome Kern, rinse off to something snappy by Sondheim or Bernstein. I like to bee in Amhaireekha. I clap and stomp and try not to slip in the tub. There have been times when Georgie has abandoned her cereal, pulled off her pajamas and joined me to jiggle around under the shower spray. She has come to know lots of the words and does the complete "I'm Getting Married in the Morning," in a cockney bellow impossible not to admire.

This morning the program is devoting a full hour to the

music of *Kiss Me Kate*, and George and I, in the shower, act out
parts from it, contriving gestures for all the words, something we
call the Eensy-Weensy Spider School of Singing. On "I Hate Men"
we soap each other's shoulder blades and scowl. ("If they can
send one man to the moon," Eleanor's always saying, "why can't
they send them all?") On "Why Can't You Behave" I shake my
finger like a good, offended mother-slash-lover, and on "Too
Darn Hot" Georgie giggles and stands behind the angle of the
water and fiddles with the faucets and the temperature, which is
when I say, "Yikes, this is where I get out," push aside the curtain
and drip out onto the bathmat. Georgie is in a giggle fit, like a
little girl who hasn't laughed for a long time. When she, too,
finally steps out, she puts her hands on my hips and says, "You're
getting fat, Mom. You're turning into a hippie!" and she giggles
some more and I say, "Gee thanks," and her eyes are wet with
laughing, her skin pink from steam and heat, her tiny nipples
like two thin slices of hot dog, and we powder each other's backs
with a blue-gingham powder mitt, which was on sale last week at
Woolworth's, wrap our heads and bodies in red, clean towels, and
return to the shredded wheat downstairs in the kitchen, bring
bowls out into the living room, turn on the TV, and watch
cartoons.

At around noon the phone rings. It's Darrel.

"Hi," he says.

I tell him I'm watching Saturday morning cartoons, all
space heroes and ray guns, and he's clearly impressed. He wants
to know if I'd like to have dinner tonight, and because I really
want to spend tonight with Georgianne, I say no but can we
make it for next Saturday? and he says all right how about seven
o'clock and I say great.

I like Saturdays. Now that I'm a merry widow, they feel happy,
aspiring. When I was married, my husband and I would always

fight on Saturdays: That was when we had the most time. I remember one Saturday, after *The Best of Broadway* had done 1776, and after my husband had declared twice in a loud voice "I cannot abide this musical," he asked me to get his glasses from the bedroom, since I was closer. I said no, and told him he was lazy and presumptuous and had no sense of moral outrage at anything, at which point he bolted up and said loudly, "You needling bitch, if you really believe I'm so despicable then you're a masochistic scumbag in love with my prick." Our marriage, I suddenly realized, wasn't going well.

I hadn't heard the word *scumbag* since I was a kid. Eddie across the road had yelled it at my brother Louis once and Louis had yelled it back. I stared at my husband. This was a man who could say *subpoena duces tecum* like it was soup. *Scumbag?* It terrified me. My heart did a fast crawl out and onto the hilly dirt road of aloneness and escape; it's an image I have: a wide dirt road which undulates like a roller coaster. I think it's somewhere in Lebanon.

Later we had an argument about his involvement with a woman at work, and I stormed into the dining room and took the plaster bust of George Eliot he'd given me for Christmas (George's middle name was Eliot; this was his sense of humor) and broke it against the stereo he'd given me for my birthday. Two birds with one of the birds.

We were rotten and cruel. Especially on Saturdays. We'd say things like, "Blow it out your ass, Bingo-Boots," though I'm not sure why.

The rest of the afternoon George and I clean the house. I wash the dishes and run the vacuum cleaner quickly through the living room. Georgie dusts: "These cobs sure do make webs," she says. She thinks this is fun. Her friend Isabelle Shubby from next door is helping her dust, a volunteer from the neighborhood. The

Shubbys' house is separated from ours by two driveways and three trees. It's a big turquoise split-level, the only one on a street of brick and stucco. Her parents have noisy parties, which they invite me to so that I won't get annoyed and call the police. I've never gone, however, though someday I just might show up in lace and emeralds or something. Isabelle has brought her Labrador, Adams, and we put him in the bathroom with newspapers on the floor. I don't like dogs, large bumping dogs. They have a crowd behavior like humans: They gang up and go straight for the genitals. Besides, Adams doesn't like the vacuum cleaner, which I keep turning on and off and moving from room to room.

In the living room *Mme. Charpentier and Her Daughters* is crooked. It is dry-mounted and unframed and I have to balance it between push-pins. I turn off the vacuum, go to re-align it, and notice a small dark scribbling, as with a black felt pen, in the left corner. It looks like the sort of thing Georgie used to do to books and papers of mine when she was little.

"Georgianne," I say. "Did you do this to the Renoir print?"

She comes closer. "Don't yell at me," she says. "How do you know it's not Gerard? He coulda done it." She looks at the black squiggle, then moves on, dusting the TV, her little arm making circular movements with the rag. Isabelle has stopped to look at a magazine.

"I'm not accusing you, I'm just asking you." Neither of us says anything. After a minute I add, "What makes you think Gerard might have done it?"

"I dunno," she shrugs. She's still concentrating on her darkening dustcloth. "He was looking at it." Isabelle glances at me fearfully. She says she's wondering if Adams is okay.

"I'm sure he's okay," I say.

The dark line on the Renoir looks like a miniature of the crack on the side of the house, the seam of a jigsaw puzzle, a tear in the blue of a dress.

. . .

The news tonight is about Congress and about polyps, both threatened by man. We watch, glued, frozen. We have ice cream for dessert. After the news George and I watch a sociologically minded talk show whose program tonight is on talented, autistic children. One of them, Donna, is in the studio audience, between her parents. She looks only twelve, but is seventeen. The host makes a mistake, tells the world she's fourteen, then apologizes. Her black eyes dart around, and then she retreats into the sweatered hump of herself. Autistic or not, she knows this is a humiliation: to be called fourteen in front of millions of viewers, when you are really seventeen. Her mother next to her, I can see, in the corner of the screen, tries to console her by squeezing her hand. Donna has made something of a national reputation for herself drawing greeting cards. The silver-haired host bends down to compliment her, as if she's a lobotomized dwarf, a midge, a worm; her features suddenly relax when the host says again, "Donna, you're really very talented," and her mouth and eyes fall into all the right places, and the voice that says "Thank you" is a low, strong, woman's voice.

It's as if I know the girl. She almost has my name, and I bet we know things about each other: slipping behind the hips and shoulders of our mother, squeezing her hand, we don't want to talk to this silver-haired man, we see things clearly, we can sit here all day locked up yet seeing, our mouths unnecessary, though they may smile to be polite. I have been her: the darkness, the slump, the fat splotched cheeks, the frumpish skirts. People talk past us, we are invisible; when they say our name, if they really look at us, they don't mean it, they only want us to say anything, anything stupid, but our dark woman's voice, we know, would terrify.

Sometimes anything but cartoons is too real for me.

. . .

Sunday is always a bad day. A sort of gray purgatory that resembles a bus station with broken vending machines. God is dead, and denied the last word on things, is acting like a real baby. Sunday is some sort of revenge. "And on the Seventh Day he was arrested," Gerard likes to say.

Before class on Monday the teacher, who smelled of Emeraude and faintly of onions and who felt herself perhaps the sort of woman doomed in middle age to be always taking other people's children for walks in parks, read a giant stack of student poems. The ones by a black student named Darrel Erni were the most interesting, mostly about women he'd known in Vietnam. The teacher picked at the sweater lint caught in the ragged edge of her fingernail and then stirred her coffee with a knife.

In class she grew dramatic. "You need to ask yourself questions," she told her students in something that resembled a hiss. "I want you to ask yourself, 'How is writing a public act? What does poetry owe the world? Are we all vagabonds at a cosmic dump or are we just not paying attention?' " Then she stomped around back and forth in front of the class and spoke of nuclear protest, presidential petitions, throwing pies with lots of whipped cream. "Do you know whether this college has investments in South Africa?"

Outside, the leaves that had not blushed or died were doing a dazzling fade, the gold, paper money of pirates.

"I want you to think about the sick luxury of your being," she said. And then she lit up a cigarette.

Tuesday is a train station with one working vending machine filled with nothing but Mars bars. I meet Gerard for a fast breakfast. I walk in a little later than usual and he looks up from a newspaper and an ashtray full of cigarette butts. He smiles. "Didn't think you'd be here today." I climb into the booth, look at him from across the table and gently take his cigarette from his fingers, helping myself to a long drag. Then I too smile. We're friends. I'm relieved.

I glance at his newspaper. "What's happening in the world? Do we still exist?"

We don't talk about Thursday night—another undiscussable, like Darrel's war, or Gerard's long ago restaurant: We leave them alone. There's still something tense between us, but it's tense like hope.

Gerard folds the newspaper. "Do you suppose this planet is hell and we've all been sent here from somewhere else because we fucked up, and we don't realize it?"

I smile. This is how we talk when we're happy. When we're depressed we spout forth irrepressibly about our love lives.

I look at the paper again. The human race is dying. We are all dying and we are sitting up in our beds smoking cigars and making dying jokes, an impressively, compulsively vaudevillian species. Monkeys with spiff.

"The coffee's like mop water today. I don't know what happened." Usually Hank's serves the kind of coffee that makes you talk real fast and then sends you knocking around the room, breaking things.

"And look at these eggs," says Gerard. Yolk has bled and dried all over the plate. Gerard always likes his yolks cooked more. "I hate them when they're all embryonic like this. The waitress is new. The last time she walked by here I said, 'Excuse me, could I also have some Band-Aids for these?' and she just walked away." Yolk has dried into Gerard's beard like wax.

"Who wants to tell me what a sonnet is?" asked the teacher. "Lucy?"

"No, it's Joyce."

"Really? Gee, my seating chart says Lucy. Oh, I see. Lucy

Joyce Brondoli. Why are you called by your middle name? Is
there a long story to that?"

Lucy Joyce Brondoli shrugged and spoke slowly, in a diffident deadpan. "The dog was named Lucy, so they had to call me
Joyce."

"The dog was there before you and got your name?"

"I forget."

"I don't understand. Why did they name both you and the
dog Lucy?"

"I guess they liked the name. A sonnet is fourteen lines of
iambic pentameter ending in a couplet and the rhyme scheme before that goes ABAB,CDCD,EFEF. Like that. Shakespeare wrote
a lot of them."

"But why didn't they just call the dog Joyce? It doesn't make
any sense."

"I get sidetracked," I tell Eleanor. We slurp coffee together in the
lounge. "I get fascinated. I think people spend most of their lives
just trying to adjust to their names. When you're eighteen months
old, you learn what it is, one of those huge, immutable abstrac-
tions in life, and from there on in it's all recovery from the shock
and indignity of it." My father had wanted another boy after
Louis. He was hoping for a Benjamin. That's partly how I became Benna. The other part involved my mother who, in looking
through a book called *Names for Your Child*, became very dis-
tressed to see that if you were a boy your name usually meant
"Almighty One," and if you were a girl you were probably "a wee,
faithful thing of the woods." My mother didn't want me hanging
around in the woods. "Well, Nick," she said to my father in the
hospital, "looks like we have a little Ben*na*." Which was the beginning of a lot of confusion. My father sometimes called me
Ben, complicating my childhood in the obvious ways. And in the
second grade I got thirty valentines, all with my name spelled

differently, everything from Bean to Donna. No one could get it right.

"My name was always such a hideosity I finally had to take up yoga to relax," says Eleanor. I smile, slurp, and accidentally burn my tongue. "You know," says Eleanor, "if I were to write a book, it would be filled with women sitting around having lunch, talking like this—about God and diaphragms and *Middlemarch*. After every lunch they'd all take out their compacts at the table and reapply their lipstick together. What yould you write?"

"Oh, I don't know. Maybe I'd call it *Split Infinitives* and load it up with a lot of divorces. Then at the end I'd have it be like *To the Lighthouse*, where all human life is suddenly lifted up out of the book and vanished, only an old house at the end, with English weeds tapping at the glass."

Eleanor nods and smiles. "That's depressing."

"Yeah, I guess if it was too depressing I'd add a knock-knock joke."

At night it's cold and I sit out on the steps of my front porch, listen to the leaves drop, like the beginning of rain. I suck on my cigarette, its false restorative, the dry papery sponge, the sucking finger of love. I exhale in the direction of the streetlight and what I see, what is formed, is a sort of halo, a luminous flower, splayed ghostly starfish! for a moment and then it floats off into the hydrangea. I repeat this, breathing on my cigarette, blowing upward into the light: At night all ghosts, all angels, haloes, luminous flowers are this nicotined dust against the streetlamp.

When I told my husband I hated him, we hadn't been married long at all. It was when he was taking my picture with his new camera, narrowing his eyes, adjusting the shutter speed, posing me at various angles until my smile felt aching and absurd.

We were in the living room. He had asked me to take my shirt off and I'd obliged. I'd been standing there by the mantel awhile and it was getting cold, the hairs on my arms standing on end, my nipples erect. "Got your high beams on," said my husband, like a college kid, camera to his face. Finally he pulled the camera away from his eyes. "Light's bad," he mumbled and walked off without taking the shot. Stunned and topless, I followed him into the dining room where he began taking pictures of the porcelain monkey-head lamp my Aunt Wyn had sent us for our wedding. "The light's hitting this great," said my husband. "The reading's perfect." His camera was clicking away.

"The monkey-head lamp?" I said. I would never understand photography, the sneaky, murderous taxidermy of it. Three times before, my husband had asked me to pose with various articles of clothing removed. Once in the bedroom wearing only boots and one of his ties. Once in the bathroom with a red towel draped strategically to miss one breast. Once in the kitchen in just my bra. And today. I did this because I loved him, I supposed, but maybe I did it because I'd grown up in a trailer and guessed that this is what people did in houses, that this is what houses were for. I'm not sure. Maybe I did it because I had only five pages of a dissertation on Miltonic echoes in nineteenth- and twentieth-century children's literature. Each time my husband had never actually taken the picture. He had put the camera to his face, squinted his eyes, bared his teeth, and grown dissatisfied. This day, however, this day of the monkey-head lamp would be the last. I stood there, naked from the waist up, fury spreading up from my gut into my face, as fury does, and when my husband turned around with only a vaguely apologetic half-smile, I punched him in the neck. "I hate you," I said, and then went back into the living room and put on my shirt. I turned around, buttoning, and he was standing by the sofa, wide-eyed, the camera hanging from its long black strap, resting against his torso like a dark, outsized belly button, like an insect that had crawled into his abdomen and was poking its head out to look around.

"The litter bag on our honeymoon was bad enough," I said. We had driven to Cape Hatteras. He had made me put the car litter bag in my pocketbook so it wouldn't stink up the rented Plymouth. I have always felt that life was simply a series of personal humiliations relieved, occasionally, by the humiliations of others. But compared to my husband I had no imagination with which to fight back, with which to construct indignities. "This is the last draw," I said. From the time I was a child I always thought people were saying "draw" not "straw." "I despise you." I walked toward the front door. I was going for a walk.

"I'm sorry," he said. I stopped and turned to look. He had kind of a vegetable glaze, the look, I imagined, potatoes got in their eyes. His neck was red. "Shoot me, if I'm such a shit. Shoot me." And then, apparently, he became quite taken with the joke, and handed me the camera, dancing around in front of me, singing, "Shoot me, shoot me."

"George," I said. "You're losing it."

"Shoot me!" he persisted, and he started taking off his clothes. I grabbed the camera and took off out the front door, across the lawn; perhaps I would throw the camera away in a trash can somewhere. "Shoot me! Shoot me!" I could still hear George cry behind me, and I turned and he was bouncing up and down on the front porch, ludicrous in his underwear. "Shoot me!"

And I shot, and the picture I took and still have, shows him ducking back inside the house, one side of him still caught within the doorframe, half of a pale blurry body embedded forever in the long dark marrow of that entrance, deep inside unseen and grinning, a monkey-head lamp in perfect light, a present only an aunt could give.

.   .   .

You cannot be grateful without possessing a past. That is why children are incapable of gratitude and why night prayers and dinner graces are lost on them. "Gobbles Mommy, Gobbles Grandpa . . ." George races through it. She has no reference points. As I get older the past widens and accumulates, all sloppy landlessness like a river, and as a result I have more clearly demarcated areas of gratitude. Things like ice cream or scenery or one good kiss become objects of a huge soulful thanks. Nothing is gobbled. This is a sign of getting old.

"Writing is a safari, dammit," exclaimed the teacher. "It means going out there and spotting, nabbing, and bringing home to the cage of the page the most marvelous living stuff of the world."

Timothy Robinson sat right in front of the teacher. He was doodling scenes from Conan in the margins of his notebook.

"But those cages are small and expensive," the teacher continued, searched, groped, not knowing quite what she was talking about.

Conan's pectorals were like concrete slabs and in Timothy Robinson's margins Conan's biceps and triceps had begun to make his arms look like large croissants. Now he suddenly was getting sunglasses. Now striped thighs.

"Don't bring back any dim-witted mooses," she said. "Don't put a superfluous dumb cluck of a line in your poem." She had used her lifeboat simile in the last class: A line is like a lifeboat— only a limited number of words get to go in it and you have to decide which word-lives are most valuable; the rest die.

It was ridiculous, but the only thing she could think of to say.

When no one said anything in response, she stared out into the center of the room and said, "So, Tim. How the fuck is Conan?"

. . .

The small, dingy P&C by campus is unusually crowded and not just with jean-jacketed students buying beer, bananas, hamburger. There are even families in here, as if from some other neighborhood. Perhaps there's a sale. The three available shopping carts by the door are gritty with black grease, spangled with lettuce bits like a rabbit's cage. They are all jammed into each other, a copulation of stainless steel. I unhitch the one with the least grease but the most lettuce and proceed to wheel it into the mayhem. People are crashing into each other in the narrow produce aisle, scrambling zigzag for plastic bags.

"Excuse me," says a male student in a white turtleneck. He doesn't have a cart, only a beige knapsack of books over his shoulder. He isn't interested in produce. "Excuse me," he says to me again. "I saw you outside and followed you in here because I thought you were beautiful and I wanted to tell you that."

"Oh, my god," I say and turn away, suddenly startled into a weird sort of terror. I fumble with the cabbage heads. Who does this guy think he is? I try to glide voicelessly away.

"Are you a student here?" the guy persists.

I can feel myself pale, jittery, glaring at a point slightly to the left of one of his ears. His heart, I know, is all chutzpah and photography. "No, I'm an instructor." I try to pronounce it like a baroness, but it comes out faltering and wrong. "Excuse me," I say to the student, then squeeze past him, between a center-aisle mustard display and someone else's cartload of dog food and frozen orange juice. I cross the aisle to the apples.

The student follows. "I hope I didn't offend you," he says. I keep my back to him, studying the apples. "My name is John. I'm an archaeology major," he says, examining, I can tell, the tweed back of my thrift-shop man's coat. I examine apple after apple, taking out my reading glasses, putting them on, and then peering out over them, saying, "Hmmmmm." I pretend to be an apple scientist. I'm unable to tell him straight out to get lost.

"Well," says John, finally. "Good-bye," and he ambles away.

I remain at the apples, counting, counting. I can feel my face splotch with red, my mouth clamp into a hard line. I breathe deeply, run my hand through my hair, return to my cart and quickly wheel it around, head for the checkout line, like someone who needs desperately to be alone, to be in bed, to be taking a bath, somewhere far away, conjugating verbs, memorizing dynasties.

The ants are still trafficking around the place, seemingly undisturbed by the weather's getting colder. Georgianne keeps singing her own misheard lyrics to a Bob Dylan song: "The ants are my friends / They're blowing in the wind." The crack has moved a few more inches, taking a slight upward turn like a kind of graph, an optimistic poll. The plumbing, however, is sluggish, acting up, the toilet slow and undignified, churning the toilet-paper, stewing, shredding things finer. This is what it's like to live in a house.

Georgie has dinner and a bath, and Mrs. Kimball comes over and I say good night and drive over to Gerard's apartment. We are going to have drinks there and then go off to the Dome Room at the Holiday Inn where he will play and I will sit in an elegant booth and mark up student poems all evening. And listen.

He is in the kitchen pouring bourbon over ice.

I pace idly about his apartment. Over his bed Gerard has placed a cheap gift-shop placard reading MISERY LOVES COMPANY. One of his Greece posters on the same wall is starting to come down. A tack is missing and the tape on the back is fuzzy with lint. "Hey, Gerard, where do you keep your tape? I'm going to fix your Kythera poster."

"Try the drawer in the nightstand there," he calls, making ice cube and glass noises.

I open the drawer. It's crammed with a jumble of things— old sheet music, dice, masking tape, regular tacks, carpet tacks, unopened packages of condoms. I take out the masking tape. Gerard has come in with drinks and hands me one. I notice he has missed a belt loop. I slip the tape roll over my wrist like a bracelet and push the drawer shut with one hip.

"Cheers," says Gerard, smiling.

"Go team go," I say, former alternate cheerleader at Tomaston High. We drink slowly, deliciously. "Tell me, Gerard. Why is it that you keep your *condoms* in the same drawer as your carpet tacks and tape?"

Gerard slurps and swallows. "How else are you supposed to keep them on?" he says.

The Holiday Inn is more brightly lit than most places Gerard plays in. There are pink glassed candles on the tables, but the whole windowless place is a bright amberish yellow and the candles are merely gestures, splots of silly complementary colors, like decorator pillows. Gerard takes his drink, sips, places it on the piano up front. He has arranged for a free glass of chablis for me, and the waitress comes over, places it in front of me, smiles, goes away. I have connections. It's all small town and rink-a-dink, but I have connections with celebrity.

I pull out student poems from my bag. I think about Gerard wanting to be an opera singer, his hunger to have something grander than this, the arrogance of a hunger.

"Good evening, ladies and gentlemen." It's Gerard, adjusting the microphone. A spotlight flips on and Gerard squints into it. That, too, wanders around like a searchlight, getting adjusted, and Gerard, along with Charlie by the speakers who is supposedly in charge of the lights, goes into some five-second Berlin Wall pantomime: expressions of chase and horror, arms thrown in the air. They laugh, then resume a more responsible mien.

"Good evening again, ladles and gentlespoons." This time he strikes a few chords. "Welcome to the Dome Room"—two more, ascending tonics. "At the"—chord. "Holiday Inn"—big chord and glissando. I've seen him do this dozens of times. Usually he launches quickly into a lot of bad lady-cannibal jokes, prefaced by "Where's the dome in this room? What a dome name." At least, I console myself, he does this for money. Tonight he introduces himself: "I'm Gerard Maines. I know some of you were expecting Tammy Wynette, but these things happen." Then he starts in with "Just You, Just Me," his own jazz rendition, never looking at the keyboard. In front of me I have a poem about an alien. From another solar system. I have forbidden any poems about aliens, but sometimes students beg me—"Please, just *one* alien"—and they slip in. Now Gerard stops to banter with the audience: "What? You're from *where?* Belittle, New York? You would live in a town with a name like that?" The people up front by the piano are loving it, the good-natured ribbing, they are starved for it. It's still a weeknight and the place isn't that full —only every other table has someone at it. Mostly businessmen, some couples, a group of women in their early twenties, smiling hopefully at Gerard then turning and whispering to one another, hands to lips. Gerard often attracts women like this. They come up to him on breaks and at the end of the night to chat and gush and ask him questions about the way he sang a certain song and what he does during the day. Sometimes they come up to him in pairs, stand there, hands in pockets, bodies leaning, sunk into one hip. Other times they come individually, a gesticulative drink in one hand, undulating cigarette in the other. Often, he's confided, he's gone home to bed with one of them, both of them awaking the next day, never in love, not always remembering last names. There was one woman, however, Hermione Miller, only nineteen, who had kept calling him, crying, showing up naked on his doorstep holding lighted candles, breaking into his car and sleeping in the backseat. He would spend whole hours talking to her, calming her down. She insisted she loved him and would go mad without him or at least have a hard time grocery shopping. She would phone him at Carpet Town and keep him on the phone, pretending she was interested in something in a lilac shag. Finally she fell for another musician, someone who worked the Double Bubble Hour at Howard Johnson's.

"When I was in high school," said Gerard, "I was moral and virile and sweet and trying to change my name to Buff, and no one would have me. There wasn't a girl in Queens who would look at me."

I don't really believe this. It's all part of Gerard's poor-boy-in-Queens mythologizing.

"Now I'm a carpet salesman in an upstate suburb, a rat playing the piano, drunk with operatic aspirations, and people I hardly know say they're in love with me. Christ." He paused. "Middle age is dangerous."

"Middle age? Gerard, you're a year younger than *I* am."

"I know," he said.

Gerard's still on the first set. He has another drink coming. The waitress leaves it on the piano. Someone near me at the bar is eating Vaseline. He has a jar and a spoon and is just eating. I try not to stare. I try to turn my attention to the stuff I've brought. I try to find things to cross out or circle, so I can feel like a teacher, like someone who knows things. This afternoon I was listening to the kids out in front of the house—Isabelle Shubby and some others—playing games, that timeless legacy of hop-scotch and jumping rhymes children bring to one another, mysteriously, without adults, and I wondered, Is there a secret world of knowledge that adults know, that gets passed on from one generation to the next, the way there is with children? I think not. I think you're blurped out into the world, you get a few jumprope rhymes, and from there on in you're on your own. Nobody tells you anything. Nobody shows you how.

"Hey, you in the back doing my taxes," shouts Gerard into the microphone. I look up and he winks. "This is for you." I wait to hear what it is. "I Want Money." I nod and smile. I'm now part of Gerard's act. A few people turn to look at me.

One of them is Maple up near the front. I didn't see him come in and now we wave enthusiastically. Maple stands, says "Excuse me" to a few people in chairs, and attempts to make his way over to my table. It takes a while before he is sitting next to me.

"So, this is your song?" he says.

"Not really." Growing up we always said "Not hardly," and I find myself almost saying it now. We also said "kranz" instead of "crayons," and began all sentences with "Anyways . . ."

"How've you been? Lots of work, I see."

"Oh, yeah. How about you?"

"Gotta new job," he says. "I'm a waiter at a veggie and granola place on Roosevelt. I'll have more time for my dancing that way."

"Be careful. You know you can never really trust people who don't eat meat."

Maple smiles. "It's better than clerking at Howland's." He turns his profile to me. He has three amethysts in his ear. He combs back his hair with his fingers, eyeing the piano. "I'm worried about Gerard," he says. "He's drinking too much." The music has stopped. Gerard's on a twenty-minute break. I see him start to wend his way over here but get waylaid by a woman in red slacks.

I try to think. Is Gerard drinking too much? Am I? Have I really noticed? "You think so?" I ask. And the waitress brings over two glasses of white wine.

"This is from Gerard," she says.

"You know he's going to audition for opera companies?"

"Yeah, I know," I sigh, all weariness and concern, and then neither of us says anything. We tap our fingers, gaze down, gaze off. "Do you realize," I say at last, "that there's a guy sitting at the bar eating Vaseline?"

In class the teacher was teaching poetic forms. She defined *villanelle, sestina, limerick.* Last night she had looked up *terza rima* in the dictionary; it followed *tertiary syphilis,* something she'd always suspected.

Saturday dinner with Darrel is at the Fitchville Souvlaki House, where Gerard and I first went years ago. There's a permanent sign on the door that says CLOSE ON MONDAY, and I worry that somehow Darrel and I won't be.

This is where Darrel wants to go. He likes the checked tablecloths, the accents flying around in the kitchen. You can hear them when someone pushes in or out of the door in back. I look around the place and wonder who all here's on first dates.

We order recklessly. I'm not sure what we're getting. Darrel tells me that the Greek name for stuffed grape leaves means liar eggplant.

"Personally," I say, "I've never put much store by honesty. I mean, how can you trust a word whose first letter you don't even pronounce?" I light a cigarette and try to look sophisticated. I am that afraid of the world. Really, I have never gotten out of Tomaston High.

Darrel smiles and says that before he was in Vietnam, he was in Italy for six months, a weird mix of orders, and, on leave

for a week, he went to Greece, island-hopped, learned a few
phrases, never slept at all. He describes things: some fishermen
he met, a village woman, a disco on the beach.

"What about the Acropolis?" I am into the authentic par-
taking of foreign countries, not ever having been to one myself,
unless marriage counts.

Darrel describes the Acropolis, and, yes, it sounds like marriage: high, stunning, stony, and old with a gift shop at the
bottom. He goes on to talk about neolithic architectural sites, the
ancient Epidauros amphitheater. I feel ordinary and ungrammatical, and as always blame the trailer, blame growing up in a
trailer.

When dinner comes we eat it. I'm not concentrating. Why
is it that I can't quite describe or picture Darrel? I close my eyes
for two seconds and try. Is it that I'm not paying attention? I
think of him as tall and strong, but perhaps he's not really.
Does he have a mustache? I open my eyes quickly to check. No,
he doesn't.

"Do you feel okay?" asks Darrel.

"It's the liar eggplant," I say cryptically.

Darrel is looking at my teeth. "You have nice teeth," he
says.

Afterward, at home in my living room, we drink wine, but
we don't kiss. Behind him, like a movie screen, I see the war, the
muck of the paddies, swoop of helicopters, the hollers and cries.
I suppose that is why we do not kiss.

But perhaps the reasons are not large and public but small
and personal. Perhaps it's simply that I'm too unattractive, older,
perhaps my body has forgotten how to do things, my lips no
longer firm or flip, my nipples no longer pink as calamine, my
tongue no longer newly, nimbly amphibious but a thick, thrashing fish-muscle. Now I'm middle-aged: hairs sprout, skin sags,
my mouth grows stupid as a boot. How can I make it work? I

try to think about Congress and about polyps: how they make currents with their lips in order to receive food.

Darrel is talking aesthetics, poetry, voice, my thesis, and at the mention of the last all I can think of is how my whole life all I've ever really wanted was for my small, bug-bite breasts to heave seductively up over the neckline of my shirt, like a scientific wonder. Perhaps one might learn it with practice, discipline, commands: Heave! Heave-ho! "Do you like Joan Baez?" Darrel is saying. "I think her voice is more beautiful than any other singer I can think of." I burst into a medley of all the Joan Baez songs I know. Darrel sings an old army thing about Nixon, set to the tune of "Hark the Herald Angels Sing."

Our laughs grow louder and hazy. Soon we are kissing. Soon we are unbuttoning. I haven't kissed or unbuttoned in a long time and it's like, at long last, a meeting of friends, falling into a familiar, ineffable dance we've both learned elsewhere, long ago, but have revived here, a revival! perhaps like Agnes DeMille's *Oklahoma!* something like that. It is as if our separate pasts were greeting each other, as if we were saying, This is how I have been with other people, this is how I would love you. If I loved you. Everything always seems to boil down to Rodgers and Hammerstein. Off you would go in the mist of day and all that.

"You know, I'm probably old enough to be—" but here I stop for a second. "I'm old enough to be older than you," I whisper. "Don't look at my body. Don't say anything about it."

Darrel smiles. "I wouldn't dream of bringing it up at a time like this."

And soon we are upstairs, pulling down the bedspread, something in us pounding and accommodated, a mashing of hips, a pressing of faces, a slow friction of limbs and chests and lips against the sheets, this argument that is sex. Sometimes his chest moves up from mine with a soft sucking sound from the damp, trapped space between our sternums—something wet and reluctant, like marine life or a heart that can't stop beating no matter how it tries. We are gasping, quiet, in the dark, and then the wash of violet and night tornadoes through my legs and up behind my eyes, plumbs and spirals my spine, and I know if I can keep feeling like this I'll be okay, if I can feel like this I'm not dead, I won't die. Life is sad. Here is someone.

The next three Saturday nights we sleep together. They are full of chuckles and whispers and much munching about the neck and shoulders. They are sweet and gentle, not at all like my marriage, where my husband used to laugh and slap me on the back after I'd had an orgasm, like a buddy, like I'd just hit this crazy home run. I don't remember feeling such relief at the start of an affair: I'm not afraid. It's like the joy of meeting someone who knows your favorite cousin—everything proceeds from this momentous, bridging fact. Like two Maine license plates honking and waving on a California freeway: the warmth of shared exile; two ugly step-siblings meeting at a ball, smiling and waltzing and, having no fairy godmother, not having to rush off in a tizzy like Cinderella who was all jitters and economics, foot small as her bank account. *We* don't have to rush home, we can dance all night, curfewless and happy, our feet warty and huge as skateboards.

"You're out of your mind," says Eleanor, not smiling. "Your professional position is precarious enough. Why jeopardize things further with another affair with another one of your students?"

"What do you mean, *another*?" I ask warily. She has said it twice. I've noticed. "It's not like I sleep around with my students. Look, you don't know Darrel. He's great. He's the sort of guy who tells you just the edge of his whole tragic life story, then smiles and leans over and sniffs your hair."

Eleanor shrugs. "It only matters how things look."

"Now you sound like my husband, Mr. Photography."

"To *them*, to *them*, it matters." The invisible them. The them upstairs with offices and foot-long pens. Eleanor is exasperated with me. She goes out to get a drink of water and doesn't come back.

When I pull into the driveway, it is late, five o'clock, and the Shubbys next door are having a happy-hour party. Despite the autumnal nip in the air, the guests have spilled out onto the front porch, shouting, dancing, waving cocktail glasses.

"Hey, Benna," Mr. Shubby calls to me, as I get out of my car. "Come on over."

"Thanks, but I really can't," I call back, though for a split second I consider going. What could it hurt? Some small talk about the New York Film Festival and what I do for a living? I'm not in the mood. I slam the car door and walk across my lawn which is already scaly with leaves. An orangey crimson is settling in all along the street. The cork-bark in the front is in a cold, deep blush.

"Okay, be that way," Mr. Shubby shouts back. He's being good-natured. He's being the life of the party. My arms are full. I smile and shrug. Mrs. Shubby comes out on the porch and signals flirtatiously to her husband. "Irv, you're needed in here to open a bottle." She spies me on my own front steps, fumbling for keys. "Benna, dear, why don't you come join us." The "dear" is to make me feel like a girl, a foolish girl, an unwed mother.

"Thanks, really," I say. "Maybe next time." I find the keys and by this time the whole Shubby porch is waving and calling. "Join the party! Come on!"

"Can't, sorry." I slip inside my front door, close it, sink back against it. The party sounds now are distant, deeply buried rumbles and squeals, like something wrong with your car though you can't figure out what.

The ants sniff and speed around the window frames. They are frightened: It's October. Like all things without recourse, they scurry, veer off into the walls of their own overpopulation, their own destructiveness, looking for a way out.

Georgie has a note from the school nurse. She might need glasses. I'm supposed to take her to an eye doctor. "I can't see, I can't see," she says, stumbling around the house, deliberately bumping into furniture, arms outstretched and groping stupidly. "Where am I, where am I? Is this the bathroom?" she says, staggering into the kitchen, her eyes squinted almost shut. I am mincing onion for Quick Chili, my own very personal recipe.

"Cute, George," I say, looking back at my onion. And then because she doesn't say anything else, I say, "Tell me. What do you think of Darrel? Do you like him?"

She has opened her eyes and is playing with the buckle of her shoe, which she has taken off so she can fly it around like a spaceship. "He's okay," she says. "When's Gerard comin' over?"

The last argument I had with my husband was about intelligence and sexual fidelity in marriage. "An intelligent person does everything with ambivalence," he said. "Strictly speaking, fidelity can never be a given." We were in front of a drugstore. In the window was a Russell Stover candies display. I couldn't believe my ears. Was this the difference between men and women? That women could never believe their ears?

"No!" I shouted. "That's just not true. An intelligent person has an intelligent faith, and when an intelligent person decides to do something, it's done unambivalently, unequivocally, intelligently. Why the hell did we get married? Sexual fidelity must always be a given!" Strictly speaking strictly. Whenever I'm furious, the only vocabulary I can come up with are words that have been spoken in the last thirty seconds. My sentences become anagrams of the sentences before. "Intelligent people are not ambivalent people." He was being an asshole, so I would be one too. I would ask him to love me unambivalently, to love me in theory, to love me unambivalently in theory as I shouted at him in front of dozens of persons, persons in cars, persons with newspapers under their arms, and Russell Stover gift boxes and friction pour le bain in bags coming out of the drugstore, sick, ailing persons with unfilled prescriptions going in, persons walking by, putting up umbrellas, persons turning on their windshield wipers. How could he help but be ambivalent about our marriage? I think, in fact, that right then and there, in front of the drugstore, was where and when his ambivalence ended. I think that is when he became unambivalent and unequivocal and decided he didn't want to be married to me anymore.

We never made it into the drugstore. I forget what we were going there to get. We went back to the car, to our Rabbit bandaged in bumper stickers. It was starting to drizzle, and we each slammed doors and didn't talk to, look at, or touch each other. I stared at the glove compartment knob. He started the car, started the windshield wipers, and we drove home. He twitched in his jaw; I could see it in my peripheral vision. There was a purity to the hate, to the determination. It continued for twelve hours. Then, the next morning when both of us were in the bathroom, brushing our teeth and dressing for work, he said, "I never want to see you again," only I misheard him at first and thought he'd said, "I want to see again."

When I was little, I didn't understand that you could change a few sounds in a name or a phrase and have it mean something entirely different. When I told teachers my name was *Benna* and they said, "*Donna* who?" I would say, "Donna Gilbert." I thought close was good enough, that sloppiness was generally built into the language. I thought Bing Crosby and Bill Cosby were the same person. That Buddy Holly and Billie Holiday were the same person. That Leon Trotsky and Leo Tolstoy were the same person. It was a shock for me quite late in life to discover that Jean Cocteau and Jacques Cousteau were not even related. Meaning, if it existed at all, was unstable and could not survive the slightest reshuffling of letters. One gust of wind and Santa became Satan. A slip of the pen and pears turned into pearls. A little interior decorating and *the world* became *her twold*, an ungrammatical and unkind assessment of an aging aunt in a singles bar. Add a *d* to *poor*, you got *droop*. It was that way in biology, too. Add a chromosome, get a criminal. Subtract one, get an idiot or a chipmunk. That was the way with things. When you wanted someone to say "I love you," approximate assemblages—*igloo, eyelid glue, isle of ewe*—however lovely, didn't quite make it. "You are my honey bunch" was not usually interchangeable with "You are my bunny hutch." In a New York suburban bathroom, early in the morning, a plea for sight could twist, grow slightly, re-issue itself as an announcement of death.

"You want to see again?" I asked, incredulous. His vision had always been fine. And he looked at me. He was standing in front of the sink. Then he looked into the drain, the stopped-up drain. He shook his head and said, "I never want to see you again."

"Oh," I said, three syllables short, where had they gone? Zapped by the ray-gun of a mumble. "Oh. I thought you said, 'I want to see again.'" And I grabbed some Merthiolate from the medicine cabinet and went back into the bedroom and painted peace signs all over my thighs. A few minutes later he came in and, looking like someone about to spit, lifted our largest red

Samsonite bag down from the closet shelf and loaded it with as much stuff from his dresser as he could. He never came back for anything else. I had turned into a bitch, and he had turned into a man with a fire-engine-red suitcase marching off toward the commuter train, looking as if he might spit. The last thing he said was, "What the fuck are you doing to your legs?"

I did cry. I didn't think I'd really turned into a bitch. I thought he was in love with someone else. And the Merthiolate took three days of hot baths to come off. Six months later, when he was dead, I knew that life had been unfair to him.

Georgie and I go to Woolworth's to buy barrettes. We walk almost aimlessly up and down the aisles, Georgie singing a song she thinks she's heard on *The Best of Broadway:* " 'When you walk through a store hold your head up high . . .' "

In the housewares aisle she teaches me songs she has learned at school. Most of them have trees and flowers and animals in them. I think at peace talks and arms negotiations all those magisterial, overweight men should be forced to sing such rounds of "White Coral Bells" and "Lady Bug, Lady Bug." It might save us. How afterward could those same men lumber gruffly off to go press buttons, lily of the valley decking their garden walks, checking their misfired testosterone.

I have fantasies. Such plans, such hopes. Walk on, walk on with holes in your heart.

George pulls a damp Band-Aid from her pinky and shows me the crinkled fish skin beneath. "Little white fish pinky," she sings and dances it in the air, her finger sticking upright like a startled periscope.

At Hank's I ask Gerard if he scribbled on my *Mme. Charpentier.* He looks at me and his mouth drops; a small cave opens up in his beard. He is clearly appalled. "Why the hell would I do something like that?"

I'm sorry I've asked him. I don't dare tell him that George suggested it. She, of course, is the logical suspect.

"Sorry," I say. "I wasn't really thinking, I just thought I'd ask, I wasn't really serious." I try to change the subject. "How's the singing going?"

Gerard beams widely and I'm relieved. "Just the news I was going to break. I've landed a part with the Free Verdi Company. I'm Don José in *Carmen*."

"But that's not Verdi."

"That's not the point. Jesus, Benna. You're supposed to say congratulations. I get to kill the soprano."

"Congratulations," I say. "You're going to be great at it. I can feel it in my bones." I lean over the table, my sleeve dragging in some coffee, and give him a kiss.

Thursday I take George to Dr. Nintz, the eye doctor. George has grown suddenly frightened. She doesn't understand how she's supposed to look into the eye machine. Dr. Nintz smiles and shows her. "Tell me what's in the top row," he says.

"A, F, T . . ." Her voice is a whisper, a speck. For someone just beginning to read, the wordless arrangement of the letters must be scary, jumbled together like a foreign language, like the names of Indian tribes.

"You'll have to speak louder than that, dear," says the doctor.

Afterward we go to the optician's with Dr. Nintz's prescription and pick out frames. She tries on five different kinds and looks in the mirror as if she's not really seeing. Perhaps she's perplexed at her own reflection. She doesn't seem to care what frames she gets.

"Which do you like best, kiddo?"

She shrugs. "I dunno. Mom, you choose."

"I like these." I point to a pair of clear whitish frames with silver hinges.

"Okay," she says.

I remember having to get glasses when I was young, though my mother always took me to an eye clinic for examinations. I had to stand in line with about a dozen other children, and then we were raced through the eye charts, holding, in turn, one hand over each of our eyes. We had to indicate which way the E was going by indicating up, down, left, right with the hand that wasn't covering up the eye. I always thought that the E stood for "eye" and its different positions were the four different ways your eyes could be impaired. (That was also back in the days when I thought the ice cream man lived in his truck.) My mother had once worked at the clinic; she thought it a fine place. I hated it. Later, as an adult, I tried to justify my hatred philosophically if not economically: a clinic was an unfortunate symbol of our entire society, a stark, fluorescent hieroglyph; every experience and institution was a virtual clinic, always looking over its shoulder, saying "Next?" and diminishing us all; whether it was love or art or graduate school or genetics or history or Auschwitz, there were always too many forms, too many people both ahead of and behind you in line, so close you could hear their gurgling and breathing and the impatient shifting of their weight from foot to foot. If George had been scared at Dr. Nintz's office, I certainly wasn't ever going to take her to an eye clinic.

Five days later we pick up the actual glasses. She wears them out of the optician's office, unsure and clutching my arm. "They feel funny, but I can see better, Mom. Wow." And she begins itemizing things, the rags of leaves on trees, on sidewalks, the headlights of cars.

"You look very pretty," I tell her.

. . .

From the backyard I am taking in the evening: The trees on the horizon release the moon, upward, the electric egg of the moon in a slow ovulation across the sky, lone as a diamond, as one bad eye roaming.

The ants are my friends. They're blowing in the wind.

When Darrel stays over, we don't talk about our ex-spouses or the war or anything. We compare Donald Duck imitations.

"Yours is good," I say, lying next to him, naked and goose-fleshed. Duck-bumped.

"Here," says Darrel. "I'll teach you how to do Donald Duck when he's mad," and he lets loose with a blustery duck noise that vibrates the whole bed. "Try it," he says.

"What do you do?"

"You just do the same voice, only you shake your head back and forth real fast."

I try, but it comes out with a lot of spit, and Darrel laughs at me. "Oh, well," he says.

"Sorry. This is the sort of thing I'm usually quite good at. I must be having an off day." And then I do my imitation of Julie Andrews at the automat—which Darrel finds quite astounding in its way.

I am walking to my last class of the day, my Darrel class. The October air is breezy and clear, like a day at the beach. The trees have shed a large crunchy tea all around campus and a few students are lying out on it, faces closed and aimed at the sun. The dogs love this kind of weather. They are out, also, frolicking around, nibbling at each other. I'm afraid of them and hope they stay where they are and don't romp too close to the sidewalk. You can't trust dogs. They always look like they're smiling. They spot each other from blocks away and dash to put their noses in each other's groin. They know things about you that no one else does, things you haven't told them but that they sense—that you are menstruating, that you are scared—and they take advantage.

In class the teacher distributed a student poem which began: "The autumn of adulthood turneth brown." These kids thought they were writing the Bible. It madeth her ill. It madeth her lie down in green pastures, it madeth her that ill.

In the back Darrel said something to Melanie Masters and they both laughed. She was young, dainty, pretty as a *Seventeen* magazine. She needed practice in the art of missing belt loops. The teacher felt herself flush, her heart pound, and she looked away, at someone else, at someone else who had his hand raised and was about to say that when talking about getting older you don't need to say both autumn and brown, one implies the other.

How had this happened? One Kafkaesque day she'd woken up and discovered she was a teacher at a community college, the perpetrator of a public fraud. The faces all about her seemed suddenly to alter and flicker in the light like mother-of-pearl. She had nothing to say to them. She had nothing to say and ended the class early.

The teacher walked across campus toward where her car was parked. She was going to have her hair trimmed. Sometimes all her existential crises became focused on her hair; she would look in the mirror and see it zooping out all over the place and say in a level voice, "I don't think that I can go on." And then she would try to rescue her life, herself, by a visit to a beauty parlor.

She passed a student she had had last year, and smiled, said hello. The student, however, looked at her blankly, as if he'd never seen her before in his life. How is it, thought the teacher, that I can remember this guy—his first name, his last name, his ottava rima about "the chicken pox of the soul"—and he seems not to recall me at all?

In the hairdresser's I smile at Yvette. I assume she remembers me, she's done my hair before, but she seems to smile right through me, no ripple of recognition. Yet we'd worked up a kind of intimacy once, hadn't we? We'd talked about men and ovaries and the effect of smoking on hair follicles. Now she doesn't seem to know me from Adam. She massages my scalp, just as she did then. "What will it be?" she says. She runs her fingers through and through my hair.

At night my insomnia lies next to me, on the floor by the bed, like a cousin come to visit.

"I know you're really crazy about me, kid," I say to Darrel, who is also there and who doesn't seem to notice the cousin. Darrel is on his side, turned away from me. I rest my head on his hip. "I know ya really are." I have worked up a fake voice for this. It's part Mae West, part pain reliever commercial. His eyes are closed. He turns to hold me, whimpers softly, then lets go, says nothing, rolls with all the blankets and slips promptly into sleep. I feel as if I'm in a war, lying in a trench with a dead person next to me, while the sky peels open in bright browns and reds like surgery.

Already we have settled into the tomb and heavy sleep of premature marriage. We brush our teeth in front of each other. We floss before bed.

I clasp my bare breasts to make sure that they're still there.

Oh, where is the snooze of yesteryear?

Where are the negligées downtown?

II

"You have a choice," she told her class. "The whorish emptiness of lies or the straightlaced horrors of truth." On the board she wrote the words *horror, nothingness, onomatopoeia.*

There are reasons why Darrel and I don't talk about the war, not the least of which is my own past. While he was off fighting and choking and hurling cognac against walls, I attended one campus sit-in, chanted "Hell no we won't go" a lot, and then went home and read *Mademoiselle* magazine. I never threw things, I never said "pig," I voted, my first time ever, for Humphrey, which later I was told was consummately unhip ("Benna, he was Johnson's stoolie!"). Two friends of a friend of mine were trotting around New York with pocketbooks packed with homemade bombs and leaving them at government buildings. I, too, hated the war. But I drank too much beer and took midday pajama naps. I memorized passages from *Romeo and Juliet*. I actually liked the song "Cherish." I had a loose yarn bag with a long shoulder strap and in it I kept only Kleenex, a comb, blusher, and a pack of Salems. On our way to Woodstock my college boyfriend and I got stuck in traffic and never made it to the festival. We turned around and went home, had supper at a dairy bar. To this day when I think of the sixties, I think of ersatz jazz renditions of "A Taste of Honey," of Sergio Mendes's "Fool on the Hill," of dairy bars with vanilla egg creams.

In the windows of health food stores there are advertisements for Vietnams. Or so it seems at first glance—as if whole decades were just odd, imperfect anagrams of one another. George watches

Dan Rather and at night asks me about the Vitamin War Memorial in Washington. "Vietnam," I correct her, and then I explain it to her carefully, the birds and bees of America. "Hush," I say afterward and hope she'll go to sleep.

I'm just checking on her before I go to bed, but she hears me and stirs. "Mom?" She's all creamy and rose with sleep. Her nightgown smells of Tide. "Can I have some honey milk?"

Honey milk is what I make when the weather gets cold: warm up some milk and add honey. "All right," I say after some hesitation. I know sometimes I'm not a good parent. "But then you have to go to bed for good." Milk, I rationalize, is a mild soporific.

"Goody," says George, leaping out of bed with astounding energy. Maybe she was never asleep at all.

Downstairs we sit at the kitchen table and drink honey milk, me and the little minker mumper. She holds the mug with two hands and it covers most of her face. She talks into it. "We're going to Beruba after Christmas, right?" I can barely hear her.

"Maybe," I say. I've been halfheartedly to travel agencies, checking out package deals. I've priced the bus versus the train to New York, the cab to Kennedy. I've scrounged around and finally located an unused passport and my birth certificate in a shoebox full of appliance warranties.

George's attention span is flibberty. She yawns. "Mom, what can I be for Halloween?"

When I was thirteen I bought a long black fall and went as Joan Baez. No one in Tomaston had ever heard of her. She was only just starting out in Boston cafés then, had only two albums out. Everyone thought I was a witch.

Gerard smiles at me. "You could make a belt out of old spice tins and go as a waist of thyme."

"Thanks." I'm drinking too much coffee, I can feel it.

"Or stick yourself all over with romaine and go as a honeymoon sandwich."

"What's a honeymoon sandwich?"

"Lettuce alone." He slaps the table and guffaws.

"These are pretty bad, Gerard."

"You could get a giant gray veil and go as an innuendo."

"I could Scotch tape pretentious words and literary references to a fuzzy sweater and go as a book review."

"That's good," he says, all positive reinforcement. "We could both dress up as puppets and sing 'Zing Went the Strings of My Heart' and 'You Made Me Love You.' Then we could beat each other up."

"What would that be, besides weird?"

"Punch and Judy Garland!"

"Oh, my god." I have to put my head down in my arms to get control of myself, I'm suddenly laughing that hard. "What's wrong with us?" I've come back up for air. Hank is looking our way and smiling, shaking his head.

"Or," Gerard is saying, "you could dress all in green and sing 'In the Ghetto.' "

"Good grief, who would that be?" I can barely get the words out.

"Elvis Parsley!" Gerard's pleased he's entertaining me. My laughing is noiseless like pain. I accidentally knock over a water glass.

"God, Gerard. I think I'll just cover myself with spots and go as a social leopard. Something like that."

"What do you think of my villanelle?" asks Darrel. "Do you like it?"

"I do. I like it," I say. One of the repeating lines is about the tongue of the tongue. I can't read poetry anymore. I don't know what to say. I don't know what it means. Darrel glances sheepishly up at me from beneath his eyebrows. He does this on purpose. "What do you think of this line here?" He points to the second line of the poem. It has a nice image in it, an ant trying to get to the other side of a bathroom mirror. He's good.

"You're good," I tell him.

"I have a series of poems about insects in your bathroom."

"You're kidding. You've found inspiration in my bathroom?" Insects, yes, but inspiration? Among the plumbing and the creams and the tweezers and the friction pour le bain? In that embarrassing shrine to my insecurities? In that church of What Is Wrong with My Body? How could he have done it? Though once, now, I recall I did see something remarkable in the bathroom: A big fly buzzed right through a spider web and instead of getting caught in it, the fly ended up dragging the spider along on about six inches of spider silk torn from the web; they flew around the bathroom like that together all day, the spider a kind of astonished kite trailing behind. The whole thing seemed emblematic of something—though I wasn't sure what.

"Remember that groggy wasp last weekend?" Darrel is saying.

In fall my house is particularly susceptible to insects looking for summer, confused, wondering where it has gone. When it gets cold outside, they reel, stumble, come into my house to die.

Darrel, with a grin, reads me a new poem. It's fraught, apparently, with meaning. He's lost his diffident eyes. He leans back and gives me a twinkle. " 'To Bee,' " he reads. " 'Though sometimes I believe you're black I'm told / you are a wasp / graceful, tiny, tired bird / I am afraid of you / your thrumming / and have you trapped / between my inner window and my summer screen / banging lady-quiet / at the wired sun / the difficult checkerboard of day / and dying green.' "

There is a long quiet.

"Good," I say.

In the morning Darrel fumbles with his clothes. I lie in bed watching him. A sock falls from his shoulder. He turns his shirt right side in and underwear drops to the floor. "What are you doing?" I ask.

"Magic tricks," he says.

" 'Ah, love, let us be true / To one another . . .' " The teacher was reading this aloud, pointing out the significance of the commas. Stacy Harold and Tracy Fay were sitting to her left, trying on each other's jewelry. (She recalled Tracy's soul—it had been shaped like a lavaliere.) They wore sweat shirts and strings of pearls. Stacy's crystal earrings refracted the afternoon sun. In every class the teacher had taught at Fitchville, there had been a Tracy or a Stacy who liked to try on other people's jewelry in class. And a guy named Joe or Jim or Tom who slept, chin against chest, occasionally startled awake by something in his own dreams though never by anything happening in the classroom. Then there were those students who sat and listened and nodded like angels. They took notes. They were so wonderfully attentive it embarrassed her. She loved them. She was grateful. She wanted to buy them things—candy, pencils.

A black student named Darrel was late for class. He pushed open the door, nodded at the teacher, saying "Good afternoon," then strolled the length of the class, nodding and saying "Good afternoon" to no fewer than five other students, until he reached his usual seat in the back. Everyone smiled at him. They liked him. He was popular.

"What are you doing, Darrel?" asked the teacher. "Running for president of the student council?"

Darrel took his coat off, sat down, and then leaned back in his seat. "I'm just being my usual friendly self." He winked, and the teacher hoped no one had seen it.

Every year Fitchville has a Halloween parade, replete with band, floats, horses, and costumed schoolchildren. On Saturday I take George and we walk to the corner of Fitch Boulevard, the street of the parade. The crowd along the curb is fairly large. George taps me on the leg: "Is it coming, Mom? I think I hear it." The wind blows hair into her eyes, in behind her new glasses. The autumn sun glares off the lenses, distorting the look of her face; she appears lost, or handicapped, a sweet, tiny, telethon child. I lift her up for a few minutes so she can look down the street over the heads of the people. Something is coming, an orange and black crepe paper dragon with people's feet. "I can see a monster, Mom," she says. People turn around to look at us and smile. Some of them have children, some of them don't. I see the Shubbys with Isabelle about fifteen yards away, and I wave.

Because George is too heavy, I finally have to put her down. I stand her in front of me and play with her hair, tucking it behind her ears because I know she likes that. She leans her head all the way back and looks at me upside down, giggles. Behind the dragon are cowboys and horses whose hooves are shoed and clack heavily on the pavement. The palomino closest to us lifts its tail and defecates onto the street, never missing a step. George opens her mouth, covers it with both hands, looks up at me in delighted horror. Behind the horses come the ten winners of the children's costume contest, and one of them, a very authentic-looking Heidi, while waving to her parents in the crowd, marches through the pile of manure. She looks down, visibly dismayed, and tries to shake clean her shoes and socks, scraping and scuffing her soles along the road, trying not to lose the beat. We can hear a band coming up, and soon it's loud and upon us. It's the Fitchville High School Marching Band, and the percussion section all wear masks—E.T., Ronald Reagan, state-of-the-art stuff. We march in place and put our fingers in our ears. The parade is badly paced, however, and after the band is by us there is a strange lull. The band and humdrum have passed quickly. The trumpets now honk faintly in the distance to our right, like a memory, and the drums are a far-off thunder. What cars and floats remain behind, minutes later, trundle forward and by us in a slow, chilling quiet, an unfestive lag, a huge, guilty ooze like age.

For a moment a cloud passes over the sun and there is a short shower, a sprinkling of rain. We hold out our hands, palms up. We pull our sweaters tighter and squint up at the sky, until the sun suddenly bursts through again, lighting up the trees like an idea.

Halloween night I go trick-or-treating as the Bride of Frankenstein, and George goes as Joan Baez, with a small plastic guitar and peace-sign pins. The neighbors chuckle and put candy in our shopping bags and send us on our hypoglycemic way. We've gotten an early start. The Shubbys tell us we're the hit of the street. George says, "Who's Joan Baez again?" and walking along the sidewalk I teach her the words to "Kumbaya," a cinch, and "Pretty Boy Floyd," a bit harder. "I like Joan Baez," she says. The air is cold and I hug her. We only do two streets.

At home George lays all her candy out on her bed and counts it.

Gerard phones on a break from the Ramada. "It's wild here," he says. "Someone's dressed as a condom and someone else here who is six-feet-six and three hundred pounds is Nancy Reagan. Quick, guess what I am?"

"An opera singer." I say it too quickly, without thinking. It's unkind.

"Right," he says and hangs up.

Eleanor calls from a party at her house. There is a lot of noise, like a television set. "Aren't you coming?" she yells. "You should see me, I'm costumed as the Dean of Sophomores!"

"You're kidding."

"Yes, I'm kidding. Actually I'm dressed up as the Dissertation Muse. I've got a giant bedsheet around me and rhetoric books and job lists and cigarettes and photocopies of abstracts dangling around my neck. It's very complicated. No one understands it. They ask me what I am and then say 'Oh.' You're not going to come rescue me?"

"I don't think so I—"

There is a sudden click and we are disconnected.

Darrel, too, calls from a party. "All kids at this party," he says. "It's a drag. I feel like an old man."

"Why don't you stop by here," I say. "I like old men."

"I just might do that," he says. "I'll be the one with the paper bag over my head. I'm going as the Unknown Negro."

"What's that supposed to mean?"

"I don't know. I couldn't come up with anything else. I haven't thought about it that deeply."

"Shall I give you a trick or a treat?" I can hear him consider this. Someone, a woman's voice in another room, shouts "Hey Darrel." I want him to say, "Baby, *your* tricks *are* treats." Something like that.

"Hmmmmm," he says instead. "Let me think about this." And he hangs up.

Only a few more trick-or-treaters come by: punk rockers, the requisite pirate, a Rudolph the Red-Nosed Reindeer, and a tiny, tiny child on whose head someone has put a huge and hideous rubber mask of Richard Nixon. The child hovers by my knees thrusting out a small twine-handled bag, the little hands squirmy and pink as shellfish.

"Have a nice night," I say, giving them all Hershey bars. These are better than the cough drops and Northern Spy apples my mother—all sternness and cold prevention—used to give out. With Hershey bars, I feel I'm finally normalizing my life, making something up to the trick-or-treaters of the world.

The Shubbys come by with Isabelle. They are all dressed as rabbits, large and small. Irv Shubby actually looks the most like a rabbit.

"Say thank you to Benna," says Mrs. Shubby, with her pink nose and painted whiskers, coaching Isabelle.

"Thank you," she says, a pip in the night.

When I first went trick-or-treating I went with my brother Louis, and stayed at the very first house we went to, not understanding we were supposed to move on. I went into the house and instead of hovering in the doorway, getting my candy, and dashing out, I sat down in one of their chairs, quietly waiting and chatting a bit, as if I'd been invited for tea. My brother Louis ran on ahead to the next house, impatient and oblivious (the houses were fairly far between, there was no time to spare), which I thought was a bit rude since we'd been invited in and given candy. Some sort of conversation seemed in order. I stayed for over an hour before these neighbors, sweet and bemused, escorted me back home. "Where did you go?" I asked Louis when he came back, loaded with enough candy to last until Christmas.

This has been my problem in life: I don't move on well. I don't trick-or-treat well. I don't understand. I sit in the sludge of my life and stay there. In a drawer somewhere I have six index cards for each of my former lovers, and I've drawn pictures of their souls there, wispy and dark—a thin stack: I believe in thin stacks, I believe it's important to keep these things, like credit card bills, under control. The word *number*, I realized when I was ten, can be pronounced two ways. "You haven't slept with enough people to understand that none of it means anything," said Gerard to me once, showing me a dictionary definition of *fuck* that read "in the present part., a meaningless intensive."

But I had read in a novel when I was fourteen that more than seven and your soul goes.

At midnight when Darrel finally rings the bell, I open the door, step out and slip my head up under the paperbag with him, and we kiss, standing in the doorway like that.

"Are you crying?" he whispers. "What's wrong?"

"No. I don't know. Nothing." And we go upstairs, leave our underwear dangling from doorknobs, Darrel whispering things while I try to speak while crying, doing the garbled hyena of weep-speak.

I awake at dawn, and it's a beautiful irisy sky, like a movie set you don't believe for one minute. Darrel reaches for me sleepily, all potion and skin, and I roll back into his arms like a child, this slow lovely grind that is love, that is the secret of bodies, private as grief.

"Are you mad at me for last night?" I ask Gerard on the phone. He is watching a football game on TV and this is half-time. Gerard says TV football is like watching cells under a microscope, that it's all about conception and contraception.

"No, why? Are you mad at me?" he asks, as if puzzled. This is how we work, via amnesia.

It is All Saints Day evening. I sit on the edge of the bathtub, drying off Georgianne, marveling that the human race has managed to create such comforts for itself as the warm fluffy nubs of towels, the squirming, nearsighted silk of daughters.

"We're going to Beruba for Christmas, I know," she says, fogging the air with baby powder. She's trying to bully me.

"How do you know?" I look at her and squint my eyes into small incisions.

George shrugs.

"Do you *want* to go?" I ask, rubbing her head dry, fishing for affirmations.

Beneath the moving towel she scrinches up her face. "Do *you* want to?" she squeaks, in imitation of someone, something, I don't know what, and she tweaks my nose, my skinny merink, my bony pumpkin.

"Whatever happened to that little niece of yours?" asks Gerard.

"Niece?" I ask, disoriented.

"Yeah. Anna or Annie. The little one, your brother's kid who used to come visit you."

"Oh, Annie." I'm quiet, take inventory, and then zip on ahead. "She and my ex–sister-in-law are off in Michigan. My brother Louis couldn't even get joint custody. It's very mysterious. Everybody misses her." I lower my eyes. There's a long silence. Gerard leans over and tweaks my nose. "What is this nose-tweaking jazz?" I grumble. I toss back orange juice like a gargle.

I am sitting at home with a pile of student poems. I have put the more interesting ones, usually the housewife poems, on the bottom, with Darrel's at the very bottom, as a sort of reward. But now I'm looking at them in front of me, on the dining-room table, and I can't read any of them. I have nothing to say, nothing to write, nothing registers in my brain. All these student lines fly away from me, scatter like pigeons in Venice, rise up around me like locusts. I can't begin to get through this pile of poems. I would rather eat them than read them. I would rather do anything than read them.

Today is my husband's birthday. He would have been thirty-six. I wonder what he would have looked like. I wonder if he would have been happy, if we would have been friends.

I go right to Darrel's poem. It is called "Dolphin."

> *With my clicks and whistles*
> *and 30,000 years*
> *of history, the Iliad*
> *and Minaoan prayers*
> *and kisses hardened, curled*
> *inside me like a coral reef,*
> *it is music, the waves,*
> *not the grinning angularity*
> *of corners, coroners, sandwiches,*
> *that washes, courts, and wins*
> *me and my child's rhymes. We*
> *glide and scarcely touch for now,*
> *desiring just the slick, silk share*
> *of speed, the drink of seas,*
> *oh love, the drink of seas.*

I wonder if it's about sex. If it's about me. If it's about why he's not in love with me yet or never. Words, I think, words are all you need for love—you say them and then just for the hell of it your heart rises and spills over into them. My idea in a love affair is that if everyone makes enough declarations, one of them is bound to come true. Words are interesting that way.

But these words—I don't know. I circle *Minaoan*, which he's spelled wrong, and write "Good!" at the top; then I turn off the light and, terrified of literature, go straight to bed.

The teacher was at her office hours in the Union, sipping coffee, staring off into space. She leaned over to get something out of her bag on the floor—a pen wrapped in a Kleenex in case it leaked.

Looking up from her bag, she saw a young black woman in jeans and a red sweater, standing beside her.

"Ms. Carpenter?"

"Yes?" Benna sat up. She had never seen this woman before.

"I'm Ruby Olson. Can I bother you for a minute?"

"Sure. Have a seat."

Ruby sat down. "This really will only be for a minute." Ruby placed her own bag on the floor. "I'm here as a sort of emissary from the Black Women's Equality Group."

"Black Women's Equality Group?"

"Yeah. BWEG." It sounded like someone spitting out food. Ruby smiled. She was pretty. Dancing, almond eyes and good jewelry. "There's only twelve of us, but we're devoted."

The teacher smiled back.

"The reason I'm here is this," continued Ruby. "Do you know how many white women at FVCC are going out with black men?"

The teacher resisted the urge to look quickly into her coffee. She hated Fitchville. She hated this college. She hated coffee in Styrofoam cups. She could feel her cheeks burn. She took a deep breath and stared back at Ruby, stared at her with an intent to poison, wither, dismantle the eyes and jewelry. "Nohowmany," she said, flat as medicine.

"Six," said Ruby. "Do you know how many white men are going out with black women?"

"What is this, a quiz?"

"Zero. It just doesn't happen. With white women taking virtually eighty percent of the black men on this campus, and white men just plain not interested in anything but a white girl, we black women are stranded."

The two women glared at each other.

"Maybe your complaint should be with the black men," said

the teacher. "Or with the white men. Maybe you shouldn't be taking this out on other women."

Ruby shifted in her seat impatiently, then shouldered her bag as if to leave. "Sociologically it's complex. Look, Ms. Carpenter, you're a cool teacher. I've heard you are. I just thought I'd come to you with this. My basic point is that we women have to stick together."

"And that," announced the teacher, as Ruby stood up to go, "would be exactly my point as well."

"Ruby Olson's right," says Eleanor.

"Oh great," I say. "I'll stop seeing Darrel because he's black." Perhaps everyone, when you got right down to it, was a racist.

"I'm not saying that," says Eleanor. She inhales and blows smoke out through her nose. "I'm just saying think of the black women on this campus, that's all. All twelve of them. I mean, this town is an Aryan breeding ground. Think of their situation."

"But what about *my* situation?"

"Kill two birds with one stone. Dating a student, Benna, you're probably the talk of dozens of impromptu department meetings held in the restrooms of both sexes."

"You mean, kill one bird with two stones." Everything conspires. Everything feels dizzy to me now. My voice has shrunk to a gaspy whisper. "Besides," I say, helplessly. "Darrel's way too old for Ruby Olson."

"Look, you know how awful everyone is here. You should just watch yourself. The tenured shall inherit the earth. And even the crummy courses you're teaching."

"What should I do?"

"Actually," says Eleanor, walking over to where I'm seated and putting her hand on my shoulder. This is what I need. This is what I have her do. "I'm not sure."

.   .   .

I'm in bed with Darrel. On a cold night a bed is a warm recoil, it is a pearly place, like heaven.

I am average in love. I say things like "I love you" and "I need you I really do." I say them too quickly, like an asshole.

I don't tell Darrel about things Ruby, Eleanor, or George have said. I don't want to discourage him. I want us to figure things out for ourselves. We have become nocturnal animals. We coo wise things out into the night like owls.

"What the hell's the matter with you?" I say in the dark. We can't see each other. He doesn't want to hold me. I wonder if I should get a bunk bed, a bed full of bunk—why not: The truth never sets you free.

Darrel is stalled. Stalled out and away from me, paces away from words, from love, from love words. God, only someone with no imagination would get stalled out there.

"I don't know," he whispers. "Benna, sometimes I just don't feel capable of love—not the kind you're talking about and want."

"Oh, great," I say. "That's just what I need." I know these kinds of men. They're afraid you want to marry them or in some other way own them so that you can then provide them with a running commentary about the way their false and sniveling characters might be improved. They have a tendency to look at your hips in disgust, to take off through traffic without looking sideways.

"Benna. I'm sorry. I'm not sure what you need from me, but I feel numb, I've felt numb for years."

"You're *numb*? Don't tell me you're numb when I'm lying here falling in love with you and jeopardizing my job to boot."

"Don't be melodramatic."

"Well, then, don't be numb." I lie there, jiggling my legs. "Don't think I couldn't be numb too if I didn't work so damn hard not to be. Numbness! That's the easiest thing in the world. You don't think I could be numb if I wanted to be?"

"No, actually, I don't," Darrel says slowly.

My voice is a whispered shriek. "Numb? You want numb? I'll give you numb," and I cross my arms tightly, cross my legs, throw my head violently back into the pillow, squeeze shut my eyes, fold in my lips, and burst into tears.

"How are you doing these days, Gerard?"

"I'm okay. I'm being Don José and getting a lot of shit for my high notes. The performance is December seventh."

"Carpet Town going okay?"

"Hmmmm?"

I think he has a hangover. He's perspiring and one eye is wandering. I smile. "Carpet Town? Remember that place you work? That's going fine?"

"Oh yeah," he says. "That's a breeze compared to the rest of my life."

"They shoot breezes, don't they?" quips Eleanor. She's in a weird mood today. She's dressed in a strange feathered hat and purple parachute pants. She feels like chatting; neither of us is concentrating. I'm clothed in brown and a sort of army green, the idea being camouflage. When your life's a mess, I say, wear neutral colors. At either end of your life—infancy and old age— you can get away with reds and turquoises, but when you're navigating the tumult in between, it's best to blend into the landscape. Walking down a country road, for instance, you are more likely, if hit by a manure truck, to be lost, shoveled, scooped up without a trace, which would be the idea, which would be the essential point, which would be the best thing for everyone.

"Eleanor, you have to be more selective about your vices. You can't be overbearing, self-righteous, dress like a maniac, *and* tell bad jokes. That's being a hog. That's like grabbing up all the best sections of the *Times*."

"I'll try to control myself," she says. "Don't you think they should paint this lounge a decidedly different shade of orange? And why don't you come over for dinner sometime next week."

"Sure," I say. "Just let me know."

"Great," she says. "See you. I'm off to go *aerobe*."

Why is Darrel numb? Why is Gerard drinking? What is the essential difference between men and women?—somehow I feel the answer to the first two, to almost all problems, lies there in the last, though I have no answer. Is there really a difference at all? And if there is, what should we do about it? Limit your answer to one page. When I was seven, Billy Adelsen screamed at me from the field across the street, "Boys have wieners, girls have popos." No one I've met since has had it quite so clearly worked out and understood. Billy, however, as with all confident and shameless proclaimers of truth, was punished. His mother, who had been visiting my mother, heard his shouts through the screens of our porch and came charging out down our front lawn, off into the field, through which Billy had turned and fled. When she caught up with him, she dragged him by the ear as he howled the one hundred yards home. I've never heard the word *popo* since, though sometimes, still, I think about it. My mother was a nurse—social worker and always used the correct terms for things, like *vulva* or *B.M.*, names that sounded like foreign cars. When I'd been home sick from school and needed a written excuse from her, she would write mortifying things like "Benna had loose bowels" instead of "She wasn't feeling well," which is what the other kids' mothers wrote. Unlike Billy's mom, she never punished us but only pretended she didn't understand when we used another more informal terminology. "*Bupper?* I don't even know what you're saying. These are your *buttocks*." My father didn't care what we said. He was an underpaid, underworked fireman, a victim of downward social mobility at a time when for most Americans that was an impossibility. He had grown up in a large house in Philadelphia and was now raising his children in a trailer with additions: a porch and a family room. "Leave the kids alone, Jan," he'd say. "You're not letting them be kids." This, I had to gather, was the difference between men and women.

There were other differences, too. Once I asked my mother what a Communist was. This was in 1957. "It's a person who wants to help poor people," she said, and then quickly turned her back and started washing dishes. I stared at her apron and thought about this. A week later I asked my father the same question. He scowled, sat me down at the family-room card table, and set up an exhibit using two cookies. "Here, Benna," he said. "This cookie's yours." He placed it in front of me. "And this cookie's mine." He placed the other in front of himself. "An American says what's mine is mine, and what's yours is yours, right? A Communist, though," and my father gazed intently at me to make sure I was paying attention. I was hungry. I was thinking about the cookie. "A Communist says, 'What's mine is mine and what's yours is mine,'" and at that he snatched up both my cookie and his and shoved them in his mouth and chewed. I didn't cry out, though I wanted to. Something was wrong. Maybe only lady Communists helped poor people. Men and women were different. I understood that. Men drove the station wagon too fast, and women said things like "Slow down, Nick. Your gonads are taking over." Men were also more likely to complain about the cooking, and women were more likely to serve skimpy TV dinners in revenge —for three whole weeks or until the apology, whichever came first.

These were clear.

But these were little things and long ago. As I got older, I grew even more confused.

·   ·   ·

The eight o'clock class was doing a group sestina. When in doubt, Eleanor always said, do a group sestina. The six end-words had been chosen by the students themselves: *arm-hair, Spam, motorcycle, plié, lounge, crash-helmet.* The teacher wrote them on the board. The in-class assignment involved writing on a sheet of paper one line with the appropriate end-word and then passing it to the left. By the end of the period they would have twenty sestinas and everyone would have contributed. The members of the class were having a good time. The teacher could hear their giggles and their scribbling. It was a party game. It was ludicrous. It was the only way she knew how to teach.

The ten o'clock class was doing a group sestina. The six end-words had been chosen and written on the board by the students themselves: *paste, haste, drinking, typing, erasing,* and *mame,* spelled like the Broadway musical. "What is this?" howled the teacher, pointing at the last. "*To mame?* Is that 'to coax the husk right off of the corn'?" And for a moment she burst, frighteningly, into song. "You've got to learn how to spell," she said finally, "or it will make me hysterical."

The teacher took a walk before her afternoon class. Near the campus were several old houses rented by some of FVCC's full-time students and from them blared radio jabber and stereo music. That is the difference between the young and the not-so-young, she thought. The young keep their windows open so that the world can fly in and out. By the time you hit your thirties, you're less hospitable; you start closing up the windows. You've had enough of the world; you have, you think, everything you need for the wintry rest of life. You can't let anything else in, for you will never understand it. And the nightmare, of course, is that as you slowly start shuttering up your house, you turn and suddenly see, with a gasp, that you are the only thing in it.

. . .

The two o'clock class was doing a group sestina. The six end-words had been chosen: *race, white, erotics, lost, need, love, leave.* The teacher wrote them on the board, stretched them out in a long horizontal list.

"We don't get to choose our own?" asked a student named Herb.

"You've got seven words there," said a black student named Darrel, who always sat in the back by the window.

The teacher had to erase one. She hesitated, looked along the list, considering, putting her hands on her hips, a gesture of nonplussed authority. Then she reached over and erased *love*, but changed her mind again and wrote it back in. Then she walked over and erased *white.*

The students began writing the first line of a sestina.

The teacher looked out the window. It was too warm for November. They were having a spell of Indian summer. Outside in the sun there were dogs. A male dog had just hopped atop a female dog, piggyback. The female dog just stood there patiently, looking alternately glassy, bored, embarrassed. The teacher turned away. She chewed on a cuticle. "Men are outrageous," she said to herself.

There is a thread dangling from the crotch of my jeans. I grab it tightly and yank it to snap it free.

"What on earth are you doing?" says Eleanor.

"This is my penis envy," I say, holding up the thread.

"You'll have to do better than that," she says.

"Who've *you* been hanging around?" I construct an exaggerated wink.

Eleanor has made a wonderful fettuccine carbonara. We sit in the dining room of the half-of-a-house she rents. We chat amiably and, amazingly enough, manage not to bring up the subject of our lovers (it's as if our sex lives have embarrassed us somehow, dragged us through indignities) until just before dessert.

"Trouble in Newton-land," says Eleanor. Newton is the biochemist she's been seeing for over a year now. "He's having an affair with someone. He says he feels rejuvenated with her."

"Oh, Christ. What is she, another biochemist?"

"No," sighs Eleanor, stacking up dishes for the kitchen. "She works for AT&T."

Sympathy is important at a time like this. "God," I finally say. "I'm so glad I have MCI." And then I take out a pen and a scratch pad from my purse and draw her a picture of a woman with large breasts and a t-shirt that reads AT&T: YOU BROKE US UP, NOW WE BREAK YOU UP. One needs to be a girl about these things. Graduate school can knock the girl out of you, and, really, sometimes you just need to be a girl.

Eleanor smiles restlessly. She says she knows we're both doomed at FVCC. She wants to pack it all in and travel for a year. She has saved money. She's thinking of Italy.

"Do it," I say. I tell her I'm planning a trip to the Caribbean with Georgianne. I realize, after I've said it, that it sounds tacky and meager, not the same as Italy at all.

For dessert Eleanor serves cherries jubilee flambé. I watch the blue flame dance around the ice cream, quick and berserk. When it's out and the ice cream's melting, I dig in.

Eleanor watches me and smiles. She holds up one sticky cherry between two fingers. "No matter how many you eat, Benna," she says, "you'll never get it back."

I wash dishes, she dries.

I need an annual check-up. I decide to go to a new gynecologist Eleanor has recommended. Eleanor is a woman who faints at the sight of a Q-Tip; she wouldn't steer me wrong. "Don't go to the clinic, whatever you do," she said. "Last time I was there they told me I had a crook in my vagina and when I said, 'Well, get him out, for godsakes,' they didn't even laugh."

In the waiting room I read *Good Housekeeping* along with two other women. Occasionally we all glance up furtively from our magazines, smile, then look back down. An elderly woman comes into the waiting room and sits on the sofa next to me. "Is that you on the cover?"

"Excuse me?" I say. She is leaning over onto her lap, looking at me and then at my magazine.

"Is that you on the cover?" She smiles hopefully.

I turn my magazine over. A pretty brunette woman is beaming and holding triplets. "Oh my goodness, no," I laugh politely.

"Oh," says the older woman and pinches in her mouth. She smooths her skirt and looks straight ahead.

I resume flipping pages.

"Have you ever seen it rain on only one side of the street?"

I turn my head and stare. Her lipstick is on crooked. It's a bluish pink and bleeds out beyond the lines of her mouth. "No, I don't think so," I say.

"I have." She nods, very pleased. I, too, bob my head and together we bob our heads.

In the examination room Hazel Doyle the doctor presses my abdomen. "Some water retention," she says, smiles, keeps pressing.

"I'll do anything for retention," I say. Now she starts to poke and prod a birthmark below my left breast. It's a mark that I myself have never paid much attention to. I want to ask her about having a baby at the age of thirty-four, at the age of forty, about infertility, about artificial insemination, about test tubes.

"I think it's a third breast," she says. "Hmmmm, this is interesting." She glances at me to note my reaction, which is not good. "You see, it's in perfect line with the nipple above it." She's excited by this. She calls in two of her assistants who also bend over me to look at it. Everyone smiles and ooohs and aahhhs. It's only a flat little beige thing I never much thought about. But now I'm upset. I don't know why Eleanor has recommended this doctor to me. I pull my shift back on rather rudely and hop off the examination table. "Excuse me," I say. "I'm due at the circus in three minutes."

I drive home near tears, and when I tell the story to Gerard, he smiles and puts his arm around me. I tell Eleanor her doctor's the hound of hell and she says "My word!" and I don't breathe a note of it to Darrel.

My mother died when I was nineteen. She had some sort of strange disease where her organs began, mysteriously, to dry out. When the doctors caught it, she was gangrenous throughout her intestines. She was the one who told me about it first, sitting up in the hospital bed, strong, rigid, tall (she was a head taller than my dad), trying to fight the grogginess of painkillers, and using all the exact names for things. None of the names she told me registered. I sat down on her bed and cried into my knees. Then she lifted me up and we both cried together. When she brushed my bangs off my forehead I could smell garlic still on her fingers, in the grain of them, like a kitchen cutting board, that's how fast she'd been rushed off. From the discovery of her illness until the funeral service was only six days. My father drank the whole time. Afterward Louis and I got him a dog—half-beagle, half-collie—to keep him company. I went back off to college and fell immediately and tearfully into the arms of my boyfriend. Ten days after my mother died I made love for the first time. Perhaps I'd been waiting for her to die, this woman whose slips I'd worn for childhood dress-up games, the bodice hollow and droopy like old breasts, this woman who in the name of perfect posture allowed her children no pillows. Perhaps I'd been waiting for all that terminology, that correctness, to die so that at last I could relax, with my sloppy carriage and careless parlance, my thrice-kissed shoulders, and my one pair of black nylon tricot under-wear—of which she'd never have approved. Though she might have smiled and shaken her head about the underwear, standing there at the laundromat, holding them up. She might have said, "And whose fancy underlinens are these?" She might have done that.

Saturday morning and I have to call my father. I have to find out what's he doing for Thanksgiving. He still lives alone in the trailer in Tomaston. He's named the dog Elizabeth (for five years she was just "Dog"), and she is now so old she does little but sit in the family room and breathe, her whole body moving in and out, her eyes looking up at you, a glassy black.

The last time I spoke to my father he was talking about finally getting circumcised and about having all his moles re-moved. For health reasons.

"Dad? Hi, guess who this is?"

"Now let me see. Is this my favorite daughter?"

We always do this. "This is your only daughter. How's it going?"

"Just fine. How are things in Fitchville?"

"Okay. I'm calling to find out what your plans are for Thanksgiving, if you'd like to come down here for dinner. I'm planning a big turkey with chestnut dressing."

There is a pause, then some muffled noises. "I've got some news, Benna," he says. "I've got a girl friend."

There is a dictionary on top of the phone book, and I flip through it nervously, as if looking for something to say: My father has a girl friend, my father has a girl friend. In the dictionary, after *sild*, a type of sardine, comes *silence*.

"Oh, my goodness," I manage. "Congratulations." That is,

I'm certain, what my mom would say. She would say it in a hearty voice and thrust out her hand. *Quid pro quo* comes just before *quiescence.* "I hope, gee, that doesn't mean the two of you won't be coming here for Thanksgiving?" There's some scuffling and some clicking noises.

"Hello, Donna, dear." There's now an older woman's voice on the other end of the phone. She sounds like the woman in Dr. Doyle's office who thought it was me on the magazine.

"Hi, who is this?"

"It's *Benna*, Miriam," coaches my dad in a loud whisper. "Benna," he says, "this is my girl friend, Miriam. Miriam-Benna, Benna-Miriam." Being introduced on the phone like this, what is one supposed to say? "Delighted I'm sure"? I never really knew what that meant. Delighted, I'm sure, *what?* "Nice to meet you"? I can hear my father say, "Here, Miriam, now you speak." They must be passing the receiver back and forth, two old people who have pulled up card-table chairs by the phone. I can see them leaning forward, heads cocked, faces sparkling with holiday.

"Hello, Benna, dear," she tries again. "This is Miriam."

"Hi, Miriam."

"My, you do have a sweet voice. Your father's told me all about you."

"The part about the awards and prizes is true." I've just made this up; I don't know what else to say. I can hear a hand, like a seashell, over the phone.

"She says the part about the awards and prizes is true, Nick. What part about the awards and prizes?" Miriam then gets back on the phone. "Hello, this is Miriam."

"Hi, Miriam. Only part of the part about the prizes is true. And I was just kidding about the awards."

"Yes," she says. "Your father and I are planning on taking a lovely trip to Florida for Thanksgiving, aren't we, Nick?"

"Yes, that's true," says Nick, my father.

"How nice," I say.

"My son and his family are down there and they love to have grandma for holidays, you know how that is."

"Of course." I'm feeling lost, floating.

"Nick, do you want to say more to Donna?"

Afterward I put on a sweater and go for a walk. I try to breathe deeply and can't. My breath won't catch and turn over; it stops prematurely in a panic and I have to breathe shallowly, off the top of my lungs. My nose has gone numb. Though it's sunny for November, my nose has gone cold as meat. I touch the tip and it feels not like a nose but like a strange, fleshy bump, like a cervix through a diaphragm, a distant knob. I feel a pain in my chest and in my head. I wonder if I'm having a stroke. I keep walking, thwarted and dizzy. A girl is trying to roller skate in the big chunky gravel of her driveway and can't. She stumbles around, an image of all the impossibilities of everyone's life, ridiculous and heartbreaking. I used to do that, skate around like that in the driveway and fall, stones sticking in the pus of my scraped knees, like something necessary.

Even walking I am disoriented. I must get outside of myself, I must extend myself, communicate with the world. I stare at a squirrel up ahead and, without thinking, call, "Here, kitty-kitty-kitty."

"What is this scar?" I'm tracing a long, pale train track along Darrel's leg. "Is that from the war?"

"No. I was in a bicycle accident when I was ten. I smashed into the bumper of a car and landed on pavement and glass. I had to have fourteen stitches."

"Oh."

"Sorry to disappoint you."

"You didn't disappoint me."

"Of course I did."

"No, you didn't."

"Yes, I did. I know what it is you want me to be."

"No, you don't."

"I'm figuring you out, Carpenter."

I look him straight in the shoulder blade. "No you're not," I say. "Buster."

When I think of my father dying, both of my parents gone, it somehow becomes important to remember my childhood and that's when, of course, I can't. It all becomes evaporated, like a doomed planet in a science-fiction movie. Sometimes, though, I remember bits and it's like finding a few odd pieces of lost jewelry. I remember visiting my father at the fire station, trying on his hat; playing dress-up with my mother's old lingerie (I sometimes modeled for my father when he was home); trying on secondhand things my cousin in Boston had outgrown, sweaters with Filene's and Jonathan Logan tags. My mother would stand me on a chair —"Ta-da!"—and we would have a fashion show.

These are all connected with clothes, with trying to be some-one else; that's mostly what people remember—that effort to leave themselves. Although there are a few other things I re-member, odd lodgers in the rooming house of my recall. I remem-ber my paper route, my trombone lessons, summers spent squeez-ing open the throats of snapdragon blossoms and pretending they growled and really snapped. I remember a friend named Sarah Garrison coming over to play, fascinated that we lived in a trailer. She stayed for dinner, and when her mother came to pick her up, Mrs. Garrison came to the door with a pale, bewildered face: "Is Sarah there?" The trailer appalled her, maybe frightened her. Here, I knew, was an adult I was stronger than. I showed her my monster finger puppet. "This is a snap dragon," I said.

And I remember playing with Louis: Flying Horses, Astro-

naut, Wedding. When we were flying horses we would flap our
wings and whinny and gallop down the road. The neighbors
worried. We would make nests in the field across from where we
lived, and we would lay eggs in them and then spring up and
rejoice in horse language. We would do little dances with our
hooves and teach our babies how to look for worms in the ground.
For Astronaut we hiked a hot mile and a half down the road to
the junkyard, where we climbed, like gleeful astronauts, into the
old abandoned cars, steering them, making motor noises, squeal-
ing tires, squinting out through the smashed windshields which
had been splintered into stars. When we played Wedding, we
would go out into the woods with gauzy curtains draped over our
heads. Louis consented to this mostly because he was lonely and
had nothing else to do. We were both brides. We would pronounce our ersatz vows to one another and throw our fern
bouquets (made by grabbing the bottom of the fern and moving
our hands slowly up the stem, denuding the entire fern). I would
sing the wedding music—something I deemed romantic, a song
my father had learned in the army and would sometimes sing
around the house: ". . . She's got a pair of hips / Just like two
battleships / Hot dog, that's where my money goes."

But even these bits drift away from me, even now after I've
conjured them. It's because they don't fit anywhere, so I can't
keep them still, can't connect and possess them. They make only
for a jagged fuzz of a past and a father getting old and eating
giblets in Florida.

My life, what I've lived so far, crumbles across its very center and the pieces float off a slight distance and just stay there,
jigsawed, glueless, and dead.

My heart is raucous as a tea kettle. I have stopped by Gerard's with
Chinese food for a quick chow-down. I eat and rant at the same
time, sitting cross-legged on the floor against the couch. I point-

lessly hurl throw pillows across the room. "What are you doing?" he asks. "Throwing cushion to the winds?" I curl my lip. I tell him I want to pretend. I want to pretend there's such a thing as requited love. As the endurance of love.

"Endurance is a country in Central America," says Gerard. "It has nothing to do with love. As for requited, that has nothing to do with anything. Except, my dear, you and me." He extends a long, curving arm. He kisses me. I say good night, I have to go, I have to go home and make honey milk.

Gerard walks me out to my car. It's dark already, and the night sky is beautiful and cold. Gerard points up to it. "You see the sky?" he sings to the tune of an old Herb Alpert song. "The sky's in love with you . . ."

I hold up the tail end of an egg roll. I look Gerard straight in the beard. "I am a wok," I say, "I am an island." Then I get in my car and drive away.

Darrel has keys, I hear the jangle and thud downstairs, and soon he has slipped into bed beside me.

"Did you say something?" he asks. He glides his hand down the side of my ribcage.

"No. Why?"

"I thought you said something."

"No," I say. "Did you?"

"No," he says.

This morning I get up to correct papers and it's still dark outside, the streetlights still on. I put some water on for coffee, then wander out into the living room. I glance out the front window, and there's a woman in slippers and a robe standing in the middle of the street, grinning and waving at me as if she'd been standing there all night just waiting for me to look out and find her. I shut the curtains, terrified, then peek out again to see if she's still there.

She is and gives me a glorious, gregarious wave. She sees me, recognizes me, knows me—how does she know me? Oh my god. I walk to the kitchen and back. I peek out again. Only the frozen gray street—she has vanished.

The greatest number of accessory mammae was reported in 1866 by Neugebauer, who found ten in one woman.

Many images of Diana, the virgin goddess, portray her as polymastic, having over a dozen breasts. They look like clusters of tropical fruit; she doesn't look too displeased but then she's a goddess why the hell should she.

Tonight Gerard plays at the Ramada in the Nickelodeon Lounge, a space lit with dusky rose lights, the ceilings dangling coleus and mingy philodendra and spidery antique fans which are motionless and probably don't work. With a small stack of student poems, I sit in one of the booths that line the far wall. The upholstery is a sort of crooked Aztec, the table waxy polyurethaned cherry. Gerard is at the piano up front in a coral-hued spotlight, swaying from side to side, fingers dribbling along the keyboard while he chats exuberantly at the audience, various members of which look up occasionally from their veal cutlets and fried mushrooms to nod, clap, or laugh with their mouths full. I give him a subtle wave and a broad wink, and he smiles, armlessly directing one of his jokes my way: "What did one lady cannibal say to the other lady cannibal? 'I don't know what to make of my husband these days. Could I borrow a recipe?' "

The audience likes it, likes the idiocy of all this, though one woman near me has glanced down at her stroganoff and complained, "Please, not while we're eating." Gerard begins singing the *Cabaret* medley, his high notes occasionally strained and misshapen. When he gets to the song "Married," he stops singing for a moment, his hands continuing in some bland arpeggios, and he says, "My wife: She's one in a million. I just have to make sure she doesn't find out." A large white-haired man to my left, part of a two-couple foursome, guffaws loudly, then gets swatted in the arm by the woman next to him. Gerard smiles at me and moves quickly on through to the end of the song, the musical-comedy bliss of marriage. Gerard has never had a wife. Sometimes I think he knows too many philanderer and lady cannibal jokes to ever have one. "What did one lady cannibal say to the other lady cannibal?" he's now asking. " 'Boy, is my husband in hot water!' " He bangs out some loud chords, there are some amused groans. Another lady cannibal joke is about how to make a husband stew. With onions.

I'm not sure why he feels so brutalized, or why he's directing so many of these my way. Perhaps this is my self-centeredness, my failure to really know Gerard.

He finishes up the *Cabaret* medley. I applaud vigorously, and he nods, says thank you, keeps playing. He is trying to appear tireless. He creeps a ways into a Louis Armstrong song—"I went down to St. James infirmary / Met my baby there / Saw her laid out on the table / So sweet, so cold, so bare"—and then quickly moves into a Fats Waller tune, "Keeping Out of Mischief Now," a weird, dark wit to the juxtaposition. This song is pretty, and Gerard sings it with his eyes closed, his electrically haloed face raised toward the ceiling, a religious painting in bright colors on black velvet. I think for a brief, glowy moment that even though people are getting up and heading for the salad bar, loading up with pickled beets, pickled corn, pickled beans—kidney, string, wax—that they appreciate Gerard, that he really is talented, that in some endless way I too will always be in love with him.

The song is over, but his fingers still linger on the keyboard, a salad-bar tinkle.

At the break the spotlight goes off and he comes over and

sits at my booth. "More freshman poems?" He riffles quickly through the pile, a polite curiosity.

"Yeah, I keep thinking of leaving them at the salad bar. Next to the croutons, like an alternative lettuce."

Gerard smiles wearily, then buries his face in his hands, a pianist's hands, leathered trees of knobs, dour veins, branches of fingers. I reach over and touch his forearm. He feels embarrassed working here. The salad bar gets to him.

"I can't come out," he says, not removing his hands. "Not for at least ten minutes."

I feel superfluous, a giant, wet flesh match in a sweater I just bought on sale this afternoon. "Okay," I say, and we sit there, silent, sad, his shoulders heaving twice, his face vanished into his palms until finally, a long finally, he wipes his hands down slowly off his face and though pink-eyed and sleepy, he looks all right again. He has used up most of his ten minutes, and the spotlight has come back on, and no one is in it, a signal that Gerard's break is over.

I take Gerard's hand. " 'But soft, what light through yonder window breaks?' "

"Shit," says Gerard, glancing over his shoulder. He picks up my empty drink and chugs it back. The ice cubes knock against his teeth and upper lip. " 'Churl,' " he says, putting the glass back down with a clunk. " 'Drunk all and left no friendly drop to help me out?' "

When we are depressed, we quote Shakespeare, to put things in perspective. Between us we know about five lines, which limits our perspective.

"How come you're always Juliet and I'm always Romeo?" I moan.

"That, my dear," says Gerard, getting up, "is the question of the century. We shall take it up anon."

"A nun?" I bat my eyelashes, place my hands in prayer position.

"You have a silly brain," he says, and tweaks my nose, this new habit of his.

"*I* have a *silly brain?*" I act appalled. I cross my eyes, spread my lips crazily, pull my hair up on end. I want to be happy.

"Bonne nuit," he waves and shakes his head. Some of the pink has left his eyes. He is smiling.

"Ennui." I wave back.

"Mom?" Georgie has switched the light on in her room.

"Yeah?" I walk in and she is sitting on the edge of her bed with nothing on but her underpants. The edges of her hair are damp and sticking to her face like the chic hairstyles of 1930 or 1963. Her skin is white and warm as bread.

"Why did you take your pajamas off, honey?"

"Did Mrs. Kimball go home?"

"Yes, she did. Aren't you feeling well?" In sickness and in sickness, till death do us part.

"I can't sleep," she says.

"I noticed. How come?" I locate her nightgown underneath her pillow and smooth her hair back with it, like a towel.

"I dunno."

"You don't know?"

"Uh-uh. Mary Merwin is going to have a baby brother or a baby sister."

"Who's Mary Merwin?"

"She's a girl."

I help her get back into her nightgown. "You know, it's turning into winter out there."

"Mr. Winter-binter."

She's not sleepy.

I stand up and do my Statue of Sleep-Liberty imitation. Yawning and holding a torch: " 'Give me your tired, your poor, your huddled masses yearning to breathe free.' "

George smiles and I lean over and give her a *puffle*, something my mother used to do with us: press mother's mouth against child's neck and blow out air. It's warm and wet and tickles. George tenses, shoulders up by her ears in anticipation, her whole body in a scrinch—then she giggles and relaxes. "Do it again," she says, and I do it twice more.

"See you tomorrow, schminker-schmunker," I say, love dissolving language into funny sounds, non-words.

"See you tomorrow, schminkie-schmunkie," she giggles.

I wrinkle my nose, make a face. She sticks out her tongue and makes a humming sound. I blow her a kiss from the doorway, and she does a Bronx cheer in parody, an arm puffle, and I turn off the light.

Herman—

    Nice poem. I like especially the part about the "bouquet of irises gooey and rotted like the dead heads of birds" and the way "limp panting tongues" resonates at the end. Technical point: You cannot say "to lay down" unless you mean to copulate with feathers. You must learn lay *from* lie *before you can graduate. (In addition to the swim test there will be a lay detector test.) Otherwise, fine.*

                            B.

Gerard is having some hot affair with a woman named Merrilee. He thinks he may be in love.

"Arouse by any other name is still arouse," I say. "Can I get —yeah, the ketchup. Thanks."

"She ought to have a sign across her pelvis that reads 'Abandon all hope, you who enter here.'" Gerard stuffs an egg into his beard.

"Personally, I always liked the one in *The Wizard of Oz* better: 'I'd turn back if I were you.'"

Gerard looks at me from over his coffee cup, sets it down with a chipping clink, and sighs in joy. Gerard never sighs in joy. "I swear, it's like sleeping with a *Playboy* magazine." He smiles contentedly.

"Yeah, my brother used to do that," I say. "Only with him it was really a magazine." Under his bed my brother Louis had more pictures of nude women than an art museum. I remember hearing my mother say to him once in a loud, scolding whisper: "Louis! Don't play with your genitals!" which I thought was the same word as *gentiles*—leaving me greatly bewildered as to whom we were supposed to play with.

"Well, Gerard," I say, leaning back and fishing through my purse for cigarettes. "Congratulations."

I am driving home from the supermarket. It took much longer than I would have liked. George wandered off by herself to stare at the candy, while I loaded up on canned goods and had my fruit weighed—something vaguely sexual-sounding, something that Eleanor might say. I also had to spend too much time in the meat department, having a turkey sliced in half (also something Eleanor might say). Roasting only half a turkey and freezing the other half is a trick I learned from my mother, something for small and/or budget-impaired holidays. The butcher takes it in the back room, where there are carcasses, fish smells, and lots of white jackets, and where he has some sort of electric blade that whips through the bones and the plastic wrapper. Then he loosely ties the two halves back together with string and brings them out and grins and thrusts them at you.

By the time we get home it's a dark, denimish twilight. George has chocolate in the chap of her lips.

"Georgie, can you help me with the groceries?" I lean over and unlock the door.

"Yup," she says, putting her mittens on.

I get out, go around back, unlock the hatch. I hear the telephone ringing in the house, grab a bag, and bound up the back steps into the kitchen. I put the bag down on the counter and it slips and falls into the sink, but no matter.

I want it to be Darrel. "Hello?" I'm breathless, I think from the dash in.

"Hi, it's me," says Gerard. "I was just about to hang up. Did you just get in?"

"Hi. Yeah," I say, trying to hide my disappointment like a venereal disease, like someone sick from love. "Listen, can I phone you back? I'm bringing groceries in right now."

"Actually, Benna my love, in about sixty seconds I'm leaving town for a family Thanksgiving with Maple at his parents'. I just wanted to phone and say bye."

"Yeah, well: Have a good Thanksgiving, Gerard."

"You, too," says he. And then we hang up. I sigh and begin to pull groceries out of the sink, when I hear Georgianne crying outside. I hurry back out and see her sitting on the steps in the cold, sobbing into her knees. "Georgianne, honey, what's the matter?" I say, sit next to her, put my arms around her and she tilts and leans into me, sobbing harder. I look and see that the bottom of a grocery bag she has struggled with has apparently ripped and various groceries including oranges and the two turkey halves, now unstrung and separated, have formed a small scatter about the driveway.

"Mom," wails George, lifting her face and pointing out at the driveway. "Mom, I broke the turkey!"

Thanksgiving itself is not so cute. Almost everyone I know—Darrel and Gerard—have gone visiting moms and pops.

For dinner at my house it's just Eleanor, George, and I. George is cranky and doesn't set the table properly. "George," I remind her, "the forks go on the left."

"They don't have to if they don't want to," she says, all knuckles and recalcitrance and averted gaze.

I've spent five hours peeling and chopping chestnuts for stuffing, while various parades have been blaring from the TV in the living room. Eleanor arrived an hour ago and has been helping me; now she's at the table stirring chives into the sour cream so that we can eat elegant baked potatoes. My cuticles are shredded and sore; I shake a finger at Georgianne. "Don't give me any lip, young lady."

George makes a face. "Don't give me any lip, young mleh-mleh."

I put down the nutcracker I'm holding, bend over, grab her wrist, drag her near. "Do you *understand?*"

George pulls her wrist and shouts, "Ow," howls as if she's been mortally wounded, something she's staged for Eleanor's benefit. Then she runs to Eleanor's chair, stands next to it, and both of them are just there, staring at me from across the table, their eyes swirling far away like the surfaces of four complicit moons, four sour apples, four angry gods, four angry oh-my-gods, with their arms hugging, their mouths hung open, rubbery with flabbergast.

"Are you all right?" Eleanor asks later.

"I'm fine," I snap, lift plum pudding out of the oven, mix hard sauce with difficulty, drinking most of the brandy myself.

We eat dinner uncomfortably, a ritual we are bad at; all dissembling and irony, we are doing imitations of other people at Thanksgiving and we do them feebly, looking around, like kids from Tomaston not knowing what fork to use.

After dinner George and Eleanor play cards in the living room. They talk in low tones. I'm in the kitchen and can't hear what they're saying.

When it starts to get dark outside, Eleanor has to go. She

comes into the kitchen and puts her arm around my waist. "Do
you need any help?" and I say no. We hug and she says she has
to get going, George has destroyed her in twelve straight rummy
games, the girl's a killer.

"I know," I say.

George and Eleanor say good-bye by laughing and pretending to sock one another in the stomach.

By nightfall George is still not speaking to me. She has gone
outside, gotten on her bike, driven to the edge of our property
and the Shubbys' and remained there, arms folded.

"George, get in here," I call from the front door. I have on
only a light sweater. George has crookedly donned earmuffs and
an unzipped jacket, no mittens.

She refuses. She re-folds her arms and tells me she's running
away. She's straddled the bar of the bike; it's too big for her.

"On your bike?" I shout.

"Yup, and I want my bank book this instant," she shouts.
"I'm not on your property, so don't worry."

"George, please." My knees are rags, my head mush, my life
chestnut dressing chopped for hours and hours. Is this my daughter? I don't recognize her. I close the door, but don't lock it. I
leave her, go upstairs, and climb into bed with my clothes on and
my shoes.

At five-thirty in the morning I'm up, downstairs, boiling water
and pouring it over oatmeal. Though rumpled I am already
dressed, this is easy, this amuses me. In the living room Georgianne is on the sofa, asleep with her earmuffs still on.

I look out the window. She has left her bike fallen on the
Shubbys' property. The streetlight is still on. I start to turn away,
back to my oatmeal, when I see her, the woman with the bathrobe out in the middle of the street again, with two children and a
dog, and they are waving, though the dog sees something and runs
after it and the children say something to each other, take each

other's hands and walk off in another direction, and the woman is left standing alone, still waving, dauntless, happy to see me.

November twenty-ninth is my birthday. I have an ache in my wisdom tooth. Darrel is supposed to be back from his parents' house in New Jersey and is supposed to take me out to dinner.

 I count too heavily on birthdays, though I know I shouldn't. Inevitably I begin to assess my life by them, figure out how I'm doing by how many people remember; it's like the old fantasy of attending your own funeral: You get to see who your friends are, get to see who shows up.

Eleanor has to be away for the day but she drops by early in the morning to give me a beautiful piece of pottery with zigzags. It seems expensive, as solid solitary objects often do, though I know nothing about pottery. Georgianne has smiled at me, kissed me, made me a card. It has three construction paper panels: The first has a flower in a flower pot; the second has the same flower in a flower pot, only this time the flower has grown; in the final panel the flower has grown so much you can't even see it—only the stem and the pot. At the bottom she has scrawled in crayon: "My love just grows and grows and grows for you. Happy Birthday. Your Daughter, Georgianne Michelle Carpenter." It's the exact same card design she used last year—an idea filched from a children's magazine. Apparently she thinks I would have forgotten that she gave it to me, assumes adults don't really take that much notice of children and that therefore she can get away with this theft and redundancy. I kiss her. I thank her. We are friends again, funny friends. I nibble on her head and say, "I chews you." She giggles, brings her shoulders up to her ears in a lovely shrug-hunch.

 In the kitchen we eat ice cream. I can't get it together to make a cake.

.   .   .

Darrel gives me a kiss with much rump-rubbing and torso-pressing. I haven't seen him since before Thanksgiving; this feels nice; and though he could have phoned at least once this feels like love what do I know.

"I missed you," he says in what I deem a heartfelt way.

We are in the car, driving. Darrel's driving.

"Where are we going for dinner?" I ask. It's getting darker earlier these days. "You're not losing an hour, you're gaining a sun," I always tell my classes in the spring when the clocks get set ahead again.

"A little place out past the mall. We just keep going straight."

"I hope it's not that cynical Chinese place."

"What cynical Chinese place?"

"That place with the ferns and all that cheap French wine."

"No, this is a new place. I'll tell you: It's called Fig's."

"Oh, Gerard's been there," I say. "He says it's nice," and then suddenly I know what this is: a surprise party. I know it. I'm sure of it.

"Is this a surprise party?" Now I will watch Darrel lie. When he says no, I will study him, watch how he does it; from here on in I will know what he does when he lies, how he sets his face, how he moves his mouth, I will know his lie look, his lie voice, his lie words, though he won't know I'm gathering this intelligence; nonetheless, I must gather.

"No," says Darrel, and because we're stopped for a light I can turn and see his face fall into a configuration of mature concern, of heartfeltedness. He reaches over and attempts to squeeze my left buttock, though mostly the car seat's in the way.

"I just want to take you to a place you've never been to before."

"Did you sleep with someone over Thanksgiving?" It's a long light, and I watch his face.

"Benna," he scolds. And then smiles, slightly self-conscious, shakes his mature, concerned, heartfelt head, and pinches me gently in the hip.

"Surprise!" shouts everyone. There is Gerard and Maple and some people I don't know, some friends of Gerard, why does Gerard always have friends I don't know. They wanted to go to a party; I'm only the excuse; I feel bashful and hide my face in Darrel's sleeve as if I were Georgianne, then lift it out again. There are a few affectionate laughs and "Aw's." I look along their faces, and suddenly I see Verrie. She looks beautiful and stands and we hug tight.

"God, you look great," I gasp.

"It's California," she says. "I hate it. Hate brings out my youthful glow."

"Not me," I say. "Hate makes weight," and I puff out my cheeks and laugh but I have indeed gained weight should I care.

Fig's is orange and square with several cigarette machines. It looks like the FVCC faculty lounge. My eyes feel scrappy and splotched. Verrie's in town for a day, she says.

Gerard kisses me, brings me a chair. "Happy Birthday, Benna. Were you surprised?"

"Oh, yeah," I say.

Gerard gives Darrel a friendly tap. "Good work," he says.

"It was nothing," says Darrel, all male conspiracy. I feel manipulated, described in the third person. Regardless of how you try to love them, men always return to one another in the end.

Eight people around a table. Introductions. Names like Pooky and Cappy. (No Merrilee.) Drinks like scotch. Presents like books. Food like steaks and chops. Why was Joan of Arc luckier than Mary Queen of Scots? Because Joan got a hot stake and Mary only got a cold chop. Cappy howls, spills a drink. Jokes like that.

There is a birthday cake. Candles like spikes in a large *34*. Now being in my thirties is getting serious. Now the second number is larger than the first. Someone gives me a card that says, "You're not getting older, you're getting bitter." Darrel leans over and kisses me.

Gerard also leans over and kisses me, apologizes for the birthday card, reminds me not to drink too much I have to teach tomorrow, says, jokingly, "You're almost as drunk as I am," and soon Gerard and I are up and doing Motown Shakespeare. Verrie has requested it. "As you from crimes would pardoned be / Let your indulgence set me free why don't you babe." We do footwork and spins like the Temptations.

All the world's a stage we're going through.

The ants are fewer, sluggish and wintry, perhaps swacked with schnapps. Some of their bodies are tinged with gray. They stumble under worm husks, still scale the stucco. The crack has reached the rear kitchen window, and the sky spits snow. Madame Charpentier has a new black tangle at her throat. Her children have mustaches.

Eleanor is back with Newton and has changed her mind about Italy. I tell her again about going to the Caribbean with George. "Wanna come?" I ask. "It might be fun."

"Not me," she says. "I'll throw the going-away party." She toasts me with her coffee cup. "Happy going away."

"Please, I'm not going away *yet*." I nibble at my cuticle.

"Sorry," says Eleanor, proposing a new toast. "Happy will be going away."

We sip our coffee. We smack our lips. "Yes," I say. "That is probably true."

Gerard says he bombed out at the Met auditions. He says he doesn't want to talk about it. I oblige him but then wonder what sort of complicity with his demons and my own weak, ignoble ease that entails. Tomorrow night is his big debut in the Free Verdi Company's *Carmen*. Some directors of various opera company apprenticeship programs are supposed to be there. Perhaps they'll come backstage afterward and give him their cards.

"Wait until you see it, Benna. The best Don José ever: Carlo Bergonzi meets Neil Sedaka meets Zelda Fitzgerald." He regales me with some vocal calisthenics that sound inhuman, worse than fog horns. He laughs at my wince. Hank shambles over and asks him if he could not "make these such noises."

"I have to have a wisdom tooth removed this afternoon. I've scheduled it now while I'm still employed and have insurance to cover it, so I suppose I should," I say to Gerard, my mouth gluey with egg.

"Poor you."

"But listen, I'll be there tomorrow, munkface and all. I'll come backstage and give you a rose and a cough drop."

"Thanks," says Gerard.

Darrel offers to pick me up from the dentist's office, but I tell him nah, not to worry, I'll be fine.

"Are you sure? I'm actually fond of dentists' offices. They've got great chairs."

And I say, "Sure as squash."

He narrows his eyes. "I'll try to be there just in case."

The air downtown is slate cold, Christmas-shopping air. I step into Dr. Morcutt's office (*"Morcutt?"* hooted Gerard. "You would go to a dentist named Morcutt?"), and it's stuffy and chemical, as if the place had just been painted and no one had opened the windows. It gives me a slight headache. I walk up to the receptionist and say, "I'm a little early for my appointment. Should I come back, walk around in the fresh air for a while, rather than wait in here?"

The woman at the desk, a Mrs. Janice Felds, according to a bar pin high on her left breast, looks at me, suddenly concerned. She stands up and presses my hand between both of hers. "You don't look well," she says, probing my eyes with hers, attempting to locate something in them, something serious in them, she'll never find it. My face feels hot, my stomach bruised, my back clammy as a dock. Mrs. Janice Felds presses her hand against my forehead like she's the school nurse.

"Come with me," she says, and leads me into one of the examination rooms.

"Really, it's no big deal," I'm saying. "It's only just the paint smell."

"Sit down. Lie back," says Mrs. Janice Felds, and I sit in the big dental chair, lean back while she cranks it into a horizontal position; someone walking by could see up my skirt.

The examination room looks suddenly odd to me. Instead of being crammed with dental equipment, it is big, with one long empty counter on the side—like at a vet's, where everything is put away, out of sight, protected from the thrashing of terrified animals. It feels like a roller skating rink with just this spare dental chair at the center.

Now there are other people in the room. There is murmuring. I detect it. Someone presses a cold wet washcloth to my forehead. I begin to feel foolish, begin to sit up. "Really," I say. "None of this is necessary."

"Just rest," says the other nurse, and I am made to recall a lover I had once who also hovered over me and commanded things: Here, here, no here; relax, damn it. I look up and see three sets of nostrils and an ebony birthmark. The dentist comes in and takes my pulse. I close my eyes wearily.

"Really," I continue to protest. "It's only that you just painted in here. I sometimes get a little dizzy around fumes is all."

Dr. Morcutt is troubled. He looks at me, like Janice Felds, searches vainly for a trace of substance in my face, in the smudgy, silly, crayoned and stained-glass windows of my soul. "But we haven't just painted in here," says the doctor. "We haven't painted in here for two years."

The extraction is a rape. Or a Caesarean. Some sort of untimely rip. Due to Dr. Morcutt's concern for what he calls "patient management," I'm given only the minimum local anesthetic, no general, no laughing gas, no funny business. He's afraid I may have allergies.

"Hey. Do I have allergies," I say, though I really don't. I have fears.

It's only one tooth, but it takes an hour to get it. Not only is it impacted, it's committed as hell to remaining with the rest of my body and rather than surrender, it self-destructs, crumbles into twenty tough little bits and slivers, and the doctor sweats, says shit, chomps his fruit gum harder. A nurse behind keeps pulling up on my jaw, as if its attachment to my skull or neck were an irritating superfluity. To communicate my body's complete disapproval of these goings on, I make low groaning sounds, which after a while I'm afraid sound like sex, so I stop. The tugging, scraping, snapping in my mouth is a war, a huge mean war, this is what it is to die, to be fighting dying, to be snatched, gouged. I keep thinking I'll swallow my tongue or even that I already have. My jaw aches and bends. "Her jaw can't take this," the nurse behind me warns. "The bone's giving way."

"Uuuuuuuhhh," I say in agreement, will I faint I may faint. After it is all done, the dentist and I look at each other: We've been through something together.

"You have the bones of a woman twice your age," he says into my eyes.

"You don't like that?" I ask softly. He rubs a smooth finger naillessly around in my mouth, like a lover.

"I'll call you tomorrow," he says. And he walks through one of the side doors that leads to an adjacent room with another patient in it, a blonde maybe, someone from Radcliffe with a completed thesis, awaiting his services.

I rinse with water. I spit. Then I stumble out of the chair, turn, and shake hands with the nurse, whose eyes are all atwinkle. "Take care of yourself," I say.

Darrel is in the waiting room. He sees me and stands up, extends an arm my way. I have a prescription for codeine clutched in one fist; I can feel my bangs damp against my temples. I must look funny, swollen and bedraggled, for Darrel gives me a gummy, toothy grin, and shakes his head, like I'm cute, like I'm not his teacher. He puts his arm around me. "You okay?"

My tongue's dead in my mouth, thick and swollen, like something hit by a car. There's Christmas music in this room, piped in from the ceiling: and quiche lorraine forever and ever. Hallelujah! Hallelujah! I lean my head against Darrel's arm. It is slippery with nylon; already it is parka weather. "Why, it's one of the three wise men," I say, trying to smile. I look up at him. "And I think I know which one." I wonder if I should have the tooth put back in. "I love you," I say. Forever. And ever.

Darrel smiles. "You're on drugs," he says.

Hallelujah! Hallelujah!

"Poor mumpy-mom," coos George when she sees my swollen cheek. She wants to touch it, the way people always want to touch the stomach of a pregnant woman. She brings me a glass of milk. "Can I look inside?" she asks.

"It's like giftwrap," I say, and I open my mouth so she can look at the black threads.

"Eeeyow." George looks both mesmerized and ill. "Does it hurt?"

"Uh-uh," I shake my head, my mouth still open for her to see.

George turns away. "That's enough," she says and I close my mouth and she takes a sip of my milk, peering out at me from over the glass rim. Like an owl. Like a suspicious owl.

"Hello, Mrs. Carpenter?"

No one calls me *Mrs.* "This is Benna Carpenter, yes."

"Mrs. Carpenter, this is Rita Milnheim from the Lertoma Club, and we'd like to know if you'd be interested in donating eighteen dollars to send four mentally retarded children to see *Hansel and Gretel* performed by an authentic New York theater group."

The voice is chilly and mechanical. Eighteen dollars sounds like a lot. "The what club? What's the name of your club?"

"The Lertoma Club, Mrs. Carpenter. We also have the nine-dollar plan which will allow us to send two mentally retarded children to see *Hansel and Gretel*." Once an insurance salesman came to my door. "Mrs. Carpenter," he said, shaking my hand, "my name is Dick Helm and I'm here to find out if you're covered." I stared at him. Then I glanced down at myself. "Gracious, I think so," I said. At which point I sent him over to the Shubbys. Which is a habit I have.

"Well," I said, "the nine-dollar plan sounds a little better, but I just had a wisdom tooth removed and can't really talk very well. Could you send me brochures or something? I would just like some more information on your organization before I give any more money away."

"Certainly. Thank you very much for your pledge, Mrs. Carpenter. You've made two handicapped children very happy. Good night."

She hangs up before I get to protest. First of all, I haven't officially pledged anything, and I resent being rushed, bullied, misunderstood into it. Second of all, why would two retarded children ever want to see *Hansel and Gretel*, a play about the abandonment of children? What if I refused to give the Lertoma Club my money. Certainly most of it benefits the theater group and not the kids at all. Why not nine dollars for, say, beer and M&M's? If I were retarded—hell, even if I weren't—that's what I would want. What if I don't pay? Would two kids be left standing out in front in a lobby somewhere, teary-eyed, wondering why Missus Carpenter didn't send in the money? "We don't like Missus Carpenter! We don't like her!" they would chant in unison. Would they be stuck there while all their friends went on in? Would this be the real *Hansel and Gretel*? Would this be what they should see?

"Mom, a long time ago I put a tooth under my pillow, but the tooth huvvah didn't come and give me anything."

Huvvah is Georgianne's baby word for fairy. I don't know where she got it; I think it just kind of developed on its own, like marsupials in Australia. For some reason we've kept it in circulation.

"Really?" I say, wondering if I should wrench her out of infancy, get rid of this tooth-and-money jazz. My mother had told us right from the start that there was no tooth fairy, sorry kids, and that Santa Claus was simply a spirit in your heart that prompted you into present-giving. The Easter Bunny, however, I knew really truly existed, though he was crucified on Friday and had to wait until the third day to rise and pass out jelly beans. What could I say to Georgianne? "Honey, there's no such thing as the tooth huvvah"? It wasn't compelling. It wasn't a spirit in your heart.

"Why don't you try again?" I suggest and cup my hand over my jaw. "The tooth huvvah owes me quite a bit of money, too. Maybe the tooth huvvah will come visit tonight." Maybe Darrel, I thought, was the tooth huvvah.

"Nah," says Georgianne.

"Why not?"

"Cuz in school I made a ring with it."

"A ring?"

"Yeah. Wanna see?" And she whips out from behind her back a tiny pipe cleaner twisted and curled into a circle. Glued to it, rather precariously, is her tooth, the blood in it now brown as a body part. It looks like some horrible thing that got done in Vietnam and people never talked about until ten years later.

"My," I say.

George slips it on. "It's very pretty. I just have to be careful."

"What did your teacher say?"

George shrugs. "She said I just shouldn't wear it to church. But I tole her we didn't go to church, we went to Donut-O-Donut, and she said, 'Well then I guess you could wear it there.'"

The dentist calls, as he said he would.

"How are you?"

"It's supposeta hurt, right?"

"*Uncomfortable* is the word we use."

"I'm uncomfortable then. Yeah. I'm okay."

"Good. Glad to hear it."

"How are *you*?"

"All right, thanks." He pauses. "After you I had five more."

I think about this. It sounds like something I said once to my first boyfriend, in a bad coffee shop, over beers, in my imagination, in New York: *After you I had five more.*

But what does one say to a dentist?

"Eye-yi-yi."

"That's teeth for you."

"Yes," I say, "it certainly is."

"Come in on Tuesday, and I'll remove your stitches."

"That sounds interesting."

"Yes. Well. See you then."

"Right," I say. This is like every divorce. You get tears in your eyes and think, "God, all that oral sex and now we're talking to each other like bureaucrats."

My face is puffed up like a boxer's. I know Darrel secretly finds me irresistible this way but just isn't letting on. When I mention this he rolls his eyes and exhales in an exhausted fashion. Then he, too, asks to see my stitches.

Benna Carpenter's morning classes had nothing to say about poetry. They had nothing to say about sex either when she switched the subject to that. They merely wanted to be told what to know. They wanted to know what they should be writing in their notebooks. "This class is supposed to be full of lively discussion," she said to her eight o'clock class. "I'm going to start bringing in pots of coffee." To her ten o'clock class she said, "It's people like you who were responsible for the Holocaust."

The Free Verdi Company performs at Baker High School, a few miles outside of Fitchville. I arrive a little late and have to tiptoe into the auditorium, which is a large room, perhaps used in the daytime as a cafeteria, with a stage at one end and rows of folding chairs, unfolded and arranged in meticulous lines. The cast is already on stage, singing. There are no costumes, no sets, no orchestra: This is what the Free Verdi Company means by *free*. There is a piano, and the cast reads the music from books they hold in front of them. And *Carmen:* This is what they mean by Verdi.

The auditorium is only half-dark and half-full, mostly, I assume, with friends, parents, senior citizens who in the middle of Carmen's arias squeak in their chairs, or readjust them loudly across the floor. The woman singing Carmen is a pale, wheat-haired woman named Dixie Seltzer. She tries to look seductively Spanish, but ends up steamily emoting like a Kansas housewife with the vapors. Gerard hasn't really prepared me for the amateurishness of this production. Mediocrity alone never surprises me, but this particular example, unheralded by the usually shrewd and cynical Gerard, comes as a painful surprise, like a car accident. I'm probably being unkind. I adjust to my seat, slip off my coat, re-cross my legs. Perhaps it's not all that bad. The rest of the audience seems to be enjoying it, smiling and applauding and glancing down at their programs to see who's singing whom. Perhaps it's just my unpreparedness for this that has made it seem so quickly awful, or perhaps it's the Jewish mother in me, wanting only the best for Gerard ("My son! My son the musical genius is drowning!"). What the hell do I know about opera?

The lights go up. There will be three intermissions. The cast is allowed to meander the corridors, linger at the water fountain, chat pleasantly with relatives. An older man, strikingly white-haired and in a red turtleneck, brushes by me, in a hurry to leave. He has his car keys in his hand. "I for one am not sticking around for the rest," he says to me meanly, stagily, because I am the nearest person at the moment. He stops and smiles at me, as if I'm supposed to agree. I look away. I look for Gerard, spot him by the stage door with his back to me, scurry up behind him and then give him a big hug. "You're terrific," I say, though I've hardly heard him sing a line yet. "Act two," I remember him saying, "act two is where I turn into Placido Domingo."

Gerard turns and beams. His eye wanders off to one side like a haywire satellite. "Thanks for coming. Let's walk." He takes my arm and we march loudly off down the corridor to the left. It's one of those hallways with a long glass wall on one side. Outside it's night and bushes. "I just need someone to pace with," says Gerard, and our legs are close, brushing and in step, identical, like pals, like siblings. "Two siamese twins," says Gerard. "Tragically joined at the hip."

"I like this," I say. "I'm absconding with the leading man. I think it's something that with a little practice I could learn to do very well." Gerard isn't really listening. He seems nervous, a slight rose flush behind his forehead and eyes. "Are you nervous?" I ask. "You don't really seem nervous."

"There's a guy in the audience from City Opera. It might be nice to impress him, you know, shake his hand backstage, all that gladhanding stuff. He's got white hair and is wearing a red turtle-neck—I saw him from the stage. Did you happen to notice him?"

"No."

Gerard looks at me, clearly tense, this the ravage of ambition. "You think this is all bush league, don't you?"

"No, of course not, Gerard."

"Where's my rose?" he grins.

"Damn. I forgot it. I'm sorry." We have stopped walking. We are both looking at each other's feet.

"Well," says Gerard, looking up, hopeful as a fisherman. "I still say this is better than the Ramada. What's wrong with your face?"

"Thanks a lot, Gerard."

"No, I mean your cheek. It's swollen."

"My wisdom was removed. I told you about that."

"That's right," he smiles. "Now I remember. You taking funny pills?"

"Yeah, but they're never funny enough. This morning I told my students they were responsible for the Holocaust. They never looked up, just wrote it in their notebooks. I'll buy you a drink after you kill that bitch Carmen."

"I'll need one," he sighs, and then we walk back up the corridor. When we get to the stage door, the corridor is emptying and I take Gerard by the elbow and say, "Well, good luck!"

"I don't believe in luck," he says. "I believe in miracles." He stops and tucks in his shirt. "That's just part of my personality."

The chorus is really the weakest element. It wobbles around and gets way ahead of the pianist. Gerard's voice, for the most part, is clear and strong. He's a fairly confident Don José and rarely looks at the score, until a bad note undoes him. I can see him redden, hesitate, lose his place, flounder back into his book.

Nonetheless, everyone loves the Flower Song, that song of the not-forgotten rose.

Gerard keeps insisting on buying the drinks. I have to fight and argue and end up having to say belligerent-sounding things to the waitress, who refuses to run a tab. "If I ever have kids," he says, "I'm going to name them Methyl and Ethyl." He toasts and swigs.

Something's tired between Gerard and me. It's as if we have disappointed each other into irritation; we have witnessed the other's failures for too long, and it has made us cranky.

"You really thought it was okay?" asks Gerard again.

"Yes, Gerard, I thought it was okay." I am on the verge of a sigh or a snap or a shout.

We try speaking of other things, of the decline of the world, how humanity is done for, how Gerard has been seeing Darrel around town with another woman, how Gerard thought I should know, and how Gerard seems a little too eager to tell me, how Gerard drinks way too much, and how Gerard felt our goddamned friendship was about truth and honesty, and how some things are better not to know or tell like for instance the man in the red turtleneck who left early because the whole production was a joke how's honesty if you like honesty. And how I'm so volatile, and how it is that all this is happening, how I shouldn't have to sit and listen to some drunk musician tell me about Darrel screwing around, and how sorry Gerard is, he really shouldn't have said anything he just thought it would be for the best, and how Gerard is just a washed-up, no-talent Huck Finn or should we say *Hack* lounge act playing at everything and just because he's drunk he's pretending he's hurt, don't pretend you're hurt, for godsakes he should just drink himself to death, and how I just don't have the character for alcohol, it requires too much sweetness and commitment, and how Gerard should just go fuck himself, and how so should I.

And how did this happen? I never know how anything happens.

In the student union snack bar the teacher was scanning student blank verse—something different from blank student verse, she thought, but not that different. She looked up, gazed abstractedly out the window at the walk, that silly artificial promenade, that highway of undergraduate love, of sweet constitutionals. And then a student of hers named Darrel was suddenly strolling by out there with someone young and pretty and their bodies were touching, bowed slightly toward one another, and they drank from cans of Diet Pepsi as they walked. Perhaps they were having some political or intellectual discussion, thought the teacher. Perhaps this woman was a Marxist. You could always tell a Marxist: They wore the best clothes.

The teacher turned her gaze away, stared back down at the tabletop, near the edge, at something scratched into the wood. DROP ACID, it said. And then beneath it, in different writing, NO, TAKE IT PASS-FAIL.

. . .

I have always wanted to grow old with someone, to be with someone through all of life, to lie under an electric blanket together,
in the daytime, and compare operations.

Darrel is wearing a t-shirt that says APOCALYPSE PRETTY
SOON. He places his hand on my crotch. "Nice place ya got
here," he says. I don't smile. We've been talking about his future
and now he's trying to change the subject. I maneuver away,
squirm on the sofa.

"Don't change the subject," I say. "Look, I want to talk
about this. I don't get it: You *truly* want to go to *dental* school?"
This is what he's just told me again. He's smiling.

"Yeah, I like the chairs. Those dentist chairs. They're like
rocket ships."

"But *you* don't get to sit in them. That's the other guy."
The electric chair, I don't tell him, was invented by a dentist.
"You really want to be a dentist."

"Yes, eventually." He stiffens, defensive, his smile vanished.
I look for his lie look, his lie face, but can't seem to spot it. "I'm
thinking of becoming an orthodontist. I've told you this before,
Benna."

But it's an absurdity that doesn't register with me. Here
we are on the god-knows-what anniversary of John Lennon's
death and Darrel is saying he wants to be an orthodontist. Maybe
I am hearing things wrong. That sometimes happens this time
of year: People hear things wrong. The night John Lennon died
I was standing in a deli and someone burst in and shouted,
"Guess who's been shot? *Jack Lemmon!*"

These things happen this week in December. Look at the
screw-up at Pearl Harbor. Darrel has meant something else all
along. Surely he doesn't want to become a jeweler of teeth, a
bruiser of gums. It's a joke. "Yeah, right," I laugh. "I can see
you as an orthodontist."

Darrel looks suddenly irritated, screws up his leathery face into a fist, bunched like one of those soft handbags. "What, isn't that good enough for you, Benna? Upward mobility for the oppressed? Is that just not angry enough for you?"

It's true. That's what I want for Darrel, from Darrel. He should be angry like Huey Newton. Or in a wheelchair making speeches, like Jon Voight.

"You want me to be a little black boy vet with a Ph.D. and a lot of pissed-off poetry?"

"Why not?" I say. It doesn't sound bad, it's just the way he's saying it. Darrel stands up and paces peevedly about the living room.

"I can't believe it. You're just like everyone else. You want me to be your little cultural artifact. Like a Fresh-Air child. Come off it, Benna."

"*You* come off it," I say. This is the old children's strategy of retort. I've learned it from Georgianne or remembered it or maybe simply saved and practiced it. "You're being so, well . . . *bourgeois.*"

This is the word that intelligent, twentieth-century adults use when they want to criticize each other. It is the thinking man's insult. It is the wrong word. Don't let your mouth write a check that your ass can't cash, Darrel said once, and this time I truly have. Darrel's been storing up for it and leaps on it like a wild man. "*Bourgeois!?*" He's pacing quick and hard, left to right. "You!" he shouts, freezes, points at me.

"You don't have to point at me." He is my student. He shouldn't be pointing at me.

"*You*, Benna, are the most bourgeois person I know."

I wonder if it's true. Behind him I imagine I see all the other people he knows, a winding queue of ethnic celebrants, weathered hitchhikers, Vietnamese women, off-off-Broadway actresses. None of them owns a TV set. They have large peasant breasts. And though they occasionally drink Diet Pepsi, they are cool, practicing Marxists, anarchists, Trotskyites, vegetarians with finished dissertations.

Darrel continues. "I don't know, Benna. What would you have me do? Flounder through graduate school, never finish my doctoral thesis, then marry some lawyer for their money and bitch at them until they're another drunken suicide?"

My vision snaps, sails off like a kite let go. That's me he's talking about. That's supposedly what I've done. "You're wrong, buddy. You're dead wrong." Now I struggle to my feet, up off the sofa. Darrel stops pacing, turns to face me. "I'm sorry," he says.

"I don't know where you got that idea about me, but it's wrong. You don't know what you're talking about."

"I'm sorry," he says again. "It's just something that gets said, you know, around."

"*Who's* said that?"

Darrel wipes his forehead in frustrated apology. "No one in particular. It's just what's said . . . by people."

"Well, it's wrong. And get out of my house!" I'm screaming. "Get out!" I feel suddenly, terribly, old. Maybe now's the time for a group sestina. I feel the parentheses around my mouth, the turmoil of exhaustion in my gut. Here are the end words: *so, this, is, what, we, are.* My body, if a surgeon looked inside, would look like a drawerful of old socks and shoes. My eyes feel like stones in my forehead and my heart has blasted several sharp pains and disappeared entirely. I have always wanted to grow old with someone, but this is not what I had in mind.

Darrel picks up his things slowly, his coat over one arm, his books under the other. "You see, you can't operate within this relationship unless it's a little classroom for you. You need that power."

"Get out!"

Darrel heaves his coat up onto one shoulder and before he

opens and slams the door he turns and says, "I love you, but there's one thing you've gotta understand: I'm not just one of your fucking students." Then the front door swallows him up and closes like a book. I look at it for one long dumb minute before I'm out the door myself, watching Darrel get into his car, and standing on the porch, loathsome and coatless in the cold, I shout, "Yes, you are! Yes, you are! That's exactly what you are!"

And he guns the engine and drives away. There is a wind with ice in it, and the streetlights blink on.

In nature certain species, in order not to be eaten, will take on the characteristics of something that is an unpleasant meal. The viceroy, for instance, as a caterpillar looks so much like a bird dropping, and as an adult so much like the ill-tasting monarch, that birds, as agents of natural selection, as Darwinian loser-zappers, leave the viceroy alone. Similarly, the ant-mimicking spider is avoided because it appears to have the fierce mandibles of an ant, though it's really only a dressed-up spider making pretend. The function of disguise is to convince the world you're not there, or that if you are, you should not be eaten. You camouflage yourself as imperious teacher, as imperious lover, as imperious bitch, simply to hang out and survive.

I sit in front of the TV and, for twenty minutes, without turning it on, stare at a woman mechanically eating a cabbage and mayonnaise salad from a large bowl in her lap. Afterward I feel nauseated, and devour an entire pound cake, its lovely topskin soft as leather. I feel like I'm part of a documentary on evolution and I'm one of the species that didn't make it because regardless of everything else, it was just plain too stupid.

III

Gerard wasn't at breakfast, and I had to sit there and make pleasant little faces in Hank's direction to let him know all was well, the eggs were fine, the coffee hot, the silverware clean. Everything's okay. The semester is winding up. Or is it winding down.

It's Novemberish weather for December, that sort of still, ochre chill, no snow, no wind, just the old bones of trees, the damp, dead mat of leaves, the infinity of phone poles and wires along the streets. In the backyard the wrens gather and cry like kittens.

Inside the house the furnace kicks on. The living room's warm with red and dust.

I have to think of Christmas presents: what to get George, Gerard, my dad—he's always the hardest. George is sprawled out on a chair across from me, imitating me, limbs thrown out and apart, coat still on, body in the configuration of a slumped, crash-landed star.

"What should we get Grampup for Christmas?" I ask her.

"Get him . . ." She pauses, giving this great consideration. Her face looks profound and little in her new spectacles. "Get him some plates."

"Plates?"

"Get him . . . get him a new car."

"He doesn't need a new car. He never drives over thirty-five." Slow for a fireman; he's retired. "*I* need a new car, not him." My car is now one of those cars that will never go sixty except over a cliff.

Georgianne gets up, trudges over, sits on the edge of my

chair. She is a heap of layers: tights, dress, sweater, coat. I put one arm inside her coat, around her waist, hold her. She presses her face close, her glasses knocking into my cheekbone. "Give him a big kiss!" she says, and gives me a juicy smack right near my eye, saliva getting in it, my little whimper-whamper, my Christmas elf, my mush-tush.

It is December tenth, a new moon. The phone rings and it's not Darrel, it's Maple. "Gerard's in the hospital," he says.

"Oh my god." I sink into a nearby chair and switch the receiver to my other ear. My whole life I can think only of car accidents. "He was drunk, wasn't he?"

"Probably," sighs Maple. "He slipped in his tub and cracked his head open and broke a rib. It sounds appalling, but it's serious."

Gerard apparently had lain in his bathroom in and out of consciousness for about ten hours. Merrilee, the human *Playboy* magazine, discovered him there when she stopped by, after a fight, with a contrite, Yuletide loaf of zucchini bread. It is all ludicrous enough to begin with, but to have Merrilee in on it in such an heroic fashion seems preposterous, suited only to the fact of the tub, not to the gravity of the injuries, wrappings, tubes, round-the-clock watch at Methodist Central.

"You can't go in there," a nurse whispers loudly to Maple and me in the corridor. I am pulling open the Intensive Care Unit door.

"I'm Gerard Maines's brother," says Maple.

"I'm Gerard's wife," I add.

The nurse, head floor supervisor Sheila Simpson, smiles at me. "His wife's already been here."

"Merrilee, that bitch," I whisper to Maple, and bit my thumb cuticle.

"Come back tomorrow," smiles Sheila Simpson. "During visiting hours. He's already doing much better, and we may move him out of I.C.U. tomorrow."

Maple's face mirrors my relief. "That's good news," he says.

"Sure is," she says.

"Tomorrow," I repeat dumbly.

"Yes," she says. "Now why don't you go on home. It's six-thirty. You're missing the *real* news." She chuckles. She is not funny. I stand on my tiptoes and try to sneak a peek through the small window on the I.C.U. door and think I see Gerard lying there asleep, something plastic jammed up his nose.

George is watching Dan Rather and eating cheeze popcorn out of a bag. "Is Gerard gonna die?" she turns and asks; she has the face of an old, worried Yugoslavian woman, binging on popcorn. An airliner has exploded over St. Louis. The scribblings on Madame Charpentier have formed a dark, circular splot, like a black ball of string between her breasts, and horrid black shapes all over her face, like a catcher's mask.

"No," I say, and in my heart I take back everything mean I've ever said about God.

In class the teacher put her elbows on the desk and talked into her fists.

"We all have ways of erasing ourselves," she said, and then passed out photocopies of "Modern Love," "Because I could not stop for Death," and several poems by Anne Sexton. She never had been able to organize her courses well.

The hospital is all purposeful white bustle and smells more strongly than last night of soup and rubber and isopropyl alcohol. I have found Gerard's room number from the main desk downstairs and am checking out the plastic-wood plaques over all the doorways to figure out if I'm headed in the right direction. I turn a corner and finally locate 262. "Excuse me," blurts an orderly trying to wheel a cart quickly by me. I've stepped out in front of him like a dazed woman.

"Sorry," I say.

The door is heavy, knobless, and ajar. I push it open further and glance around. A white-gowned Gerard, no plastic up his nose and no beard, is propped against pillows and staring straight ahead. His head, neck, and back are in some sort of traction, part swingset, part backpack. His skull is wrapped in gauze. His arms, thin and bare, are attached to I.V. tubes like a marionette.

I step all the way in. "Hey, Q-tip head, you'll do anything for a free meal, won't you?"

Gerard glances up slowly, like someone with a huge head-ache. I imagine his head has stitches in it like a baseball. He looks fragile, smooth chin and all cheeks, boyish without his beard. He grins weakly and I can see that one of his front teeth is chipped at a diagonal. "A body in motion tends to need some rest," he says. He has a bruise and scratch on the left side of his face. I lean over and kiss him. His lips are dry, swollen lavender with cracks of red. I can taste the slightly metallic taste of blood. I want to tell him how very sorry I am. I want to make up with everyone. When I get home, I'm going to phone Darrel. "Benna," Gerard says, his voice gone soft and husky. "I'm glad you're here. Have a seat."

I drag one from over by the partition, behind which is an old man reading a magazine. "Don't mind me," calls the old man.

"Don't mind him," says Gerard.

I sit down and cross my legs. Gerard looks smaller and smaller to me, fading in and out like a quasar. "Do you hurt?"

"Not really. I'm just a little dizzy. They're probably not going to keep this apparatus on for very long. I'm okay. Maple was in earlier."

"Yeah, I know. We arranged it that way, splitting up our visiting slots. We're a two-act show."

"Even Merrilee came." He smiles, lost.

I attempt a skeptical, quizzical face, then let go of it. "Thank god for Merrilee, huh. Thank god for the staples in life." I am thinking here of the zucchini bread, though the centerfold does, of course, come to mind.

"I don't know what happened. One minute I was unlocking my apartment door, the next I'm here."

"They shaved your beard."

"*I* did that in my drunken stupor, somewhere between the front door and the tub. Not too many razor cuts even. I truly am an amazing fellow. In case you didn't know."

I put my palm to his face. He badly needs another shave. "The new Gerard," I say, not coming up with anything better. "I brought some books to read to you."

"I already know Habakkuk by heart."

"I know, I know." Gerard's right eye is wandering off to one side, as it does when he's tired, a lost Ping-Pong ball. The tooth makes him look like a pirate or a street kid. I look down at my lap; I've brought *Turkish Fairy Tales* and *Alice in Wonderland*. Perhaps my problem is that I try to turn everyone into a child.

"How's lover boy?" asks Gerard. His eyes close for a moment. The question is teasing, like a brother, but the face is weary, like an old person visited insincerely by a young one. Maybe I'm not handling the visit energetically enough and am tiring him out. I dance the books around as if they're playthings. I try to distract him. "Zoopty-doopty-doo," I sing loudly, for a joke.

"How is he?" Gerard says again.

"Well. I think I blew it. It didn't work out." I realize that that is how everyone puts it: *It didn't work out*. Like something that refused to exercise, to exert itself aerobically.

"I'm sorry to hear that," says Gerard, opening his eyes. He tries to sit up more, but it hurts.

"Yeah. I don't know whether to shower him with gifts or go steal things from his apartment." I hold up the books like an elementary school teacher. I dance them around again. "I think there must be a reason I'm going through life alone."

Gerard takes my hand and says nothing, though he smiles just slightly, just sadly.

I don't say anything either. I don't know how to talk to people. Everyone else's lives are far more complicated than mine and it makes me not know what to say to them. I bitch. I argue. I joke and clam up. I sing Broadway showtunes. I'm just an asshole from Tomaston.

"Benna, get yourself a pet," says Gerard. "Why don't you get a dog and name it Wazoo or Aretha Franklin Carpenter, something like that?"

"I don't like dogs. You can't trust them. They always look like they're smiling." I dance *Alice in Wonderland* around again. It's getting less and less funny. Not that it was so great to begin with.

Gerard persists. "You need some other people in your life. Your husband's dead, Verrie's moved and re-occupied—who've you got in this dump town?" I keep noticing the jagged white of his tooth.

"I've got you."

"No, not me," he sighs. "That's my point here. You need someone besides me."

"I've got Georgianne," I blurt out.

"Georgianne?" And suddenly I realize what I've said. The little piece of planet I've been operating on shudders and twists.

"Yeah. Georgianne." I chew on my thumb cuticle. I've never confessed it before. Now I will have to confess.

"Who, praytell, is Georgianne?"

I hesitate. I'm a Beruban cliff-diver. I take a deep breath, and my feet push off. "I made her up." I am sailing through air. "She's, well, sort of my daughter."

Gerard stares at me, uncomprehending. "You made her up? You made up an *imaginary* daughter?"

"Of course not," I say. "What, you think I'm an idiot? I made up a *real* daughter. Yeah." I can feel the sea, the heat behind my face. "I don't go around making up *imaginary* daughters." I pause. "That would get too abstract. Even for me." I think of Pinocchio. Of Thumbelina. Of the children in *Hansel and Gretel* living much of their lives as baked goods.

Gerard tries to be kind. "What is she like?"

The late afternoon light tinkerbells around the room. I want to talk about something else. I feel embarrassed. "Would you like me to read or pour you some ice water or something? You're too injured to be interested in this."

But Gerard's interested. "Do you imagine having conversations and everything?"

"Everything. Babysitters, the whole bit." I can hear the defensiveness in my voice. I wonder if he thinks I'm mad. "Since my brother got divorced and my niece Annie lives off with her mother in Michigan, I don't get to be Aunt Benna very much—so I made up Georgianne to keep me company. She's a cross between Annie and my husband George. I pretend she's his child and sometimes we talk about things. It seemed one of the few decent ways to bring someone into the world." I shrug. "I just kind of gave in to the idea of her. You know how kids can be."

"I'll bet you're very cute together."

"We're disgustingly cute together."

"Do you plan things in advance? Or does she pretty much take care of things on her own?"

I hesitate, not knowing what he's asking and whether he's asking it seriously. I twist my watch around on my wrist. "You know what the Bible says: *Even the lilies of the field, um, make it the hell up as they go along.* I also have a friend named Eleanor."

Gerard's right eye has come back and both of them are trying to fathom me, scrutinizing like a couple of old concierges. "Do I dare ask who *she* is?"

"She's, uh, a very heavily made-up woman. Heavily, heavily made-up."

Gerard laughs and I'm relieved. "What is she like?"

"Like me only with a wig. She tends to shout things like, 'What, wait until I'm forty and have a Mongolian idiot?' Things like that."

"Is there anyone else you've made up?"

People come and go so quickly here. "No," I say, doubt at my lips like an old breakfast.

Gerard lifts up one puppeted arm and places it on my knee. "You're sort of neat and sort of crazy, Benna," he says.

What he means, I think, is that I'm depressing the hell out of him. Out the window the sky has gone all hazy slate. There are churchbells playing at the Christ Methodist church across the way. "How embarrassing. I can't believe I told you." I'm determined not to cry. "I can't believe you fell in a goddamn bathtub." I put my hands to my face, then peek out at him from between my fingers.

"I have secrets, too, you know," says Gerard, growing thoughtful. "Things about my past I've never told you. I have a real nightmare that took place in a restaurant years ago. I'm surprised to this day that I can even go out to dinner anywhere. I know how it is needing to make things—"

"Gerard, you don't have to go into this. You're in the hospital, for pete's sake."

He looks at me, startled. I suddenly know what he's going to say. He's going to say, "That's it with you, isn't it? You don't really want to talk about anything, do you? You know invention and indignation and slamming car doors, but what about serious conversation, Benna? People have lives. As difficult as your own has been, there are others whose lives have been even more so."

But he doesn't say this. What he says is, "You know, don't you?" I try not to look at him. "Maple told you." Gerard's face, his bare scrubby face, grows tight and sad. He looks down at his bedsheets, then he looks back up at me, tries to look insouciantly amused. "I never knew you knew."

"I knew."

"And all this time you liked me because you felt sorry for me."

"Yup, that's the only reason." I want here to be able to tell Gerard how it is that I care for him. But I remain still, like someone being mugged, while the church chimes land on the last vibrating note of "Silent Night."

"Mom, watch me hold my breath."

"Don't hold your breath."

"Why?"

"It's not good for you."

"How come?"

"It affects your personality."

"What are we having for dinner?"

"Donuts. I thought we'd go to Donut-O-Donut." She used to love to go there for dessert. I figure if we go there for the main course, she will love me for life, though her skeletal system will suffer and fail to grow.

Instead she says, "That's no fun. Can I eat at the Shubbys' tonight?"

And though I hesitate, I finally say, "Sure," and let her go, though it's hard.

.   .   .

Eleanor, too, seems to have become unavailable. Perhaps both she and George are simply being resentful. I have exposed them, like opening an oven door on a couple of soufflés: They will never forgive me.

I phone Darrel, but there's no one home.

I go to the hospital over the weekend and read kiddy-lit to Gerard. "Dis kid Alice," says Gerard, doing a bad Marlon Brando imitation. "She really had like some life." He seems to be doing fine. They are talking about letting him out before Christmas, perhaps even later this week, though he still has tubes in his arms and throws up once a day.

The man with the magazine behind the partition is always telling us not to bother with him, to pretend he's not there. Nonetheless I read the stories loud enough for him to hear. Sometimes he asks to see the pictures. His wife has brought him a poinsettia. "Hate plants," he grumbles. The nurses call him Sal. Gerard says it's short for Salvador.

"He's had a life that makes yours and mine look like Jack and Jill," Gerard adds in a portentous whisper, though he doesn't tell me more about it, and I don't ask. Maybe I'm afraid to hear. Maybe I'm thinking about Jack and Jill, how they had it pretty rough themselves. "I know for somebody else my life might seem easy," Eleanor said once. "But for me it's extremely difficult." It wasn't stupid people who managed to be happy in life; it was people who were extra clever.

Monday was the teacher's last day of classes, and there were puddles all over the floor. Students stomped snow from their boots, and winter coats slipped from the backs of chairs. The teacher passed out cookies and cups and wine and then course evaluations. "Be as honest as you feel is absolutely necessary," she said.

"You forgot napkins," someone wailed.

An older, black student named Darrel arrived late after not having been there for a week. He spent twenty minutes filling out the evaluation and refused offers of wine.

At the front of the room the teacher was calling: "When you've finished with the evaluation you can put it face down on the front desk and go. Those of you who still owe me work, get it in by Thursday. Otherwise, have a wonderful Christmas break and it's been nice working with you this semester." She had always been told that *nice* was an empty, insipid word, but lately she'd come to rely on it quite heavily. If you can't say something's "nice," you can't say anything at all, she decided.

Someone on their way out left a carefully wrapped present and a card on her desk. She would take it home. It would be either a coffee mug or some Charlie cologne. "Thank you," she said.

The student Darrel was one of the last to leave, but when he did, he dropped his evaluation face down on the front desk, smiled at the teacher, and said, "Merry X-mas. I'll phone you in two months." Then he placed a gift-wrapped bottle of something in her hands and said, "For you." Perhaps it was cognac, she thought, something she would not hurl against the wall but drink in a single terrible sitting. For now she tried to smile in a way that spoke in part of love and in part of something else, though she wasn't sure what. She made little tentative swimming motions with her fingers, and the student Darrel did likewise, nodding, two sea anemones saying farewell.

At home the crack side of the house is drafty, so I make hot chocolate.

I look out the front window, sipping. The sky is a charcoaled cantaloupe, some oranges and pinks caught in the night clouds like gases. Between the road and sidewalk is a snow hill leading down into the driveway, and some neighborhood kids, including Isabelle Shubby, have taken sleds to it. The snow has melted and refrozen into ice. I can hear their shouts: "Ready or not, here I come!" "Hold your horses!" "Yoweee!" It has started to snow almost like sleet, and it patters against the windows like the staticky glitches in an old record. All of life seems to me a strange dream about losing things you never had to begin with. About trying to find your glasses when you can't see because you don't have your glasses on. That is what it seems.

Although she was not supposed to until after she had given grades, the teacher read the evaluations the students had written. Most of them were perfunctory, favorable, and dull. Under *What did you like best about the instructor?* someone had written "Real pretty" and someone else "Knows a lot of swear words." Someone else had written "Obsessed with sex." Someone else had written, "Your mind is a swamp. Your heart is a swamp. Your soul is a swamp." And then there was a picture of a swamp. Near the bottom of the pile from her afternoon class was handwriting she recognized. "Dear Benna," it said in the space allotted for *Other Comments.* "You don't know a flying fuck about poetry."

The rest of the night the teacher spent at an all-night diner called Hank's where she consumed coffee and homefries until her gut burned and where she sat making homemade Christmas cards that read SEASONS GRITS AND HAPPY NOWHERE or else JOLLY X-MAS FROM SANTA AND HIS SUBORDINATE CLAUSES. She drew pictures. She wrote special, little notes on the ones she was sending to her former lovers. And sometimes, in trying to think up merry little words, she would glance at the faded photo of fried chicken over the counter: six pieces, dead and breaded, arranged carefully in a circle on a plate with parsley and cranberry sauce, red and green, like Christmas.

·   ·   ·

On Thursday I get a note in my department mailbox. It is what I was afraid of: I no longer have a job. It has been necessary to cut down on the number of writing courses. The Reading and Writing of Poetry is being eliminated entirely. There's an additional informal note about my "questionable personal conduct"— it says that although that is not the reason I'm being laid off, I should be more aware of this in conjunction with future academic employment. It's signed by the department chairman, Standish Massie, a Marxist with a hilltop Tudor house that has a great view of the Fitchville proletariat.

I get out of the mailroom fast. I get out to think, to walk, to head for my car.

I'm looking forward to the unemployment checks. What is teaching, anyway? Nothing more than babysitting, like some failed, old wet nurse. You eat too much, snoop and poke around the kitchen, see what's there. Soon the parents come home. And they catch you, always, napping on the sofa in a snore and a ring of cookie crumbs.

I try to think of the proper, dignified way to depart: Shake hands with the department chairman, hug the secretary, give some books to the faculty library. The upstairs faculty library, I've always been told, is where teachers donate their books when they leave.

And so right then and there I go home, pack up a box of old paperbacks I don't want, and bring them back to campus, march them upstairs to the faculty library. The librarian sees me coming down the corridor and stands, slowly, behind her desk, like a sheriff in a western.

I set the box down on her desk and look around: The place is small, in need of books. "Here are some faculty books," I tell the librarian. The titles include *Sheena, The Case of the Grinning Gorilla,* and *How to Make Love Without Really Trying.* "Looks like you could use a few."

Close up the librarian is young and sexy as a starlet. "This is a library for books *written* by faculty members, not simply owned by them at one time."

I look at her, look toward the window, look back at her, her perfectly lashed eyes and blink. "Oh my god," I whisper. It is, after all, a library. "I'm sorry. I thought it was like a summer cottage, you know, like after you've read something you leave it for the next person."

"This isn't a summer cottage."

"Right. God. You are so right." And I take the books back up into my arms, like a mother, like a mother of books, and I turn and clunk back down the three flights of stairs, my coat over one arm, the metal fire door slamming behind me. Out in the parking lot the sky is dark and spitting snow. I stand by my car for a second, out of breath, lean the books onto the hood, and struggle with my coat. When I get it on, when I am in the car with my coat on and my books, I look up through the windshield at the square fluorescent eyes of the library. "You're damn right this is no summer cottage," I practically shout. I practically shout in my car! And without warming up I tear home through two yellow lights and a stop sign.

When I pull into the driveway, I can hear noise from a party over at the Shubbys'. It leaks out at me through the windows of their turquoise home like a fume. The Shubbys are good people, I have to remind myself. They have probably never hurt a soul in their lives. They are generous. They love life. They have a beautiful daughter. And when I get inside and can still hear their party noise I phone the police and register a public nuisance complaint—"I can't sleep," I say, "I can't think!"—and then I hang up and a minute later phone again; this time I change my voice, high and a bit southern, like a different neighbor. "They're disturbing the entire block," I say, and then I sit in the living room, with the lights out and my coat on, waiting for the police, for the flashing red lights, for the sergeant who will put them all in handcuffs, gruffly issue summonses, slap Isabelle up against the wall in a frisk, though she is only seven.

Gerard has seemed in good spirits except for today. He's no longer in traction, and they had taken him off the tubes, but he complained about the food ("the spit-pee soup") and then threw up, so they put him back on. He has gotten thin, even in just the past few days. Today he's griping more than usual about the ineptitudes and barbarisms of the medical staff. "What a medieval place this is," he says. "I'm telling you, it's like the nineteenth century in here." I wonder if this is one of Gerard's big problems, that he has a confused sense of history.

Gerard's head hurts worse. He feels feverish and nauseated.

"Merrilee's gone to California for Christmas," says Gerard. He looks gray like a prisoner of war, like mangled grade-school clay. I worry that something's wrong. He should be looking better than this. "And Maple phoned and wasn't able to come today. My back is mush from lying here. Sometimes I think I'm going to die." His eyes are off doing independent things. One eye is fixed on me, like something snapped to attention, and the other is lost and fatigued, floating toward the outside of his face like a crazy moon. He blinks, and the eyes switch, trade places.

"Shut up, Gerard. You're not going to die. Everyone says you'll be out of here soon." Though something, it's true, is wrong. I sit on the edge of the bed. Life is sad; here is someone. "I'll take care of you," I say. "I mean, Gerard, you're like a brother to me. You're like the closest brother I ever had." Gerard closes his eyes and begins to cry. I lean over and he presses his face into my breasts, the chenille of his eyebrows against my blouse. I kiss his wet eyelids and his lips shift into a sad smile. "Oh, well," he says. "Thank you, my carpenter aunt, toppler of buildings."

I don't say anything.

"You're okay, Benna," Gerard continues tiredly, though opening his eyes. "Look at you. There you are. You're okay." He is making amends. I can see him begin to drift off but fight it, the P.O.W. shadows deepening. I want to hold him, tight, but I don't. Instead, not thinking he'll hear me, I murmur to myself, "Is that supposed to be a compliment?" and suddenly one of his puppeted arms flies upward in the air, finger pointing. "*That*, my dear," he says, "is a supreme compliment." His eyes are still closed and his arm begins to drop back down, slow like a ballet of a dead bird. He smiles feebly. "That is a Diana Ross and the Supremes compliment."

And that's the last thing he says. He has fallen asleep with his mouth open. The nurse comes in and, worried, I ask her if Gerard's all right, that he just sort of drifted off, and she smiles and says he's only taking a nap, not to worry, just come back tomorrow, he might be more rested. Then she gives him an injection, and I just stand there with my coat in my arms and squeak out " 'Bye," like a mouse in a movie.

The next day is December eighteenth, a week before Christmas, and I've bought Gerard a beautiful new bathrobe from an import store. It has indecipherable Oriental lettering on the back, and I will tell him that it says "Howard Johnson's" in Korean, which is probably what it does say. I've also brought him Christmas candy, little sugar stockings and bells, in case he's off the tubes. I'm trying to feel hopeful, but today for some reason it seems hard, like a song you don't really know but fake by coming in on the last word of every line.

Maple's in the lobby by the elevator, sitting on a vinyl padded bench. He rises, walks toward me, dangerously slow, the swim of a nightmare. Something's wrong. I've done something wrong. Maple stops about four feet from me. The corridor slows down. I stop too. He glares at me. He hates me, why does he hate me?

"He was in love with you, you know. You should know that. He told me that once."

"Maple, what the hell are you talking about?" Maple's face is wincing and withering and looking away.

"The fucking bastards! They were killing him!" And here Maple's face crumples from hate to grief and rain pours out of his eyes.

"What? Maple, what do you mean?" Gerard! Gerard! I have candies! "Where is Gerard?"

Maple steps toward me, puts his arms around me, around my packages, his albino face trying to find my shoulder, the faint smell of patchouli everywhere on his clothes. I kick him, step backward, jerk away from him, almost lose my balance. The corridor flies up and down, deserted, undulating, a roller coaster in Lebanon. "Dammit, Maple, what are you saying?" I try to swallow, but I choke. "I mean, hold on here. Where is Gerard?" I've brought candies for him! I bought Christmas candy for him! and I step further away and begin digging, all alone, through one of the bags.

"There's going to be an investigation," says Maple quietly, standing off to one side, all leotard and amethyst; part Horatio, part swizzle stick; and then he brings his hands to his face, turns toward the wall, and sobs.

The teacher's packages slip, and her boots stumble, twisting her ankle. Little stockings and bells have spilled to the floor and are rolling around there. She grabs hold of a table, of a sofa arm —hold on here, hold on here—anything could fly away now. Where on earth does everybody go?

Maple is harder and harder to see; he is bleeding into the wall. "Maple," she cries out. "We'll sue!" This is finally all she can speak: the words of a lawyer's widow. "We'll sue for everything . . ." but then she is at some door, brow against glass, a small friendless girl, standing in candy and vomiting into an ashtray with sand in it.

IV

Sometimes all life felt like this: a choice between Greyhound and Rent-A-Wreck. It reminded her of a joke she'd heard once about two shipwrecked sailors who land on an island of heartless primitives. "You have a choice," says the island king to the first sailor. "Instantaneous Death or Chee-Chee." The first sailor gulps. "I guess I'll go with Chee-Chee," he says. There is a loud gong. "You have chosen Chee-Chee," announces the king, and two huge men appear and cut off the sailor's arms and legs, disembowel him, skin him, then leave him in a steaming heap to die. "*You* have a choice," says the king turning to the second sailor. "Instantaneous Death or Chee-Chee." The second sailor is pale and sweating. "I guess I'll take Instantaneous Death," he says. There is another loud gong. "You have chosen Instantaneous Death," says the king like a Las Vegas emcee. "But first—Chee-Chee!"

Benna opted for the bus, and found herself staring out the film of the window, at houses, trees, signs, as if she were starving for something. Perhaps it was all that motion within the single frame of the window, or the desire to be out and beyond the odors here, the smokey, not quite disinfected smell from the bus's hindquarters, but her eyes felt lidless, unquenchable. She pulled things in, as she had her whole life, and then didn't know quite what to do with them: the jagged eczema of snow along the river; the parsley-fur of tamaracks and pines; the clouds, which, without the anchoring ache of their dark bellies, looked as if they would wisp away. A Holiday Inn signboard on the highway read

RELAX ETHEL AND DRESSER: YOU'VE MADE IT! The parking lot was full. Benna wondered if Ethel and Dresser were happy or whether they even thought about it. In a town called Bluewaters she misread a billboard that said CARPENTER'S: YOUR OWN PERSONAL WAREHOUSE, thinking at first that it said "whore-house," which broke her stare, turned her attention inward for a moment to her knees, to her magazine, to the empty seat beside her spread with someone else's *Times*, to the old woman across the aisle who had just taken out a nectarine from a paper bag and bit and slurped and, napkinless, dabbed at the corners of her mouth with the edge of the paper bag. Benna looked back at her knees feeling that she'd been made, forever and for now, like her marriage vows, stupid with loneliness, bereft of any truth or wisdom or flicker of poetry, possessed only of the wild glaze of a person who spends entire days making things up.

The river raced alongside them, a dog barking and chasing. Ah, *warehouse*. It said *warehouse*.

Her brother Louis lived in Queens. He'd been there for two years now and she'd never visited. She was going to stay at his apartment overnight and then catch a cab to Kennedy the next morning. Her plane left at nine-thirty a.m., a silly charter flight dubbed "Carefree." A close friend of hers had died and she was getting away. She was going to the Caribbean, a package tour of desert islands, all rimmed in glitz: casinos, discos, dancing girls at the Americana. She would step off the plane and the heat and sun would hit her like a hallucination. She would eat one native tomatoey-banana dish per island; she would dance with men who spoke a halting English; she would eat canapés that looked like the asses of gibbons; she'd drink piña coladas on the rumrunner cruise; she would feed the starving, gunk-eyed cats that came rubbing around her chair legs in the cafés—she would drop them bits of roast beef. When fellow tourists confided doubtful things, she would say, "Don't make my shoes laugh," an island idiom. She would watch her purse. She would get a tan.

She slept and dreamed of a man who poked paper clips through his bottom lip.

The bus coughed and rumbled into Port Authority. She opened her eyes. The nectarine woman smiled at her and said, "Wasn't the skyline coming in just beautiful?" Benna smiled back, nodded, then heaved her bag off the overhead shelf and bumped her way off the bus. The bus driver winked and told her to have a Merry Christmas. She'd almost forgotten: Tomorrow was Christmas.

She followed signs and escalators up to Eighth Avenue, then walked the one block to the RR, the air cold and acidic. Taxis whizzed by in the slush. She had once lived in New York, not far from here, before the terminal had been renovated, and she could still remember the same half-tourist, half-resident feeling she'd had even when she'd lived here. She'd had two love affairs and had, with each of them, gone to the top of the World Trade Center for drinks.

She waited on the subway platform with two men, one of them reading a paper with a headline that said BRAIN-DAMAGED JFK HELD CAPTIVE IN SOUTH AMERICA, the other one pacing down at the opposite end, his steps echoing. Benna could hear other trains shuddering in the distance, above, but soon there was silence and only the man's echoing steps. She stared at the tracks, glanced up once in a while at the Broadway show posters.

The train arrived in a clattering din and shrieked to a stop, all those little lighted rooms on wheels. The doors banged open, and she picked up her suitcase, readjusted her handbag, and scurried into the car directly in front of her. She was not a shopper. This was how she went through life. She took the first space she saw by the door.

She positioned her suitcase close to her legs. The train

clapped shut and jerked forward. And as some sort of inexplicable dread filled her like an ink, all she could think was that she would rather be someone, anyone, else: the skinny Oriental woman rocked to a nap across from her, or the woman further down dressed in dirty animal skins and reeking of urine. She wanted to be the blind cripple with the tin, who got on at Lexington, and to whom she had given five dollars. "Merry Christmas," he said, and rolled off into the next car.

Mostly, she was surrounded by men, and soon they were all, all of them, tunneling under the East River.

She got off in Astoria, usually a festive place, she'd been told, but today it seemed foggy, even deadly. A man set up at a card table had a sign propped in front of him: HELP KILL HENRY KISSINGER. DONATE A DOLLAR. It was Christmastime. She asked no questions. She donated a dollar. Then she moved on, struggled down the metal stairs off the elevated platform and made her way up 31st Avenue toward Louis's apartment, following the directions he'd given her over the phone and which she'd written in red ink on a now-smudged three-by-five card. It was only five-thirty, but it was dark and all the stores were closed. She put her suitcase down to rest. A bus alongside her suddenly pulled away, spewing exhaust, and she held her breath so as not to breathe it. A train rattled loudly across the el above and behind her. She gasped for air then picked up her bag and continued down the sidewalk. An unskinned goat was hanging in the window of the Acropolis Butchery. Two men shouted to each other from across the avenue. "Hey, Dinny, you do this. Right?" A fruit stand on the next block was open. "You like avocado?" asked a thick-necked woman with black hair. She wore a red sweater and a green apron, an old parka draped over her shoulders. Benna floundered, groped, like a high school girl, for a personality. "Yes, very much," she said, and moved on.

. . .

"Eh, how you doing?" squeaked her brother Louis in a pitch too high for his age and body. Benna set her bag down and gave him a hug. "Merry Christmas," she said. He remained in the doorway for a long moment, one of his feet holding open the door. He seemed a little balder, a little heavier, his nylon shirt unbuttoned too far down his chest, more because it had been overlaundered and no longer fit than because of anything else. Louis kissed her on the cheek. He smelled of cigarettes and small, yellowing teeth. "Let me take your bag," he said finally, mimicking, she thought, someone else's graciousness. He nudged up his slipping eyeglasses and then lifted her bag into the apartment. She stepped into a narrow hallway which connected two rooms. The rear room was dim, musty, and bluish with a double bed and a window that looked out onto a concrete wall. Off this room, in the back, was a kitchen with fluorescent lights and a large bag of trash that needed emptying. The front room to her right had a TV, a sofa, a chair, two windows. She could hear kids outside, shouting.

"Louis, this is really a nice place." He was thirty-six, divorced, alone; this was the first apartment he'd ever had as a bachelor that wasn't a six-month sublet. "Louis, I'm serious. I'm impressed." She was, she realized, sounding like her mother, their mother.

Louis smiled and seemed pleased. He set her bag down in the dim, blue room. "It's okay," he said, suddenly rather seriously looking about.

"I brought you a Christmas present," she said. It was a sweater vest. She would give it to him after dinner.

Louis looked guilty. "I don't have one for you," he said.

"That's perfectly all right," she smiled.

"So, what's new with my little sister?" Louis self-consciously gulped from his beer can. Benna drank hers from an old jelly jar he had apologetically provided for her. "It's fine, really," she'd said. "Don't go to any trouble."

"What's new?" she repeated. She thought about telling him about her wisdom tooth. In America, two adults under forty stuck for conversation could always talk about wisdom teeth. "Well," she began, feeling the impossibility even of this. She looked at Louis. As a boy he'd always been a recluse and a moper, odd, lonely, fat. He'd sit in his little room in the trailer and eat fudge and play cards and daydream and snarl at any knocks at his door. Then he'd gotten married and it hadn't worked out, as they say. For reasons she was never told, he wasn't able to get custody of his daughter. Benna had always felt overwhelmingly sorry for him, though she knew that was wrong—distancing and finally dehumanizing.

"A good friend of mine just died." She blurted it. Lately it felt like the only thing she knew, the only thing new.

"Howdy die?"

"Excuse me?"

"How did he die?"

"Oh. He—it sounds absurd—got drunk and fell in his own bathtub. Then at the hospital they fucked up with the painkillers and the I.V.'s, and he went into a kind of coma and died."

Louis whistled a glissando of amazement and shook his head.

Benna pressed one finger into the corner of her eye. She was going to say something about its being dumb and pointless, about its being something she would never get over, but her jaw locked and her eyes were too quickly awash for her to get anything out but a wobbly "Yeah."

Louis got up, came forward, and bent over Benna to hug her, but it was awkward and made her feel uncomfortable. "Don't want my little sister to get upset now." She could feel his sideburns, his breath, his arms.

"Louis, really. I'm okay. Listen, can I use your bathroom to wash up before we go to dinner?"

Louis let go. "Anything you want, anything you want," he stammered, attempting a grand theatrical gesture with his arms.

"Mr. Host," said Benna, trying to smile.

In the bathroom there was only one towel, the size of a bathmat. It was stained a brownish gray and was draped at a careless angle on an aluminum rod.

"Louis, do you have another towel?" Benna called out the door.

"No, I don't." Louis's voice cracked sheepishly from the living room. He had turned the TV on, a basketball game.

"Oh." Benna poked her dripping face out. "Do you have paper towels?"

"Yeah. In the kitchen," he grunted.

"I'll get them." She dripped out to the kitchen, tore sheets of toweling from a roll on top of the refrigerator, and dried her face and hands with them.

"Ah, good." She found herself smiling self-consciously at Louis, who had come out to the kitchen to watch. She threw the towels away in an open brown grocery bag, next to the overflowing one.

"Where you wanna eat?" he said.

They put on coats and walked five blocks to a dark Italian steak house called The Charcoal Lounge. It was full of piped-in Christmas music and festoons of garlands, red and green. Louis kept announcing that the dinner was on him. "All right, already," she smiled, finally. She liked to say that. It was something which growing up upstate she had never heard anyone say.

Louis suddenly seemed edgy, his voice loud. "Get what you want, get what you want! Drinks? You want a drink first? Get a drink."

The waiter looked at Benna. "A drink?"

"A scotch and soda, please," she said. She put her napkin carefully in her lap.

Louis ordered a beer. "So this friend of yours who died, he was a good friend?"

"Yes," said Benna. She thought about Gerard for a minute, imagined him in a floaty pastel heaven where there was no opera, only church and church music, and knew he'd hate it there. "It's so weird to talk about somebody who's died. It seems to make them more dead," she said.

"It's rough," said Louis, shaking his head again. He reached across the table, took her hand, held it for a while. They were long minutes. She squirmed, then gently slipped her hand from his and put it in her lap with her napkin.

When the food came—salads, veal cutlets, spaghetti—Louis ate quickly. When he finished he leaned back and belched, said excuse me, and then talked about his bookkeeping job, how much he made, what it was like having a woman for a boss, how much he thought he'd make in three years, how much the government took out of his paycheck in taxes. "When we get back home," he said, "I'll, I'll show you a check stub. Three hundred dollars they take out. Three hundred dollars!" he squeaked and his eyebrows went up. His eyes rounded and his glasses slipped a bit on his nose.

"Wow," said Benna, chewing.

"Would you like another scotch?" asked the waiter.

"God, no. It'll go right to my hips," she said, although no one laughed. Louis ordered a second beer and the waiter nodded and left.

"Yeah, I'm thinking of becoming a Big Brother," announced Louis, lighting up a cigarette. Louis was the sort of person who, when changing the subject, lit up a cigarette and started his sentences with a long, drawn-out *Yeah*.

"The organization? Where you sort of adopt a little kid?"

"Yeah. I go, go for the interview next Monday."

"Well, Louis, that might be great for you." It was curious to her, this announcement to a younger sister that he was off to try to become a Big Brother, this announcement of loneliness and terror, of failure and of hunger for the most meager redemption —that of brother, even fake-brother. Benna thought of something she'd heard on a nature documentary once, something called The Stone Egg Theory, which said if you put a stone egg in the chicken's nest, it'll be encouraged to lay a real one.

"Yeah, I think it'd be good for me."

"I take it you don't hear from Annie or Fran much."

"Christmas card," he sighed. "I've sort of given up on them."

"Perhaps it's better."

"Yeah." He dragged deeply, looking at his cigarette as he did, appearing almost cross-eyed.

Some people came in and Louis looked suddenly toward the door. "I think there's someone here I know," he said, and his face went brilliant with hope and recognition. He began to stand. Benna looked over her shoulder. There was a group of people standing at the door. None of them was looking Louis's way. Benna looked back at her brother. A hesitant flicker appeared in one dark iris and then he scowled and sat back down, shaking his head. "Wope. Mistake. A case of mistaken identity."

"Oh," said Benna, and she felt disappointed for him. Someone should have been there. Someone should have waved and strode over, shook his hand, slapped his back, and said, "Louis, hey, howsit goin?—Merry Christmas, guy."

They ate cheesecake and then walked home. Two blocks from his apartment he put his arm around her. "My little sister," he said, and hugged her close to his side. She could smell the nicotine and onion sweat of his armpits, the damp heat of him beneath his coat.

.   .   .

Louis continued drinking beers. He showed Benna the paycheck
stub. They sat in front of the television for a while silently watching a bad sitcom about two people who meet when one locates
and adopts the other's lost poodle. The two "owners" battle it out
for possession, the poor dog yanked and pet-knapped and shuttled
back and forth, abused and as miserably beside the point as a baby
brought to Solomon. Her mind wandered. She thought of pets
growing tired and committing suicide, what notes they would
leave: "Dear Benna: It's all a crazy game. Farewell, Max, Your
Schnauzer."

"I'm sleepy, Louis. I've got to call the cab place tomorrow
at six-fifteen to make sure I'm at Kennedy by seven-thirty."

Louis got up. "Well, I put brand-new sheets on the bed. I
went out and bought them today."

"You bought new sheets? You shouldn't have done that."
Benna thought it odd that he'd have brand-new sheets yet no
towels.

"Nothing but the best for my sister." He lifted her hand and
kissed it, wetly, several times, like some hideous courtier, looking
out at her from over his glasses.

"Louis." She pulled her hand away. He's confused. He's
bought a woman dinner and now he's confused: He's forgotten
who I am. "Listen, I can sleep on the sofa, if you'd rather. I can
sleep here, no problem." She bent over and patted the thatchy
plaid of the couch cushion. Then she straightened and backed
away from him.

"Hey, you know your brother loves you, right?" He grinned
drunkenly, arms wide, coming toward her. She was supposed to
hug him. She attempted it, lightly, briefly, but his arms clamped
around her stubbornly. She wriggled her arms free and began
pushing him away. "Come on, Louis," she said, and twisting to
get out of his hug, she found herself trapped, the small of her
back against his spongy gut, his arms still locked now pressing

against her breasts. She squirmed and pushed down hard on his arms. He let go.

"Well, hey," he said, and stepped toward the TV and turned the volume down.

"See you in the morning, Louis," she said.

"Of course, of course," and he kissed her hand again.

"Well. Good night," she said, and he followed her into the room with the double bed and the window facing the blocked wall. She went over to the dresser, set his alarm, turned off the lights. Her bag sat by the blocked window, unopened. Louis stood in the doorway and watched. She kicked off her shoes and got into bed with all her clothes on. The sheets were rough and canvasy; Louis had bought them, but he hadn't washed them. They had the chemical popcorn smell of five-and-dimes.

"I'm going to sleep now, Louis, thanks for everything. I'll see you in the morning." She tried to act as if he weren't there still in the doorway, stubborn and lonesome and pushing up his glasses. But she could feel his largeness and breathing still close, and she pulled the covers up to her neck, squeezed shut her eyes, and retreated to someplace very far back in her head, and when she got there she sat in it like a child in a far place and said to herself over and over again, "Please, God, please."

She wasn't sure how long it was before Louis went back into the front room to watch TV, but after some time she could hear the unfamiliar TV voices turned up louder, the false, cooing women, the desperate laugh tracks, the snapping open of beer cans, and she knew then that he was there. Outside on 31st Avenue there were sirens all night.

In the morning she called the cab and it came in ten minutes. Her clothes were wrinkled and clammy, but she didn't care. Louis stumbled out of the front room, seemed tired and irritable, perhaps achey from having slept on the couch, but he helped bring her bag out to the cab anyway. The air was cold and quiet. The cabbie got out and opened up the back trunk.

"Good-bye, little sister," Louis said, aiming for some weird jocularity, inappropriate as flowers. "Have fun."

"Thanks," said Benna. "I'll send you a postcard." They quickly kissed good-bye, their mouths breakfastless and clouded with the potatoey, dishwater-breath of sleep.

"Goinda Kennedy?" asked the cabbie.

"Yeah." Benna heaved her handbag into the backseat and got in after it. On the other side of the street, to her right, some teenaged boy, up early or out late, walking by with a leather jacket and a dangling, bent cigarette, called "Hey, jiggle-butt" and waved. He looked, for a minute, like Gerard, like some teenaged ghost of Gerard.

On her left Louis was closing the door. He waved, then scuffed back toward the tiny collapsing stoop that was his. He had no socks on, and his heels were on top of his shoes, mashing the backs. He was wearing the same pants and shirt as the night before, she noticed, rumpled and misbuttoned, his coat thrown on over them. His breath floated out into the wintry morning in puffs. She watched him disappear. She knew he hadn't a friend in the world. The two of them: How had they come to this?

The cab moved forward. She suddenly realized she'd forgotten to give Louis his Christmas present, but she said nothing, and the cab turned right and kept going.

The sun was only just coming up, and the driver was still high on his first coffee of the day. He wanted to talk. "You look glum," he said. "Tough to say good-bye to that guy with the shoes?"

Benna closed her eyes, leaned back into the seat. It was Christmas. Santa Claus is a spirit that lives in your heart, her mother had told her, not believing it right to hoodwink children. But perhaps her mother had been wrong. Perhaps sitting in a taxicab like this on Christmas there was no spirit in your heart. Perhaps there was only an old man, ridiculous and fat, who came into your house through your chimney, too moronic even to use the door.

The sky's striated blush began to look like a parfait behind the apartments and stores of Astoria. The roads were empty and clear as days and days. "My brother and I," Benna said. "It's just that we never get a chance to see each other very much." Perhaps, she was thinking, there was nothing in which anyone might intelligently place their faith. Perhaps there was only rubble and sleep. *It's all hopeless*, said Fred Astaire in a movie once. *But it's not serious.* That was the only line she remembered.

"Ah, brothers," smiled the cab driver. "Do I know that. Hey, my brother and me?" He took a sharp left and double-checked the rearview mirror to catch Benna's eye. "We're like this." And he held up two crossed fingers.

V

When the train stops, the lights stop flickering, and the doors bang open, George is the first to set official foot on Grand Central soot. She stops to sniff and exclaim, "Pooey-mcphooey," in a tone that makes me wonder whether I've taught her to be polite, and, even if I have, what that means, how it really helps.

We have to grunt and lug bags out the door, over the metal ridge, onto the dank cement of the platform. We have ball bearings on the bottoms of our suitcases and from here on in it looks to be a sweatless trundle out to the hivey cathedral of the main concourse. We are off to be Beruba girls. People pour out from behind us, bumping, pushing, greeting friends and relatives with hugs and handclasps and sweaty cheek-to-cheeks. There are shouts of "Happy New Year," although it's still a week away. "It's like

Grand Central Station in here," I say to George. I cap my hand over her head and steer her in front of me like a basketball or a mail cart.

"It stinks like trains, Mom," she says over the hiss of engines. It's a harsh, queasy, burn smell, with its suggestions of hell and carcinogenesis. I think, *This* is why a woman makes things up: Because when she dies, those lives she never got to are all going down with her. All those possibilities will just sit there like a bunch of schoolkids with their hands raised and uncalled on—each knowing, really knowing, the answer.

Life is sad. Here is someone.

"Knock, knock," whispers Georgianne. She takes two steps to my one. "Knock, knock," she repeats.

"Who's there?"

"Me."

"Me who?"

"Just me!" she says and giggles wildly.

I shake my head. "You made that up, didn't you."

"Yup." She tugs at her bag. Passing the diesel at the front, we are suddenly hit with a steamy, acrid smoke billowing out from underneath it. People around us cough. George leans her head on my arm, mock-weary, Pre-Raphaelite. She is a gift I have given myself, a lozenge of pretend. *Pretend there's a child dozed between us,* wrote Darrel once, *and the city's parch and chill is not the world, and the world's not hurtful as a fist holding us sternly, always here and down.*

George fiddles with my coat cuff. "Sometimes," she sighs into the steam, "I feel like I'm right in the mist of things."

I swear, she is a genius.

A NOTE ON THE TYPE

The text of this book was set on the Linotype in a type face known as Garamond. The design is based on letter forms originally created by Claude Garamond (c. 1480–1561). Garamond was a pupil of Geoffroy Tory and may have patterned his letter forms on Venetian models. To this day, the type face that bears his name is one of the most attractive used in book composition, and the intervening years have caused it to lose little of its freshness or beauty.

Composed by Maryland Linotype Composition Company, Baltimore, Maryland

Printed and bound by Fairfield Graphics, Fairfield, Pennsylvania

Typography and binding design by Tasha Hall